How to Bake a Chocolate Soufflé

A Novel

Carly Ellen Kramer

DEDICATION

To the many fabulous women who are Famous At Abbott.
You know who you are.

RECIPES

PROLOGUE

"Every time I see these images, I am inspired anew." Tabitha Sanders, Director of Alumnae Relations, glanced again at the wide screened slide show running on a continuous loop and smiled at the crowd. Dressed in an emerald green, boiled wool skirt suit with bright red hair tucked into a perfect chignon, she was the well–spoken, highly polished embodiment of a career driven, Abbott College graduate.

Ms. Sanders adjusted the small microphone on her lapel and stepped to the front of the small stage, taking a moment to pan the room full of exuberant young women seated at skirted round tables. Energy vibrated throughout the crowd as 132 honor graduates counted the hours until their hard earned degrees would be conferred.

"A few years back, the Graduation Committee and the Alumnae Relations Office decided to combine Honors Night and the Alumnae Awards Dinner into a single, annual event. Our rationale was two–fold. First, a combined event would provide upcoming graduates with an opportunity to experience some of the ways in which seasoned alumnae share their time and talents here at Abbott College and throughout the wider community.

Second, we knew returning Abbott women would have sage advice to share with their newest alumnae sisters. In both regards, the combined event has become an annual success. Are you enjoying yourselves so far?"

Applause and a few cheers erupted from the tables, as young women supplemented their pre-graduation endorphin highs with wine poured liberally throughout the room by the roving wait staff.

"Please welcome Dean Katharine Riley, who is joining us tonight to introduce this year's top award winner." Ms. Sanders clapped her hands together theatrically as a dignified, slight statured woman wearing chin length white hair and a Franciscan cross stepped up to the podium. All 132 honors graduates stood in respect as they applauded for their beloved Dean.

"It is a real pleasure to celebrate with each of you this evening," Dean Riley began as the honor graduates returned to their chairs. "Every May, I am filled with pride over the sense of ambition, of utter fearlessness, that fills the air during Honors Night. However, it isn't simply your ambition that makes me proud. No, I could head downtown on a weekday for a noon hour lunch if I wanted to feel ambition in the air. I'm proud because I know the ambition in this room, while earnest and palpable, is tempered by the remarkably strong and personal values each of you has nurtured as an integral part of your Abbott College experience. I believe that the combination of ambition and values – a combination I feel right now in this room – is powerful enough to change the world."

Dean Riley paused with a smile as Honors graduates clinked glasses together and cheered. She waited a moment for the commotion to settle before continuing.

"You're already quite familiar with Audrey Navarro's work," Dean Riley conceded, motioning toward the slide show, "so it will not surprise you at all that Ms. Navarro has been selected as the recipient of Abbott College's most prestigious alumnae award, the Advancing Abbott Award."

The room once again broke into applause.

"It also will not surprise you that Ms. Navarro was once a student of mine, back when she was an uncertain teenager and I still had pigment in my hair." Dean Riley glanced over at Audrey, who was waiting at the edge of the stage, while light laughter glittered the room. "What might surprise you is an interesting fact about the combination of ambition and values I spoke of earlier. I learned that lesson from Ms. Navarro."

Stunned, Audrey opened her mouth and closed it again. Dean Riley continued, "Ms. Navarro's work was so successful that I blindly pushed her to run with her ambition. When I try to look at it from her vantage point, her employer and I daresay her mentor, had given her carte blanche to pursue what likely would have been a fun project. Who would say 'no' to that?

"Ms. Navarro was strong enough to say 'no.' With the complete poise and professionalism of an Abbott College graduate, Ms. Navarro explained how my ambition conflicted with her values. She pledged her full support with her carefully crafted alternate proposal, and concluded by graciously but directly clarifying that she would not compromise her values, even if it meant having to step down from the project altogether. Of course, it never came to that. What I'm not sure Ms. Navarro realized, but I'm happy to clarify tonight, is that I have never been as proud of an Abbott College graduate as I was of Audrey in that moment."

Audrey looked away, blinking back eyes.

"Ms. Navarro, it is a great honor – no, it is a personal honor – to present you with this year's Advancing Abbott Award. May your work be an inspiration to this year's Honors graduates."

Foregoing the traditional handshake, Dean Riley wrapped Audrey in a grandmotherly hug before presenting her with a handsome engraved plaque. Audrey stepped up to the podium, looked out over the tables of upcoming graduates, and waited for the applause to settle.

"Thank you. I am honored and humbled to accept this award. Dean Riley asked me to share a few words of advice with you tonight. I've been thinking about what would be important enough to discuss on the eve of your college graduation, and I've decided to tell you about my experiences baking a soufflé."

From one of the front tables, Dean Riley arched an eyebrow. Two middle aged women glanced at each other wearing matching quizzical expressions, an empty seat between them.

"I am something of a dessert aficionado. If a dish contains obscene quantities of sugar and fat, I am *all* over it. If the dish also contains chocolate, well, it would be best to just get out of my way." Several women laughed in agreement. "A few years ago while in Tahiti, I was invited to dinner at the home of a professor from *Université de la Polynésie Française*. The professor's grandmother, an elderly French woman named Aimata Baptiste, made the most fantastic chocolate soufflé I have ever tasted. After two bites, I decided that recreating the soufflé was one of my new life goals!

"Mrs. Baptiste was flattered, I think. She offered instructions in labored, broken English, which I carefully recorded on paper, seeking clarification in my own painful French as needed. Chocolate being something of a universal language, we managed.

"The next day – yes, I really am that obsessed with desserts – I attempted to make the soufflé. I followed every step carefully. Mrs. Baptiste had told me to 'exercise' the egg whites. I remember asking her to clarify, and she mimed beating egg whites in a bowl with a fork. So, when I came to that point in the recipe, I beat the egg whites exactly as I understood. My soufflé turned out, eh, not very well. The taste was pretty similar, but not spot-on. The appearance was less forgiving – it didn't rise well,

4

and looked rather unimpressive. I contacted Mrs. Baptiste, to learn what I might have done wrong.

"After a bit of English – to – French improvisation, I realized that Mrs. Baptiste didn't tell me to 'exercise' the egg whites. She told me to 'exorcise' the egg whites, or 'beat the Devil' out of them!" Laughter ensued. "On my second attempt, that is exactly what I did. I beat those egg whites until I thought my arm was going to disconnect at the shoulder. If anyone would have seen me toiling away in my tiny, ill equipped kitchen, I'm sure they would have laughed out loud. I worked up a sweat. I honestly thought I pulled a bicep. But do you know what? That soufflé was *fantastic*!" Several women in the audience began to laugh.

"The reason I'm sharing this story is because dreams are like that." The room became silent.

"You can hold onto a dream, go after it with a halfway decent effort, and end up with a fairly respectable result. Heck, that's what most people do - *'exercise.'* But what if your dream is so big you can barely hold it in your arms? What if your dream is so fantastic that it seems almost implausible? What if 'a fairly respectable result' isn't good enough? Well, then you take your Abbott College education, you take the ambition and the values to which Dean Riley referred, and you go after your dream like the Devil itself is on your heels! *'Exorcise!'*" The room erupted enthusiastically.

"That brings me to my next point, the one nobody really wants to talk about. Sometimes, the monster under the bed is real."

The room quieted down again. At a table near the podium, the two middle aged women glanced across the empty seat again, their expressions unfathomable.

"It's a taboo subject, I know. I hope you'll forgive me. The thing is, it's easy to talk about the good dreams. It's so easy, it becomes cliché. Talking about dreams loses its meaning, its potency, if we don't acknowledge that every once and a while, pleasant dreams are invaded by nightmares. Careers become derailed, sometimes due to big mistakes, and sometimes through no fault of our own. Relationships, sadly, can become unhealthy beyond repair. We grapple with illness. We struggle with loss. Taboo or not, these facts are part of the human experience.

"I want each of you, right now, to take a long look around this room. Consider the relationships you have nurtured within this college and how supportive you have been of each other's dreams. As you look around this room, who will you call when the monster under the bed is real? Who will come to you?

"I was invited to bring two guests with me this evening to celebrate this award. I could have brought my spouse. I could have brought little Arianna, a future Abbott College student, who was here earlier today. She was quite impressed by the assortment of ice cream bars in the cafeteria!"

"Is Arianna her daughter?" Quietly asked a young honor graduate seated at the table Audrey vacated, to the middle aged women.

"No," the auburn haired woman whispered with a smile.

"Arianna's her niece, in a manner of speaking," the blonde woman stated in a hushed tone.

"I could have invited my parents. But really, of everyone I could have invited, the decision was easy. Madeleine and Annie, my two guests this evening, are also Abbott College alumnae. Wave, ladies!" Audrey's guests waved obligingly.

"The three of us were suitemates, a million years ago!" Audrey beamed as young women smiled and chattered throughout the room.

"Madeleine, Annie and I have chased many fairy tales' worth of dreams. I'd say we've caught more than our fair share, including a few great big ones!"

"Cheers to that!" Madeleine exclaimed, reaching

across the empty chair to clink glasses with Annie.

"We've also found monsters under the bed. A few have been pretty darn ugly." Audrey's eyes watered as she glanced down at her table and saw Annie reach for Madeleine's hand.

"But Abbott College women stick together. We're ambitious. We're value-centered. We don't scare easily, and we don't give up. The blessing of having these two women in my life, that is a greater gift than I ever could have hoped to receive when I selected Abbott College as the foundation for my adult education, all those years ago. So, go make your mark on the world! Just don't make the mistake of trying to go at it alone."

Madeleine and Annie stood and clapped along with Dean Riley, Tabitha Sanders, and the 132 honor graduates in attendance as Audrey stepped down from the stage. The girlfriends embraced in a group hug, the strength of which made more than a few upcoming graduates marvel.

Returning to their seats, the three alumnae were peppered with questions from their young tablemates.

"Were you always so close?" One young woman asked.

"I don't know if 'always' is strictly the correct word," Audrey replied rather sheepishly.

Another young woman at the table gave the three alumnae an assessing look before speaking. "I'll be honest; I'm often intimidated by returning alumnae at these types of gatherings. They – you – always seem so put together. Is that true? I mean, after graduation, did everything go more or less as planned?"

The question caused Madeleine to choke and cough loudly into her linen napkin.

"She means, 'No, not precisely'," Annie answered with a laugh.

"It sounds as if the three of you have quite a colorful history together," a third honor graduate ventured.

"You could say that," Madeleine agreed.

"It's an interesting story…" Audrey began.

Mrs. Baptiste's Chocolate Soufflé

Grease four single-serving ramekins with real butter and dust with sugar. Set aside. Set a metal mixing bowl over the top of a pot containing one inch of softly boiling water. The bottom of the mixing bowl should not touch the water in the pot. In the mixing bowl, melt ½ cup of dark chocolate chips. Stir well. Add three room temperature egg yolks and ½ teaspoon of pure vanilla extract to the bowl and mix well. The mixture will harden a bit – don't worry, this is normal.

In a separate mixing bowl, exorcise six egg whites – *beat the Devil out of them!* As you beat the egg whites, add ¼ teaspoon cream of tartar and 1/3 cup of white sugar, a little at a time. When the egg white mixture forms stiff peaks, fold into chocolate mixture. Be careful not to mix the air right out of the egg whites!

Pour soufflé mixture into prepared ramekins and bake in a preheated, 375 degree oven for 20 minutes. Serve immediately.

23 YEARS

"Ow!"

"Hold still, girlfriend, or you'll spill champagne all over yourself."

"Then don't pull so hard. I can't breathe." Annie set her crystal flute on the antique walnut vanity and scowled into the mirror.

"Nobody said beauty was pain free," Madeleine teased as she gave the silk ties crisscrossing the back of Annie's gorgeous bridal corset a sharp tug. Annie winced.

"Sadist." Annie growled into the mirror. The embroidery and tiny beading on the bust of the ivory corset really was exquisite, but Annie's attention was quickly pulled to the labored task of drawing oxygen into her lungs while her ribcage was being constricted.

"She's beautiful in sweatpants and a ratty old shirt." a second bridal attendant replied chirpily from the corner of the room. "Wearing that," she continued, motioning to the corset and carrying over a coordinating pair of sheer silk thigh-high stockings, "she'll drop the man to his knees."

"Audrey speaks the truth." Madeleine nodded solemnly.

"Thanks." Annie smiled. "I don't mean to be such a crab. Sorry." Annie took a moment to look around the dressing room, gathering her composure. Having her two best friends so close was comforting, and the sight of her large white garment bag hanging in the open armoire made her smile. The faint organ music in the background made Annie's stomach flutter.

"Eh, you're just nervous. I would be too, if I were minutes away from devoting all of my awesome feminine wiles to one man for the whole rest of my life." Madeleine smiled into the mirror over Annie's shoulder and straightened the small blue flowers pinned into Annie's hair.

"Audrey, let's get her into this dress."

Audrey downed the rest of her champagne and set her glass next to Annie's before gliding over to the walnut armoire. As she carefully removed the bridal gown from its protective covering, a knock sounded at the dressing room door.

"If it's The Queen Bitch of the Universe, don't let her in." Audrey flashed her teeth at Madeleine.

"Shhh!" Annie giggled as she stepped gingerly into her gown.

"Who is it?" Madeleine asked in a sugary voice through the door. The last person Annie needed to see right now was The Queen.

"You're safe, but you should lower your voices, ladies. Open up."

With a relieved look, Madeleine threw open the door and hugged the smiling, elegantly dressed woman standing in the doorway. The resemblance between Annie and her mother was striking.

"The first of the guests have already been seated. Unless you plan on getting married in your underwear, you might want to pick up the pace!"

"I know, Mom. I'm just nervous, I guess. And it's not like anyone is getting married today without me."

"Don't keep the poor man waiting, dear. He's nervous enough already." Mrs. Anderson smiled warmly at her daughter.

"You've seen him? Here?" Annie looked surprised.

"Well of course he's here, and yes, I've seen him. Your father says that some of the color returned to your beloved's cheeks after he made short work of a shot of whiskey." Mrs. Anderson shook her head with an amused smirk. "Boys."

"They're *drinking*?" Annie squeaked.

"Growing up with The Queen, I'm surprised he doesn't drink more," Audrey muttered.

"Truth." Madeleine nodded.

"That's enough, ladies. You don't have to like her, but her quirks are for Annie and Bryant to work though. Eventually." Mrs. Anderson's gentle admonishment was enough to censor further criticism of Bryant's mother, at least for the moment.

"Whiskey?" Annie pressed.

Mrs. Anderson laughed. "Oh, nothing to worry about, dear. Just a typical male bonding moment between Bryant, your father, and James."

"Speaking of, I should go and see if James needs help with his tie. Or anything else." Audrey smiled mischievously, thinking of the delicious looking Best Man.

"Let it go. Bryant warned you, remember?" Madeleine lowered her eyebrows for effect.

Audrey ignored her, thinking a man severely allergic to commitment might be just what she needed right now. It's not as if any of her attempts at building a real relationship had led to anything. No chemistry. It was time for a change in strategy. "I bet he looks smokin' hot in his tuxedo."

"If James needed a kidney, Bryant would be first in line. If James needed a date, Bryant would thank the universe that he doesn't have a sister to worry about. Just don't say you weren't warned." Annie rolled her eyes at her lustful friend, and tried to ignore the nervous fluttering in her stomach.

Mrs. Anderson stood up in the mirror behind Annie. "You're all buttoned in. You're beautiful, Annie. Bryant is a lucky man."

"Thanks, Mom." Annie turned to embrace her mother, and tried to keep her tears from spilling over.

Mrs. Anderson dabbed her nose with a tissue. "It's time to get married, dear."

Candice Treymont steeled herself with a plastered on smile, took the arm of the anxious looking usher, and gave him a brisk nod. When the first notes of Chopin's "Nocturne in E Flat" began to escape from the organ, Candice was escorted with painful slowness to her seat in the second pew on the right. The flowers in her corsage emitted a nauseatingly sweet odor, and her shoes were too tight. Otherwise, she felt great... if it were possible to overlook the fact that she had been unable to convince Bryant to call off this whole charade.

She still couldn't really believe that her son, her only child, would scorn the business contacts she had so carefully nurtured for decades in Boston. Back East, she knew, he would climb corporate ladders with the ease afforded by legacy connections. But now, starting from scratch in Chicago? Because of some small town girl? Candice's investment in Bryant's years of private preparatory school and his exclusive MBA credentials would be entirely wasted. If he wanted to build a career here, Candice sniffed, he was on his own.

A moment later, Mrs. Anderson dabbed her eyes, inhaled deeply of the calming aroma of her beautiful corsage, and happily took the arm of a rather relieved looking usher. She floated gracefully down the aisle toward her seat in the second pew on the left, smiling at guests along the way. She even managed a friendly nod toward Bryant's rather constipated looking mother. While

Mrs. Anderson's manners would prevent her from ever saying so, she agreed with the title bestowed upon the woman by Annie's girlfriends. Annie's parents could hardly believe how Candice hadn't even bothered to arrive in Chicago early enough to attend the rehearsal dinner.

The instant the mothers were properly seated, the music changed abruptly and quiet laughter broke out among the unsuspecting guests. In homage to the infamous spring break vacations of their college years – just a bit of sun and sand, as far as their families were concerned – Madeleine and Audrey were walking down the aisle to Bob Marley's "One Love." 'Walking' may not have been a precisely correct term, as neither of the women took to the task of moving down the aisle with any particular reverence.

Madeleine appeared first, nodding her head to the music as she shimmied toward the front of the church. A beam of light pouring through one of the tall, narrow, stained-glass windows *(for which Chicago's historic Christ Church was famous)* caught the tiny, blue crystals sprinkled throughout Madeleine's blonde hair, complimenting her blue gown beautifully. Behind her wide smile, she wondered when it would be her turn to wear a white dress. She had been dating Andrew for two years now, and while he had been willing to move with her for graduate school, he showed no particular inclination toward matrimony. It bothered her today more than most days, she realized, and she tried to banish the thought from her head.

Not willing to be outdone by Madeleine, Audrey held her bouquet high in the air and offered a little twirl at the end of the aisle as the master of reggae continued to jam about getting together and feeling alright. Still near the back pews, Audrey waved to a rather bored looking man who managed an appeasing smile. She would need to thank him later for agreeing to this. Dancing forward, Audrey tossed her coffee toned curls over her shoulder and blew a flirty air kiss toward the front of the church.

Madeleine knew exactly where the gesture was aimed and rolled her eyes as the Best Man waggled his eyebrows.

Audrey was fairly certain this would be her only jaunt down a wedding aisle in her life, and she intended to have some harmless fun with it. She for darn sure wasn't going to be returning in a big white dress. Madeleine might take the leap someday, but Audrey glanced over at Andrew fidgeting in his seat and decided she wasn't willing to bet her next car payment that he would be standing in front of an altar anytime soon.

When the reggae song ended and the organist began the first few notes of John Denver's aptly named "Annie's Song," all in attendance rose to their feet. Bryant inhaled sharply, squared his shoulders, and locked his gaze on the entrance at the back of the church sanctuary. With her first step into the room, Annie smiled radiantly. Her elegantly simple sheath dress of eggshell silk shantung, sparkled with tiny, hand sewn Austrian crystals and complemented her tall, classically curvy figure perfectly. She wore her auburn hair in long, loose curls sparsely adorned with pale blue wildflowers that stood out against her soft brown eyes and olive skin.

Annie walked toward Bryant and their future together with joy and conviction. They were perfectly suited to one another, made each other laugh, and were well on their way to becoming one of downtown Chicago's elite career couples. Nothing would stand in their way. With that thought, she flashed a big, gaudy grin at Bryant's mother, who went a half shade paler in response. Seeing the exchange, Audrey quickly turned her smile toward the wall over her left shoulder. Next to Audrey, Madeleine sucked her cheeks between her teeth to keep from smirking and looked down to study the toes of her shoes.

When Annie reached the altar, Bryant lifted her hand, pressed his lips reverently to her fingers, and whispered "I love you." In a familiar gesture that made Annie smile, Bryant ran his left hand across his temple and through his dark brown hair before offering his arm to his bride and turning toward the wedding official.

"What self-respecting woman would drink something that color?" Madeleine said, rolling her eyes at the tray of blue martinis arriving at the table. The ruched periwinkle satin comprising the bodice of her dress shuffled slightly as she arched backward to thank the server. She reached for one of the glasses, grimacing as a sip passed her lips, and gently set the concoction on the one small square of periwinkle-hued tablecloth left uncluttered by an otherwise embarrassing number of wine glasses and empty Budweiser bottles.

"Please. Who accused you of being even slightly self-respecting?" Audrey laughed as she tipped back her own garishly colored beverage with an ease made possible by earlier indulgences of a higher proof. Her green eyes reflected the candlelight of the mirrored, floral centerpiece as she casually assessed the crowd. "Besides, Mr. and Mrs. Anderson said to have a good time – we may as well toast Annie with drinks that match these awful dresses!"

As a string quartet delivered the classic chords of Fitzgerald and Ellington, the older guests enjoyed the height of their evening and the younger crowd began to liven up. Cigar smoke and tales of business irritations intermingled with bubbly laughter and shots of college booze between the widely spaced high tables bedecked in periwinkle blue. Apparently, no expense was spared for the cocktail hour, as smartly dressed servers offered crab-stuffed mushroom caps, bites of beef tenderloin in puff pastry, brie raspberry canapés, and other delicacies. To accompany their hors d'oeuvres, neither greying uncles nor recent Abbot College alumnae were shy about sidling up to the complimentary bar.

"Maddie! Audrey! I do hope you're enjoying yourselves," they heard from several yards away. A jovial, middle age man donning a smart tuxedo with the requisite blue boutonnière approached, offering a broad smile and a warm hug to Madeleine, the nearest of the girls. "And who are these handsome men, lucky enough to enjoy the pleasure of your company?"

Madeleine and Audrey blushed silent apologies in the direction of their dates. Audrey spoke. "Mr. Anderson, it was a beautiful wedding. We're all so happy for Annie and Bryant." Motioning for the hand of the tall, somewhat uncomfortable looking young man on her left, Audrey continued, "This is my friend and colleague, Bill Dervine. We work together at Klein Bridgman & Company." The young man smiled politely and offered his hand to the father of the bride.

"It's a pleasure to meet you, Bill. Are you in public relations, as well?"

"Likewise. No, I'm an information technologist."

"IT is code for 'hides in a cubicle all day,'" Audrey interrupted. "My PR team decided that bringing more employees out into the public eye would be good for client relations, and Bill graciously agreed to participate in our first Klein Bridgman Community Day. We met, of all crazy circumstances, while painting playground equipment at the local Boys and Girls Club."

"Well, whatever the circumstances were, I'm sure Bill can see that you're a fine young lady," Mr. Anderson said, before popping an olive into his mouth and taking a long drink of amber liquid from the highball glass in his hand. "You'd better make an honest woman of Audrey, or you'll have an angry old man on your hands!"

Bill managed a weak laugh as the tips of his ears tinged pink and he examined the paisley patterned carpeting with sudden interest. Audrey looked away from both men, mortified. For heaven's sake, she had only known Bill for two months, and while he was good looking in a bookish sort of way, he was only a casual date. At 23 years old, marriage was the farthest thing from her mind. If Annie wanted to race to the altar with her graduation cap still under her arm, good for her. Audrey was happy to wear sequined hairpins and a ridiculous amount of blue satin for her college girlfriend, but this was as close to an altar as she planned to venture for a very long time.

"I believe you've already met my boyfriend, Andrew Van Heersten," Madeleine hastily interjected. "He fell in the pool at Annie's graduation party?" Andrew looked over his glasses and shot her an annoyed look, but Madeleine only laughed.

"Yes, yes, I remember. That was well over a year ago, and I imagine your entrances into the real world have tempered you a bit. Although, a few more souvenirs on this table," he chided, motioning to all of the empty barware, "and I'm afraid someone will be looking for a body of water a bit smaller and surrounded by porcelain!" Both girls pleaded innocent, while their dates chuckled.

"How's graduate school treating you, Maddie?" Mr. Anderson asked.

"It's exhausting, and my advisor is an a –, um, he's difficult, but overall it's going well."

Mr. Anderson smiled. "And your parents?"

Madeleine grimaced. "They're fine. I held up my end of the deal by completing my music teaching certification, so they're holding up their end of the deal by not telling me I'm wasting my life away in graduate school."

Annie's father smiled sympathetically. Annie had brought Madeleine home from college a few times, so he understood the backstory. He didn't understand how another father could be so unsupportive of a daughter's career goals, but it wasn't his business to interfere. Not that there was anything he could have done about it anyway.

Madeleine misunderstood his silence as chastising of her tone. "I don't mean to be disrespectful, my parents are good people. I understand their…concern… that a career as a pianist can be unpredictable. I guess it's a good thing I can teach if I ever want to."

17

"I have all the confidence in the world in you, Maddie." Mr. Anderson patted her arm, and then looked back and forth between the two young women who had become his daughter's surrogate sisters. "Please have fun tonight. It's hard to believe that a few short years ago, the two of you and my Annie were just beginning college, trying so hard to be grown. And now, just look at you, each making your own way as the smart young women you are. I couldn't be more proud if you were my own girls."

"Oh Mr. Anderson," Audrey said. "You're too sweet." Very spontaneously, she leaned forward and planted a childlike kiss on Annie's father's cheek.

Madeleine smiled approvingly. "Please, go and visit. We'll behave ourselves."

As Annie's father waved and raised his glass toward another table, Madeleine tucked a loose strand of long, pale blonde hair back into the first hairpin her fingers could find. She irritatingly observed that, for what she had paid, her up-do ought to at least hold through the evening. As she adjusted her rather uncomfortable blue heels, her ambivalence about looking so ridiculously monochromatic was overshadowed by her love for Annie. While Madeleine understood Audrey's anti-altar sentiments, they both acknowledged with ironic resignation that Annie was different. She was eager to escape the small town confines of Northern Wisconsin, and appeared equally drawn to both Bryant and Chicago.

"Did you try the lobster quiche? If I eat any more, I might burst out of my dress!" The foursome turned their heads in unison at the sound of the bubbly voice. Annie beamed.

"I sure hope not!" Audrey laughed and continued, "You have to make him earn it, babe. Bryant will be lucky not to break a finger trying to undo all of those tiny hooks and eyes!" Bill rolled his eyes.

"It's a fair point," Andrew offered with a smirk, after a healthy sip from the longneck in his right hand. "I imagine he's hoping small talk with your great aunts," he continued while motioning toward the groom and three smiling, elderly ladies on the other side of the horseshoe bar, "is not destined to be the highlight of his night!" Andrew laughed at his own remark, despite Madeleine's sharp jab to the right side of his ribcage.

"For Pete's sake, her grandmother is right behind you. Show some decorum!" Madeleine turned her attention back to the bride and softened her expression. "Does your face hurt from smiling yet?" she asked.

"Not quite, but I'd love to be able to put away the fake smile reserved for everyone who feels the need to comment on my lack of a visible title transfer."

"Annie, honey, don't take it so personally," Audrey said. "It's just tradition. People who don't understand it the same way as you aren't trying to upset you."

Annie was still simmering over her new mother-in-law's unyielding disapproval wrought by Annie's lack of a bridal veil and, more importantly, Annie's insistence on being unescorted as she walked down the aisle.

"Dad understands," Annie reassured everyone, including herself. "I just can't stomach the whole idea of women as property, transferred from father to husband. It makes my skin crawl." She sighed and shuddered. "What I wasn't expecting was the sheer astonishment from some of Bryant's extended family, and Candice especially."

Madeleine and Audrey both glanced back over Annie's left shoulder on cue, toward the tall woman in the greying chignon wearing a severely tailored black suit. Her burgundy blouse matched her flawlessly manicured nails, presently curled around a tumbler of scotch, 15-year single malt, no ice. To a casual observer she appeared professional, if a bit over-polished. To Madeleine and Audrey, she was The Queen Bitch of the Universe. To Annie, she was the baggage that unfortunately came with Bryant.

Catching their stare, Candice Treymont waved

gracefully and offered a thin smile that stopped short of her eyes. She had promised to behave herself, promised her son that she wouldn't embarrass him, but damn it, she wasn't going to act proud that her Bryant was settling for some Midwestern girl from a working class family and a second rate college. She hadn't been able to prevent the marriage but hopefully, Candice fumed, her Bryant would come to his senses before he had children, and she would be there to help him iron out the mess and move on. With a look of disgust at the specimen on her cocktail napkin and a thought about the type of people who would serve frozen quiche at a wedding, she marched outside to get some air.

Annie looked across the room in the other direction, and Audrey followed her eye. Bryant smiled at his new wife and her friends and pointed, first to his watch and then to the velvet curtains blocking the entrance to the main hall of the restaurant.

"It must be time for dinner," Annie excitedly interpreted.

"What kind of a man choreographs a wedding schedule?" Audrey laughingly questioned, her volume just high enough to suggest her level of enjoyment of the free cocktails.

"I'll tell you what kind," she continued, as Madeleine gently removed the glass from her pal's animated hand. "The kind who knows that Annie looks better with sex hair than with those perfect little flowers! The poor man wants to get this show on the road and get outta here. And who can blame him?"

Audrey slurred her words slightly as she gestured toward the bride. "She cut him off months ago, saying it would make their wedding night 'magical'."

Andrew choked on his beer, while Bill calmly surveyed the exits.

Annie blushed and turned her head quickly to see if anyone had overheard, but couldn't suppress a small smile.

Madeleine laughed out loud, and tried her best to make Audrey shut up.

"Don't forget, I've seen the underwear beneath that amazing gown. Girl, you're going to give Bryant a stroke." With that, Audrey laughed, tossed her hair again, and skipped off in the direction of the restroom. For some reason, she suddenly had to pee.

"I don't think I've told you in the last five minutes that you're beautiful and I love you," Bryant said with a quick kiss against Annie's ear.

"It's still hard for me to believe we're here, it's real, this is all for us!" Annie stammered, beaming. Locking her arms around her husband's neck, she smiled into his sapphire blue eyes and delivered a kiss that drew light applause from surrounding friends and family.

Bryant reached up to gently take Annie's hands in his. With a contented smile, he interlaced their left hands so that their new rings caught the light. "Real," he silently mouthed.

"Let's walk outside for a minute," Annie suggested. "We're not supposed to go into the hall until everyone is seated. It's tradition."

Bryant shrugged and offered his arm as they walked out a side door onto the patio sandwiched between the historic white brick building and bustling Delaware Place. It was a perfect evening, really, typically warm for June, with just enough of that famous Chicago breeze to dissipate the steam meandering upward from the grates in the sidewalk.

"I don't think I've told you in the last five…"

"I love you, too" Annie whispered back, leaning against Bryant's strong shoulder as they both took in the evening traffic flowing through the Gold Coast. It was still a bit unbelievable, how her parents had made this happen. They took the conversation about having the wedding in Chicago well. She and Bryant had met here, after all, and planned to stay in the city. Her parents' only disappointment was in not being able to host the event at the Anderson Inn. She could see it on their faces, but hoped they understood that asking everyone to travel up to Northern Wisconsin was asking a bit much. Cherry Harbor was beautiful, but it wasn't exactly centrally located.

Mr. and Mrs. Anderson had put out feelers to a long list of business contacts and, sure enough, had been put in touch with a Chicago restaurateur who was interested in working out a creative business agreement. William Gianopolous, owner of the Zagat-rated Cice Estiatorio, was planning a family reunion to include his parents and his children on both sides of the ocean. He was intrigued at the idea of spending a weekend with his family at the Anderson Inn Bed and Breakfast in Cherry Harbor, an area well reputed as a Northwoods escape with beautiful freshwater beaches. If his parents could travel all the way from Athens, surely they could manage driving just a few hours north of Chicago.

Annie's parents left no detail untended while hosting 58 members of the Gianopolous family earlier this spring. All 30 rooms of the Inn were prepared with overstuffed welcome baskets of Wisconsin cheeses and wines. Vases of Door County's famous cherry blossoms adorned every bedside table. The Andersons' guests enjoyed their wooded retreat and lavished compliments upon Mrs. Anderson for her scrumptious breakfasts of farm fresh bacon and eggs, Danish pancakes with lingonberry jam, tart cherry scones, fresh squeezed orange juice, and gallons of hot coffee. William Gianopolous was so pleased with the experience that he declared the Gianopolouses and the Andersons to be family, and professed how delighted he would be to host "his" daughter Annie's wedding celebration at his Estiatorio in June.

"We should get back. I'm hungry, and more importantly, one hundred and ninety-seven of our dearest friends are waiting to shower us with attention!" Annie laughed.

"How long do we need to stay?" Bryant joked. "I would love to shower you with attention, all by myself." He let his hand slide suggestively down the back of his bride's dress.

"Behave yourself!" Annie teased and smacked his forearm before grabbing his hand and heading toward the door.

"You can't blame a guy for trying, Annie. You have no idea what a knockout you are in that dress."

"Wait until you see what's underneath." Annie winked and couldn't help laughing when Bryant was at a loss for a come-back. The fact that he was so quick witted in most circumstances made his rare, tongue-tied moments even more charming.

"Ow!" The door opened from the inside as Annie and Bryant approached, causing Bryant to awkwardly sidestep onto Annie's foot.

"Here you are!" Madeleine exclaimed. "You do know you're missing your own party, yes? Annie, you just have to see the room. Just, go see."

With Bryant half a step behind, Annie hurried inside through the parted curtains. Cheers erupted as the band leader spontaneously introduced the newly married Mr. Treymont and Ms. Anderson–Treymont. Even Candice managed to raise her glass, though she scraped her tongue on the inside of her top teeth in a reflexive attempt to quell the bad taste in her mouth.

Of course, Annie and Bryant were familiar with the restaurant, but they had never seen it like this. Annie knew the space was beautiful on any typical evening, and knew the Gianopolous family took pride in their venue. Stemming from good manners and pragmatic simplicity, Annie and Bryant had happily given the Gianopolous family carte blanche with the décor and the dinner itself, emphasizing only that Annie adored fresh flowers, one of the attendants was allergic to shellfish, and the wedding party would be dressed in blue.

The first thing Annie noticed were the flowers, stunning bouquets floating above the center of each round dining table in tall, slender vases. That was the intention, as everything else from the linens to the dishes to the cake itself was a pure, bright white. Every bouquet was unique, and each more beautiful than the last. On the table in front of her, Annie smiled to see the large, ruffled petals of Himalayan blue poppies, their golden centers offering a second burst of color. She spotted hydrangeas to the near left and the far right, the former white with thin rims of bright blue, and the latter grey blue with rims that were almost lilac. Tall stalks of powder blue delphinium appeared in the center of the room, and dainty blue columbine framed the right wall. These had always been a favorite of Annie's, with their star shaped petals curiously inset by white bells and yellow exclamations. Finally, Annie's eyes drifted to the long, high table where the attendants were already seated. Against the white linen table skirting stood a solid, 15 foot row of the most stunning hemstitched bearded iris that Annie had ever seen. The tall, proud blooms were predominantly white, but what really caught her eye were the thin ribbons of bright blue curling upward like smoke on the vertical petals.

Rules about floral fragrances clashing with food may apply to a Tuesday meatloaf dinner, but they fly right out the window where a wedding feast prepared by a Greek restaurateur is concerned. While not the Ritz-Carlton, William Gianopolous sniffed, nobody was going to associate his Estiatorio with the dry chicken, whipped potatoes, and other unfortunate stars of typical American wedding fare. Even the rustic appetizer plates of crusty bread loaves, cured olives, feta and myzithra cheeses held up to the lush flowers. The heady aroma of the entrée course, braised and roasted lamb in a delectable blanket of fresh roasted tomatoes and halved new potatoes steeped in onion, garlic, and smoked paprika, was simply sublime. As efficient and unobtrusive wait staff filled crystal glasses with Pommery Summertime Blanc de Blancs, the best man eased his chair back and confidently maneuvered the microphone as he smirked at the groom and stood to face the crowd.

"Good evening, everyone," he offered loudly, with an easy smile. Waiting a beat and lowering his voice just a notch, he continued.

"My name is James, and as Bryant's Best Man, I have the honor of being seated next to the lovely new Ms. Anderson-Treymont for dinner, and also of offering this toast. I'm glad for the combination, as I feel much safer with the bride between Bryant's arm and my microphone." As guests chuckled, Bryant shifted slightly in his chair.

"I've known Bryant for ten years, since our hideous 9th grade year at Wakefield Academy. You might say we looked up to the members of the chess team as the cool kids. If I was socially awkward, Bryant was award-winningly so… he outgrew it though, and by our senior year could almost manage to look at a girl without passing out."

Bryant shot him an embarrassed, you-can-stop-anytime-now face, and rubbed his forehead with his thumb and index finger as Annie laughed.

"By the time Bryant left Boston to begin his MBA program at Loyola, there was a sliver of hope that he might move on from Dungeons and Dragons to women. By spring break, he appeared to be making up for lost time!"

This time it was Annie who shifted uncomfortably in her chair. Bryant shot a level warning stare at his best friend. Without missing a beat, James continued.

"When I came out to Chicago two summers ago, hoping for a few days of debauchery with Bryant as a tour guide, he instead introduced me to his recently steady girlfriend, Annie. My dreams of well-earned hangovers faded away, replaced by riveting coffee shop discussions and Trivial Pursuit rounds with Bryant, Annie, and Annie's friends."

Almost imperceptibly quickly, James winked at Audrey, who just as quickly averted her eyes.

"Not really my thing," James conceded with a bad-boy shrug, "but even so, I wasn't stupid. The way Bryant looked at Annie told me that I would be back in Chicago soon enough, wearing an exceptionally uncomfortable tuxedo, and wishing my best friend and his new bride all the best that life has to offer." With that, James tipped his head toward Annie, and tipped his beer toward Bryant.

"Cheers."

Guests clinked their glasses at the smoothly delivered and blessedly brief speech, while Bryant stood and grabbed James's shoulders in a timeless man-hug. As James took his seat, relieved that the moment was over, Madeleine and Audrey stepped up to the microphone.

"Hi Everyone! I'm Madeleine, and this is Audrey," Madeleine said, gesturing to her right with a smile, "and as Annie's best friends, we are having great fun as her Maids of Honor tonight!"

Audrey continued, "As Abbott College suitemates for four straight years, Maddie and I got to know Annie very, very well." As rehearsed, both women smirked at Annie, to make her wonder where this was going. "Of the three of us, Annie was the most emphatic about only dating men from the area, and avoiding the 'coasties' populating nearby Loyola at all costs."

Two tables away, Candice Treymont narrowed her eyes.

"So much for that!" Madeleine interjected. "Annie had a long list of 'only's.' She only dated men who were funny,"

"Check." Audrey said, miming an exaggerated X on an imaginary clipboard.

"She only dated men who showed empathy for social

26

justice issues,"

"Check." Audrey mimed again, as guests smiled.

"And she only dated men with impeccable manners."

"Che… um… what about…?" Audrey paused for drama, and almost managed to keep a straight face. Annie hid her smile behind her napkin, seeing exactly where this was going now. Bryant closed his eyes.

"Oh, that. We're getting there." Madeleine mock scolded, with mirth dancing in her eyes. "Apparently Annie decided to allow an exception. After discharging a rather impressive list of hopefuls –"

"And who could blame them? The girl *is* gorgeous!" Audrey interrupted with rehearsed Hollywood drama, waving an arm up and down a suddenly self-conscious Annie as if she were a prize on a daytime TV game show.

"After discharging a rather impressive list of hopefuls for infractions such as answering a cell phone in a restaurant, chewing gum while talking on the phone, interrupting sentences, bad breath, bad nails, or mild dandruff,"

Madeleine paused just long enough to offer a triumphant smile before Audrey took over.

"She kept her second date with Bryant even after he threw up in her car."

Annie's cheeks turned a raspberry color she laughed so hard. Bryant, whether playing along or genuinely mortified, put his forehead right down on the table. College friends who knew the story laughed and bumped beer bottles. Older guests appeared appropriately bewildered.

Madeleine wrapped up the vignette. "As it turned out, Bryant wasn't feeling well a few hours before his first date with Annie. Knowing what a lucky, lucky man he was to have this dinner reservation with our best girl,"

Maddie and Audrey smiled at Annie, who shook her head and wiped a tear of laughter from the corner of one eye.

"He kept the date. He thought an afternoon nap and a

bit of the pink stuff would help him hold his game face. As the lab tests later confirmed, salmonella doesn't care if she's the 'One.'"

Guests burst into laughter, entirely at the groom's expense. Madeleine and Annie waited for the laughter to subside, lowered their voices a bit, and softened their tone.

"Audrey mentioned that over the years, we've gotten to know Annie well. That's true, but I'm not sure that conveys it. We've become sisters. We love you, Annie." Madeleine looked away to compose herself, and Audrey gently stepped in.

"We're a little freaked out that one of us is married now," Audrey joked, looking down at her dress, "and I'm not sure I look good in this shade of blue. But no doubt about it, he's your 'One'. His car exorcism didn't scare you off, and we, fabulous trio that we are" – Audrey and Madeleine flashed wicked grins at the groom – "didn't scare Bryant away, so that settles it. We love you both, and we wish you happily ever after!"

As guests began to return their attention to their meals, Madeleine locked damp eyes with Annie, concluding in a voice thick with emotion, "Wherever life takes us, we will always be here for each other."

Lobster Quiche

Sauté one slice of finely chopped bacon and ¼ cup of diced onion until bacon is crisp and onion is translucent. Set aside (do not drain). Combine 3/4 cup milk, 2 beaten eggs, 1 cup shredded Gruyère cheese, and 1 cup diced, cooked lobster. Fold in bacon and onion mixture.

Spoon mixture into mini, pre-baked pastry shells. Bake quiche in a preheated 325 degree oven for 25 minutes or until a knife inserted into a quiche comes out clean.

24 YEARS

"Thank you for calling Baxter, Corbert, and Smith. How may I help you?"

"Audrey! Where in the Sam Hill are the documents for my 8:00 a.m. meeting with the team from Fletcher Marketing Group?"

Audrey flinched at the harsh tone as she scrolled rapidly through her planner. "I apologize, Mr. Baxter. I'll bring the documents down myself. Give me 15 minutes."

"Damn it, Audrey, I need that information *five minutes ago*. Put a move on it!"

"OK. I'm sorry, Mr. Baxter." By the time Audrey had muttered her boss's name, he had already hung up.

Audrey closed her eyes. Just a few months ago, leaving Klein Bridgman & Company had sounded like such a smart idea. After all, Baxter, Corbert, and Smith had an esteemed reputation in the world of international business negotiations. Reputation, ha. At the ground level, the only thing Audrey had managed to learn so far was that pompous, insufferable businessmen apparently lived on every continent.

Moving rapidly among the hardware in her office, Audrey managed to locate, download, print, collate, three hole punch, and bind the documents that were so urgently needed down the hall. As she sprinted toward the conference room, binders tucked under one arm and heels clacking on the marble floor, she glanced at the clock on the wall. Seven minutes, she mused. Not bad. She knocked softly as her heart raced.

"Come in."

Audrey smoothed her charcoal grey suit jacket and stepped purposefully into the room, hoping she looked more competent than she felt. "Your documents, Mr. Baxter." She set the binders on the oversized, polished mahogany table near her boss's coffee mug.

"Thank you, Audrey. That will be all." Mr. Baxter didn't bother to look at her as she turned and left the room.

Closing the door softly, Audrey turned and clipped down the inner corridor toward her office. With each step, her mood grew increasingly surly. Abruptly, she stopped outside the office door of Mr. Baxter's personal secretary.

"Jan, do you have a minute?"

"Sure, what can I help you with?"

Audrey glanced sheepishly at the smiling, impeccably dressed, middle aged woman and marveled at how Jan was able to shift her attention toward the door without slowing whatever she was typing by even a fraction of a second.

"I'm embarrassed to admit this, but I left Mr. Baxter in a bit of a lurch going into his meeting this morning."

Jan cringed and spoke to Audrey with mild admonishment. "That's the last thing Mr. Baxter needs today. We all need to perform at one hundred percent, particularly when we are short staffed."

"Short staffed?"

Jan stopped typing and looked pointedly over her glasses. "Yes. Margaret apparently felt the need for a mini vacation and called in sick today."

Audrey frowned in concern, remembering how stressed Mr. Baxter's other assistant had seemed lately.

Audrey couldn't help noticing how Margaret had been spending many of her lunch breaks on the phone with pediatricians and her son's second grade teacher over the past week or two. "Is her little boy OK?"

"This isn't about her son," Jan snapped. "This is about everyone doing the job for which they were hired. Now, what happened with Mr. Baxter?"

Audrey winced. "The thing is, I honestly didn't realize that he even had a meeting scheduled. Was this a last minute addition, or am I going crazy?"

"Mr. Baxter asked me to move a few appointments around, to squeeze in Fletcher Marketing Group today." Jan's face held a quizzical expression.

"That would be the meeting." Audrey deadpanned.

"Isn't it in your planner?" Jan asked.

Audrey scrolled through her planner again. "Yes. It's there. It looks like it was added... at 6:57 p.m. yesterday?"

Jan raised her eyebrows at the questioning tone, clearly seeing nothing wrong with the last minute change. "Mr. Baxter must have assumed you would check your calendar. You are salaried, yes?"

Aghast, Audrey opened her mouth and quickly closed it again. Salaried, yes. Enslaved, no. Realizing that the distinction was open to interpretation, Audrey remained silent. She had bills to pay.

"Is there anything else?"

"No. Thank you, Jan." Audrey stepped back into the inner corridor, and rubbed the bridge of her nose between her thumb and forefinger as she hurried toward the relative refuge of her office. After coming in early for a pre-breakfast briefing, Audrey had worked almost 12 hours the day before, skipping lunch to meet a deadline. "I must have left minutes before that planner update was posted," Audrey grumbled under her breath. "I took a bath instead of checking my planner when I got home. Shoot me." Safely inside her office, she closed her door with a gratifyingly sharp kick.

Audrey pulled a bottle of pain reliever from the top drawer of her desk and shook two tablets into her hand. She swallowed them without benefit of a glass of water, and checked the time. 8:16 a.m. It was going to be a long day.

After a typical morning of packing five hours of work into four hours of time, Audrey grabbed her coat from the back of her door and headed toward the elevators for lunch. As often as possible, she preferred to leave the building. Despite Chicago's frequent high winds and nasty winter weather, the fresh air helped Audrey to clear Baxter, Corbert, and Smith from her head.

As Audrey stepped out onto the bustling sidewalk of the Magnificent Mile, a sharp, early spring breeze tousled her curly hair playfully, causing the frazzled young woman to smile for the first time all day. She strolled right past The Grand Lux Café and never even glanced at the opulently dressed windows of The Omni, her eyes focused on a much more delectable noon hour feast. Arriving at her destination, Audrey's smile brightened even more.

"Two Chicago Dogs with the works, please!" Audrey fished around in her substantial, designer handbag for her Italian leather wallet.

"My kinda' girl!" The vendor laughed, instantly recognizing one of his most regular customers. Taking advantage of the rare lack of a waiting line of customers, he slowed his pace as he added yellow mustard, bright green pickle relish, diced onions, thick tomato wedges, a generous dill pickle spear, and a pair of yellow banana peppers to each of the all-beef hot dogs, finishing his work with a generous dash of celery salt. He passed the paper trays to Audrey in his right hand, accepted her cash in his left, and took a chance.

"When's the last time you hung out at Navy Pier?" He smiled at her expectantly, revealing a small dimple on his tan, slightly wind burned cheek. Dark hair poked out at odd angles from underneath his grey wool skullcap.

"Huh? Navy Pier? Um, probably in college." Audrey frowned at her own thoughtless remark. She glanced at his shirt. "Vincent," his name tag read.

Vincent was undeterred. "Two, three times a week you grab lunch and hurry off to the benches over there," he confessed as he waved his hand in the direction of four, wrought iron park benches surrounding a small historical marker. "Any girl who can scarf down two dogs with that much gusto would have fun hanging out – after work – at Navy Pier."

Audrey didn't know whether to be flattered by his interest, turned off by his forwardness, or mortified by his understanding of her nutritionally devoid food habits. "Uh…" was all she managed.

"Boyfriend?" Vincent offered her a face saving escape.

"No, not exactly," Audrey replied before wanting to kick herself for her honesty. Truth be told, her dating train was parked at the station, and was beginning to rust. Whenever that train took off, Audrey sulked, a wreck was sure to follow.

Vincent grinned, sensing that her hesitation was due to general awkwardness rather than personal disinterest. Being a hot dog vendor was a bit like being a bartender. You learned to read people pretty well. "Think about it, then. See you later this week!"

Audrey managed a smile. "Have a good day, Vincent." She started toward the benches, but turned back toward her office instead. She was hungry, but didn't feel like eating with the hotdog guy watching her. Heck, maybe she should go to Navy Pier with the hotdog guy. He certainly seemed more fun than the assortment of stuffed shirts with whom she interacted at work. It's not as if she had any other commitments.

Finding an open bench outside of her building and away from the hotdog guy, Audrey plunked down and savored her first few bites of lunch. She groaned at her cell phone when it rang, and groaned at her Chicago Dogs after she saw the caller ID. Oh well. It wouldn't be the first time she ate a cold lunch. Audrey answered the phone.

"Hi Gram!"

"Audrey! I'm glad I caught you. I haven't heard from you in a few days."

"Sorry Gram. My boss is keeping me on my toes lately, but I always have time to talk to you. I'm glad you called." It was true. Audrey's grandmother kept her grounded, and anyone passing by on the crowded Michigan Avenue sidewalk would have seen Audrey smiling into the phone.

"Do you still like your job so much?"

Audrey wished she could be honest. *No. No, I actually hate my job. I hate every meaningless second of hopping and jumping for people who think Chicago will crumble if anyone takes a 16-minute coffee break. Or a 7 p.m. bubble bath.* That's what she wanted to say.

"It's in my field. The pay is decent, and there's room for advancement." It was all she could say without lying. Audrey wanted to add, *if I'm willing to genuflect every time someone wants me to work a 15-hour day*, but worrying her grandmother would be pointless.

"I'm so proud of you, Audrey."

Ugh. Making her grandmother proud was one of the reasons Audrey didn't follow through on her frequent daydream of walking out of her office and never coming back. "Thanks, Gram."

"Your parents are proud of you, too." Audrey could hear the forced note in her grandmother's voice.

"If you say so, Gram. Did I tell you Annie's pregnant? She's due in November." Sometimes, changing the subject was the best approach.

"Really! Well, that's wonderful. Please send my congratulations. Audrey, your parents are taking me out for dinner next week, for my birthday. Will you come, too?"

Oh, hell. Dining with her parents would be hell, or at least the equivalent of facing The Inquisition. After the morning she had, Audrey was in no mood to even think about dealing with an evening of pointed questions about the state of her godliness, virtue, and chastity. But it was Gram's birthday.

"I have a better idea. Are you free on Friday night? This Friday? Can I take you for dinner, just you and me?"

Audrey's chest tightened when she heard her grandmother's disappointed sigh.

"Well, I was hoping…"

"Please, Gram? This will be more fun. It'll be like a girls' night!"

"Sure, Audrey. If my favorite career girl wants to take me for dinner, well, I won't complain about that."

"Thanks, Gram. It's better this way. And we'll have fun."

"I know we will, Audrey. Just remember, I don't know how to eat with sticks. I need a fork."

Audrey laughed. "Got it, Gram. Forks. Can I ask you a silly question?"

"Anytime. What?"

"Do you like Chicago Dogs?"

Rolling laughter came through the phone. "Audrey honey, why do you think I never followed my girlfriends down to their fancy resorts in Florida? Do you think you can get a decent Chicago Dog in Florida?"

In an instant, Audrey knew her stressful morning was fully behind her. "I love you, Gram. See you Friday!"

"Don't forget my fork. And don't work too hard."

25 YEARS

She heard his snow boots clomping down the hallway a few moments before the lock turned in the door. Drawing her blanket up around her chin, Madeleine did her best to unclench her eyebrows and sock away the scowl on her face. It wasn't his fault. She heard him kick his boots onto the rubber snow catch with a whump and a thud. He was still brushing the ice and snow from the hood of his parka as he entered, sprinkling droplets of icy water all over the floor.

Damn Iowa winters.

As the front door of their tiny apartment closed, Andrew took a moment to absorb the scene. The piano consuming the bulk of their living room was closed, and sheet music was strewn about the floor. Overly strewn, he noted. There was Maddie, huddled up on the couch, massaging her hands silently as a familiar, faint menthol-eucalyptus odor tinged the air. Her hot cocoa mug was on the end table, next to a bottle of ibuprofen. Steam still seeped out of the teapot on the stove, next to the tiny countertop adorned with a bottle of Bailey's Irish Cream Liqueur. She hadn't bothered to replace the screw cap.

Andrew walked behind the arm of the couch and

leaned over Madeleine to sprinkle little kisses over her hair and along the side of her neck. Reluctantly, she smiled.

"Rough day?"

"I've had better. Fenwick. I might kill him. The prison sentence would be easier than this degree program."

"Sorry." No surprise, he thought to himself, the magnificent Dr. Reynold Fenwick had managed to get under her skin. Again. He didn't understand why she put herself through this – why she put both of them through this – but he knew the routine, and spared her the lecture.

"You want to talk about it?" He asked rhetorically, as he opened the refrigerator and scanned for a pre-dinner snack. Maintaining conversation, if you could call it as much, wasn't difficult. UI graduate student housing was cheap, but it wasn't exactly spacious. If they actually set a wedding date, Madeleine occasionally reminded him, they would be eligible to apply for a two bedroom unit, tacking on an additional and desperately needed 150 square feet. Meanwhile, they were limited to the 512 square foot shoebox that passed for a single student dwelling. Andrew wasn't even on the lease.

"I'm still fighting with Liszt. Fenwick is relentless about my perfecting Liszt. He's entirely unconcerned with the reality that, while I have healthy hands as far as women are concerned, Liszt had freakishly long hook hands and I do not. I can't hit the damn tenths straight on, no matter how much he yells, or in what language."

It felt good to commiserate with her fiancé, to air her frustrations out loud, even though she knew Fenwick annoyed him. Madeleine chugged down her cocoa and stomped the six feet to the tiny kitchenette for a refill. Two long glugs of Bailey's, hold the cocoa. Andrew shuddered, silently.

As an aspiring businessman whose musical education began and ended with recorder lessons in the 5th grade, it had taken Andrew a good deal of time and patience to follow these one sided conversations. Liszt, he understood, was none other than 1800's Hungarian composer Franz Liszt, famous for his technically difficult piano pieces. So difficult were they, in fact, that Liszt himself revised many pieces twice, as pianists lacking his enormous hands – and that would include almost all pianists – simply did not have his 13-key span. Even the revisions, however, included 'tenths', or note combinations requiring one hand to hit keys ten spaces apart simultaneously. Very few pianists could manage to hit tenths precisely.

Madeleine, through years of practice, gallons of analgesic hand cream, and sheer determination, could come amazingly close. She had mastered the art of rolling tenths, or hitting the keys within mere fractions of a second of one another, so that most ears were completely deceived. Reynold Fenwick did not possess most ears.

Dr. Reynold Fenwick, Endowed Professor and Chair of the School of Music at the University of Iowa, was the reason they were here, freezing their behinds off in the less-than-bustling metropolis of Iowa City in January. Fenwick was equally famous for his brilliance as a classical pianist and his refusal to accept more than two graduate students at a time – the bare minimum required by the University to maintain his tenure. He was particularly disdainful of Master of Fine Arts students, as he very vocally considered an MFA to be a cheap substitute for a Doctor of Musical Arts degree. This attitude didn't exactly win him invitations to the dinner parties hosted by his colleagues, and he couldn't have cared any less.

Whether due to a restful night's sleep, an exceptional cup of coffee, or the unseasonably warm weather was anybody's guess. For whatever reason, Fenwick deigned to sit in on the prospective student auditions one Tuesday afternoon, three Aprils past. He scribbled and scratched rapid, arpeggiated bars of music through several brief performances, concentrating entirely on the chords in his head and not at all on either the Steinway Concert Grand sitting stage left, or the nerve-wracked hopefuls futilely seeking a smile, a nod, or a fleeting second of eye contact before scurrying away. Advisors were assigned to MFA students through a matching process, where prospectives invited to audition ranked their top three choices of faculty, and faculty ranked their top three choices of students. Almost half of the prospectives listed Fenwick in their top three and Madeleine was no exception, even though reputation held that it was a waste of an opportunity for a match.

Somewhere around the fifteenth or twentieth second of Madeleine's audition, Fenwick abruptly stopped scribbling. He paused, expressionless, for just a moment... before closing his notebook and walking out, right in the middle of the performance. From the corner of her eye, Madeleine saw him leave and was crushed. She forced herself to complete her concertina, and managed to leave with all of her grace and most of her dignity intact. What she didn't see was the scribbled note Fenwick passed to the stunned audition coordinator on his way out.

The note simply read, "Madeleine LaBlange. My student. RF."

Fenwick's incorrigible, irrational, irritable self was the reason Madeleine had begged, pleaded, and creatively convinced Andrew (in the bedroom more than anywhere) to spend his first years after completing his hard earned MBA building a résumé not in New York, or even Chicago, but in the smack middle of corn land. He loved Madeleine, but he hated Iowa. He hated Reynold Fenwick.

"I'm sorry, sweetie." Andrew placed a gentle kiss on her forehead, knowing that only time and another mug of that cloyingly sweet, creamy liquor would bring her around. "I picked up the mail on the way in. Here." He handed her a slender bundle of coupon fliers, bulk mailings, and one pale green envelope.

Madeleine absentmindedly picked through the bundle, smiling – finally – when she recognized the handwriting. Tearing open the envelope, her smile widened.

"It's their announcement card. I've gotta' admit, Annie and Bryant make cute babies."

Andrew glanced obligingly over her shoulder. "Hell of a name to saddle a kid with."

Madeleine contemplated the tiny face of Josiah Bryant Anderson Treymont, 8 pounds and 3 ounces, surrounded by a blue blanket. It was almost the same blue as those bridesmaids' dresses, Madeleine mused. It felt like Annie's wedding was last weekend, and here it had been over two years. Things had sure gone well for Annie. The last time they talked, she had already been promoted within the hematology lab at Northwestern Memorial Hospital, and arranging maternity leave had gone surprisingly well. Of the three suitemates, Annie had always been the one to speak of children with longing rather than fear in her voice. Madeleine studied the tiny face again, and reflected upon her own inability to remember to water the plant that had sat next to her piano. A few months earlier, she finally gave up and threw the pitiful brown, withered specimen in the community compost bin.

From what Annie reported in their brief phone conversation, Bryant was happy with his position at Tribune Company. Despite the famously long hours, or perhaps because of them, he was on a fast track to at least a mid-level executive position. Not bad for a guy in his mid-20s working for the largest multimedia corporation in the United States. The only dark spot seemed to be Candice, who still treated Annie like a wad of gum stuck to the bottom of her designer shoes. Annie tried to be nonchalant about her mother-in-law, but even over the phone Annie's voice revealed a desperate hope that the arrival of a grandchild would soften the woman. *Good luck with that*, Madeleine thought.

"Can you believe it's been over two years since the wedding? I haven't heard from Annie or Audrey in a long time. I wonder how Audrey is doing," Madeleine mused as much to herself as to Andrew. Annie hadn't heard from her, either.

"Then you should call them. It's ten digits each. Not complicated." Andrew settled on a leftover piece of pizza and a chunk of baked ham that, he gambled, was probably still fresh enough to eat. His tone unnerved Madeleine.

"We OK?" Madeleine asked, shifting her body so that she faced him directly.

"We haven't won the Publishers Clearinghouse Sweepstakes yet, but yeah, I'd say we're OK." Andrew made a face as he took a bite of ham, and tossed the remainder into the garbage.

"It's just… last night…"

He kissed her forehead again. "Yesterday was my rough day, like today is yours. That's all. How about you dump the rest of that mug of syrup down the drain," Andrew waved his hand at her Bailey's, "and we shake off our days at Romeo's, over fettuccini alfredo and mediocre house wine?"

Madeleine smiled. "Give me five minutes to freshen up!"

"Make it six, and wash your hands. No offense, darling, but you smell like a nursing home."

As she ran a brush through her long hair and slipped into an attractively snug, green scoop neck sweater, Madeleine couldn't shake the previous night from her mind. She had woken up pleasantly enough somewhere around two thirty in the morning, with Andrew nuzzling her neck. He felt strong and warm against her, and they had made love, slowly and gently at first. She smiled at the memory of being so comfortable against him as to resist fully waking. Their bodies fit well together.

He became insistent about looking into her eyes, jostling her fully awake with an unexpected urgency. His expression, she recalled uneasily, was unfamiliar. Much later, as he held her close and assumed her to be fast asleep, he whispered almost sadly, "Why are we here?"

What on earth did that mean?

Still baffled but feeling overly analytical in the light of day, she shrugged it off and grabbed her purse on the way out the door. Suddenly, she felt insatiably hungry.

At precisely 6:30 a.m., Madeleine entered the empty building and quietly unlocked the door to her practice room, set down her lidded mug of coffee, and stripped off her heavy wool coat. Almost immediately upon arriving at the UI School of Music, Madeleine had staked out the scratched up Steinway Parlor Grand in room 121A as her own, for the duration of her studies. The keys of the old piano were more fickle than many aspiring pianists prefer, but when handled well, the overall tone was rewardingly rich. Madeleine felt up to the challenge of coaxing beauty out of the old beast. Room 121A happened to be the nearest practice room to Fenwick's office. For that reason alone, the other music students were happy to let her have it.

Her routine was always the same. She sat on the edge of the bench in the blessed quiet, barely placing her hands on the keys, and moved her fingers in silent meditation. She played the first notes in her mind, moving her fingers without pressing the keys, over and over and over. Her eyes opened and closed, her shoulders moved almost imperceptibly, and the smooth muscles of her forehead moved this way and that, mere fractions of an inch. She had been attempting to perfect *Trois Caprices Poétiques* to Fenwick's satisfaction for months, and the first of its three etudes, *Il Lamento*, was beginning to stir inside of her. The thought that Liszt had put these notes to paper in the 1840s, and the notes had endured through generations, humbled her. She viewed her performances as equal parts art and history, and strove meticulously to honor both.

Eventually, when the music filled her head and pumped through her heart, her fingers depressed the keys and the music she had been creating for several minutes, occasionally an hour or more, was allowed to fill the air.

She was scarcely aware of the pattern. It was simply how she conceived of the music.

"May I ask what we are lamenting this cold and snowy morning?"

The familiar voice startled Madeleine so completely that she knocked over the coffee seated next to her on the bench. At least the lid held, she thought to herself.

"Do you ever knock?" She tried to look angry, but couldn't help the upward pull on the left side of her lips at the sight of him.

"Do you ever sleep?" Derrick chided in return. Derrick Haughton, who presently filled her doorway with his rangy, six foot frame and big, goofy grin, had become her dearest friend in the often catty and competitive halls of the School of Music. He was a year ahead of her, and would likely still be toiling away when she left, as Fenwick's other graduate student and the only one pursuing a doctorate.

"Not until Fenwick gets off my ass about these etudes," Madeleine said with a resigned frown.

"From what I heard, you just rocked *Il Lamento*. Your key changes were flawless, and never mind Liszt, your chromatics sounded like Chopin himself! Let's celebrate with muffins from The Daily Grind. My treat."

"Will you be my new advisor?" Madeleine asked with a sigh, and grabbed her coat for the walk to the student union coffee shop.

"Ah, Fenwick loves you, Maddie. Not as much as I do, but he's harmless."

"I'm not always sure of that, Derrick. He torments me, and is either oblivious to it or worse, knows what he's doing and doesn't give a shit. I feel like live on a seesaw of gratitude and fear. I'm grateful, usually, that the Great Reynold Fenwick, for reasons I will never understand, took me on as a student. I don't question his brilliance-"

"Nobody does, Maddie. That's why we suffer."

"I don't question his brilliance or the heavy weight of

his professional reference. He could make my career -"

"Mmmhmm." Derrick's forward leaning posture, slightly tilted head, and over attentive stare made him resemble a Labrador retriever for a moment. Or a genuine best friend.

"He could make my career, or he could break it. He can be cruel, Derrick. Callous, insensitive, OK, I can pull on my big girl underpants and deal with that. But he's so nasty sometimes. I don't understand why he took me on as a student, or why he keeps me, if he thinks so little of me."

"Is that my cue to point out the obvious?" Madeleine scowled at the bemused Labrador face. Derrick ignored her and continued. "If he thought so little of you, he'd send you back to Chicago faster than the door could hit the backside of that adorable Tahari skirt."

"It's a knockoff, $29.99 at TJ Maxx," Madeleine laughed.

"A lady never tells. In any case, you know as well as I do that Fenwick wouldn't bother to mentor anyone out of kindness or pity. He 'keeps you,' as you put it, because your talent and your commitment blow him away. It takes both, you know. I don't think he sees both very often. And here," Derrick paused for dramatic effect, lavishly gesturing back and forth between the two of them, "he has not one but two rising divas! A toast to Fenwick, the lucky bastard!"

Madeleine couldn't help laughing out loud at the absurdity of it all.

They sat together silently for a while, devouring peach melba muffins and 20-ounce lattes at the last empty table in the shop. Madeleine offered Derrick a grateful smile. He knew that Fenwick's relentless criticism of her latest repertoire additions was wearing on her, and the friendship Derrick had built with Madeleine helped her to hold on to her increasingly fragile self-confidence.

Derrick brushed a lock of toffee brown hair from his eyes and, hesitating slightly, touched her hand as she set down her coffee. "I don't mean to pry, Maddie, but is everything else OK? With you and Andrew?"

Madeleine was startled by the question, and simply opened and closed her mouth.

"I'm sorry. Really, I should shut up. It's just, well, I saw the two of you at Romeo's last night. Ethan and I went out for a beer at The Dublin Underground on Dubuque Street. We walked right past the window where you were seated, and were going to pop in and say 'hi' but, you both just looked so, distracted. I'm sorry. I've really overstepped, haven't I?"

"We're fine, Derrick, really. Between his job, which he hates, and my… well, you know my soap opera with Fenwick, it's just been a tough few days." Madeleine forced an extra dab of conviction into her reply.

"OK. In that case, I declare a game night. Why don't you bring Andrew over tonight for Trivial Pursuit and dinner? Ethan works until 6. I'm sure I can convince him to conjure up something wonderful to eat."

"Um, I'll have to check with -"

"C'mon," Derrick lightly jabbed the side of her ribcage. "We'll play girls against boys. I'll wear my lucky socks. We can't lose." He beamed at her, waiting.

After a few seconds, Madeleine gave up and let out a deep belly laugh. She remembered how, a year earlier, Andrew became increasingly annoyed with her frequent, casual references to her obviously growing friendship with some guy named Derrick. She also remembered the first time she dragged Andrew to game night, and the 'wow-am-I-stupid' look on his face when he realized that Derrick was not only attached, but madly in love with Ethan.

"We'll be there. Thanks, Derrick, for everything."

"Looking forward to it, Maddie." Derrick glanced at the giant wall clock shaped like a steaming mug of coffee. "It's almost 9. You have an appointment, yes?" He didn't comment when she closed her eyes for an extra second before scooping up her coat and the remnants of her breakfast.

Taking a deep breath, Madeleine knocked on the door marked *R. Fenwick* in large brass letters. The small, smoky glass window revealed nothing from the outside in, not that she would have dared to peek anyway. Just above the door handle, a small handwritten sign read "No custodial service. Thank you."

"Come in, Ms. LaBlange." It always surprised her that he knew who was standing on the other side of the door, without bothering to glance through the window. Then again, she supposed, he didn't receive many unexpected visitors.

His office was equal parts inviting and imposing. Office wasn't the right word, exactly. When the door closed behind her, she felt as though she were standing in a private library tucked down a long wing or up on the third floor of an extravagant home. A private library owned by a wealthy man with extraordinarily refined taste, she conceded. While the room was large for a university office, it wasn't overly expansive, maybe 18 by 25 feet. It simply felt larger, as though the décor and the man demanded and created more space.

A well-worn, honey-colored leather couch rested against the rich almond colored wall to her left, anchored with an intricately woven, slightly faded Turkish rug in shades of apricot and small, oblong walnut coffee table. A large watercolor print, unfamiliar to Madeleine, hung above the couch and was reflected in the oblong, antique mirror adorning the opposite wall. Music staff paper covered half of the walnut table, resembling something between a purposeful stack and a careless heap. An exceptionally small, obligatory desk crouched against the right wall, almost as if it were trying to hide behind the door. The metal folding chairs behind and in front of the desk were embarrassed by their own presence, and had been neglected for so long that they forgot their own purpose.

The commanding centerpiece of the room was the piano – the most heart-stoppingly magnificent piano Madeleine had ever seen. It was centered in the back of the room in front of a tall, narrow window framed in rich ivory brocade. It exuded an aura of having grown organically from the floor, as if the only purpose of the room was to provide it suitable shelter. At nearly seven feet in length, the piano appeared majestic and imposing.

Even though she had entered this room many times, the piano never failed to capture her attention. It was an antique Steinway & Sons Rococo Model B, one of the finest instruments ever built by one of the most well-reputed piano builders in the world. Knowing that Fenwick was not one for small talk, Madeleine had researched the piano herself. She learned it was built in the 1870s, as evidenced by the intricate carvings on the legs and lyre. The finish was an extraordinary Brazilian Rosewood, upon which the natural light from the single, tall window at the back of the room danced.

Madeleine suspected the ornately carved bench with the padded leather seat was custom built to accommodate Fenwick's imposing frame. She also suspected the value of the instrument was over twice his annual university salary.

"Good morning, Dr. Fenwick," Madeleine offered with a respectful nod.

"*Il Lamento* is coming along well, yes?" It was more of a statement than a question. After his verbal abuse last week, he damn well knew it would be perfect by now.

"Yes, Dr. Fenwick. I can show you how I've -"

He stood up and walked to the ugly desk while she stood in the door frame. She hated when he dismissed her like that, left her standing awkwardly for impolite stretches of time, but was used to it. Madeleine had learned enough about his odd personality to assume it was not deliberate. He poured a cup of coffee from the pot on his desk, and slowly walked over to far left cushion of the couch and sat.

He did not offer her a cup. He never did.

"Sit," he said simply.

"At the –", She gestured toward the folding chair, confused as to exactly where he intended for her to go.

"No, sit." He repeated, gesturing toward the other end of the couch.

A bit bewildered, she walked over and took a seat on the far right, with the center cushion offering a bit of breathing room between them.

"Play," he said simply. He pushed the coffee table sideways, so that it sat off center to the couch and directly in front of Madeleine.

"Dr. Fenwick, I don't –" She started to explain how utterly baffling his cryptic instructions were becoming, but he cut her off yet again. His tone, however, was more quiet and patient (dare she think of him as patient?) than usual.

"Play like you do in the morning, in your head. In your silence. Here." He gestured to the coffee table.

Madeleine felt unnerved and strangely exposed. What was he talking about? How did he know about her private routine? She glanced at him, strangely, as if she had never seen him before. She leaned forward slightly, placing her fingertips on the walnut table as if they were ivory keys. She felt completely, utterly absurd.

"I'm making you uncomfortable." It was a direct statement rather than an apology, but she noted that he paused carefully.

"I can hear in your notes, Ms. LaBlange, the careful rehearsing, but I don't actually hear you rehearse. Not frequently, anyway. That means you are rehearsing here," he tapped the top of his head sharply before running his fingers through his collar length, sand brown hair.

Madeleine noticed faint strands of silver, the only sign of his age other than the thin lines near his eyes and in the center of his forehead. He was in his early 40s, she mused. Young for the reputation he had earned and carried well throughout the music world, yet almost old enough to be her father. Sort of. Distracted, she shook away the thought.

"And here." He placed a large hand across the center of his chest, crushing the cashmere of his charcoal grey sweater. "So, play."

Madeleine shifted her attention back and began to move her fingers across the table. Tentatively at first, then earnestly, her wrists settled into their perfect form, at once perfectly balanced and appropriately relaxed, as her fingers glided across the walnut. He watched her hands impassively, and startled her with a forceful "There!"

Madeleine lifted her hands abruptly and straightened her posture.

"Back up four measures, and start again."

Unbelievable, Madeleine thought to herself. *He's actually following the score of this air piano ruse?* She was discombobulated and impressed. Mostly impressed. Hesitantly, she backed up four measures and began tapping the notes on the polished wood.

When she approached the tenth – she already knew that's where he would stop her – he whispered "Freeze." It was strange to hear him whisper, and stranger still the word he chose, as it conjured up an out of place image of children playing tag on a playground.

He slid over on the couch just a few inches, not crowding her at all, but placing himself within comfortable reach of the table. Without a word, he hovered his left hand over her right and glanced warily at her, as if seeking permission. He nudged the inside of her wrist to angle her hand ever so slightly left, and tugged down on her thumb with his little finger, creating an open space resembling a backwards L.

He glanced at her again, and she didn't say a word. In two years of study, two years of pouring herself into her art, their art, and two years of being mentored by this impossibly walled off man, she realized this was only instant in which they had actually touched. She didn't realize that she held her breath.

With his own thumb, he pushed up hard on her little finger while continuing to anchor her thumb.

"Ow!" She yelled angrily, more startled than hurt by the abrupt and uncomfortable stretch.

"A tenth," Fenwick announced simply. "You are capable of a perfect tenth. Now play the damn tenth." With that, his quiet politeness vanished and the edge in his voice returned.

Something burst inside of Madeleine, completely and abruptly. In a flash, she knew that she was going to either yell or cry, and she most certainly was not going to cry in front of Reynold Fenwick.

"You know, I'm very, very sorry you have made such a grave mistake." She looked him right in the eye, something she rarely did for more than a second or two. Her voice rose.

"Apparently you have been wasting your time on me for the last two years, as I am failing to live up to your impossible standards. You see, no matter how many hours I practice, how many hours I study, how many hours I spend trying to perform to the satisfaction of the Great Doctor Reynold Fenwick, I fall short. Shame on me," she choked, "for failing to grow giant hulking man hands in my sleep."

Her voice was red as a hot poker now, and she did not divert her eyes. He held them steady, watching and listening, his face completely devoid of expression. She continued,

"I hate Liszt. He's overly complicated and impossibly unyielding, just like you. I hate that of the thousands of composers upon which I might begin to build a repertoire, the most brilliant pianist I have ever heard and the only one whose opinion I value is completely and utterly hell bent upon my suffering through compositions that I can play, but not to his satisfaction. I'm beginning to hate the piano. I'm beginning to hate –"

"Ms. LaBlange."

He spoke only her name, very softly, and she snapped out of her rage. Instantly, her shoulders lowered and her complexion dialed down from scarlet to snow.

"Oh. My God. I'm so, so sorry."

Fenwick stood up slowly, walked to his magnificent piano, pulled out the bench, and motioned for Madeleine to come over and take a seat. Madeleine flushed again, and stammered.

"But that's... I've never... It's your... I've only played on the student pianos, Dr. Fenwick. I would never presume to –"

"Perhaps it's time you stop playing that piece of shit in your practice room, Ms. LaBlange." She couldn't help but offer a weak smile, and very nervously took a seat in front of what she fully understood was the love of his life.

"*Trois études de concert*, Ms. LaBlange." He motioned to the keys.

"Which etude?" She asked, confused and still embarrassed.

"All three. Simply start at the beginning, Ms. LaBlange."

"All –" Oh hell. She wasn't prepared for this, but she sure wasn't going to argue with him now. Madeleine lowered her hands to the keys and began to play.

She worked her way through the long and lyrical *Il Lamento*, the fast and light *La Leggierezza*, and the dramatic *Un Sospiro*. Madeleine knew the quick key changes, the transitions between tempos, and the famously complex handwork in her soul. Where Liszt wanted Beethoven, she put forth Beethoven. Where Liszt emulated Chopin, she offered Chopin. But through the entire three etudes, she created something else, an artistic sum greater than the parts of the musical score. She created Madeleine LaBlange, concert pianist. Her performance was flawless.

After she hit the final note, she sat frozen in silence with her hands still resting on the ivory keys.

"That will be all." Fenwick said quietly.

The rush Madeleine felt dissolved into a cold slap. She took a moment to gather herself, stood up with great dignity, and escorted herself to the door.

"If there is nothing else, I'll see you tomorrow, Dr. Fenwick." Madeleine didn't look back as she closed the door behind her.

Reynold Fenwick ran his hands through his hair, cursed under his breath, lay down on his couch, and closed his eyes.

Peach Melba Muffins

In a large mixing bowl, combine the following ingredients: 1 cup white flour, 1/3 cup whole wheat flour, ¾ cup rolled oats, 1/3 cup sugar, 2 ½ teaspoons baking powder, and ¼ teaspoon salt. In a separate mixing bowl, whisk together 2 egg whites, ¾ cup cream, ¼ cup oil and ¼ cup fresh raspberry puree. Add wet ingredients to dry ingredients and mix with a fork until just combined. Fold in 1 cup diced fresh peaches.

Spoon mixture into 12 standard size muffin cups lined with six inch squares of butcher paper. Top each unbaked muffin with a sprinkle of sugar and one fresh raspberry. Bake in a preheated 400 degree oven for 20 minutes. Enjoy with a friend while commiserating over a disagreeable boss or surly professor.

26 YEARS

The garage door opened with a loud rattle, and Bryant knew the clock had started. Deep breath in, deep breath out, shoulders squared, smile in place. Reaching over to the passenger seat of his Nissan, he slipped the plastic shopping bag onto his forearm and gathered both his computer bag and morning coffee mug in the same hand. He had exactly 60 seconds until pandemonium erupted.

The instant Bryant opened the door between his garage and his home, a high pitched "Wengh! Wengh! Weeeennnngggghhhh!" assaulted his ears. Peering nervously into the house, he saw Annie standing with her back to him, bobbing slightly up and down, trying to soothe the writhing, wet faced source of noise.

"Hi, honey." It came out sounding more like a question than a greeting, but he was pretty sure the smile he applied in the garage was still in place. He walked quickly into the kitchen to deposit his bags onto the counter and his mug into the sink, followed closely by his wife.

"Come here, little guy," Bryant crooned in his Dad Voice, lifting Josiah from Annie's arms. The seven month-old wore a red, one piece romper with an embroidered fire truck on the chest and two sticky Cheerios attached to the end of one sleeve. Thinking of the wail of a siren, Bryant found the outfit appropriate.

"Wengh! Wengh! Wen," the baby sniffled, quieting as he patted his daddy's face with chubby little fingers. "Da. Da. Dadada."

"Of course. Well, that just about figures." Annie rolled her eyes.

"I don't think you cry during the day at all," Bryant teased his son. A few seconds later, he realized the burning sensation behind his shoulder was from his wife's pointed glare. He turned toward Annie.

"I'm kidding, babe." He kissed her forehead. "I'm sorry you had such a rough day. What did the pediatrician say?"

"Dr. Hoover said there's nothing to worry about." Annie snorted. "She said that while most babies outgrow colic by the time they are three to four months old, a small number of babies give the gift of screaming their ever-loving heads off until they are a full year old."

"And we have a little gift giver?" Bryant asked reluctantly.

"It appears that way," Annie replied in a resigned voice. Despite the effort she put into her carefully applied concealer, light dusting of blush, and lip gloss, Annie looked flat worn down. Bryant could see it in the angle of her shoulders and the corners of her eyes. He wished she had agreed to take a longer maternity leave. He remembered the argument over her possibly risking advancement opportunities at the lab, and tried to be supportive of her new, second shift schedule. The simple fact was that the combination of two career ladders and one colicky baby was brutal.

Suddenly, Annie smiled and darted over to give Bryant a kiss.

"What was that for?" He asked, surprised.

"Rocky Road! You remembered!" Annie finished

unpacking the few items in the grocery bag sitting on the counter, pulling a spoon from a drawer to sample a big bite from the half gallon container of ice-cream before placing it in the freezer.

"Of course I remembered," Bryant stated amusedly. "A guy tends to remember when the woman he loves makes a habit of creating human beings out of a binary diet of saltine crackers and Rocky Road ice cream."

When the phone rang, Annie glanced at the caller ID and curled her lip. "I'm not touching that," she said to Bryant, lifting Josiah from his arms and walking out of the room.

Bryant glanced at the caller ID, although his wife's facial expression had already told him all he needed to know. "Hello?" He spoke into the receiver.

"How are you, darling?" His mother's syrupy voice inquired.

"Fine, Mother. I just walked in from work, actually."

"How is that little promotion of yours working out? Have they put you in a real office yet?"

Bryant clenched his teeth and ran a hand over his jaw. "My 'little promotion' came with a hell of a lot of responsibility and a nice pay raise. Some days the two don't feel quite in proportion with one another," he admitted, "but overall things are going very well. I know that surprises you, but it's true."

"Calm down, darling, I'm just trying to make small talk." Candice chuckled softly into the phone.

"How is it that every discussion about my career is 'small talk' to you? I love you, Mother, but it's patronizing. You, of all people, should know that."

"I, of all people, grabbed the best opportunities for my career whenever they presented themselves, even when I had to reach, darling."

Yes, he remembered the reaching. The moving around, constantly changing schools and saying good-bye to neighborhood friends before finally landing in Boston, so that his mother could build her blessed career.

"My best opportunities are Annie and the children. My career helps to support us. I enjoy my work, which I consider a bonus, but it's not my first priority."

"Children?" Candice asked with trepidation.

"Yes, Mother. That's why I've been trying to reach you. I wanted to let you know that Annie and I are expecting another baby, next January." He braced himself.

"Congratulations."

"Thank you. Your enthusiasm is overwhelming."

"Oh, don't act like that. If you want the responsibility of a big family, well, I'm happy for you. I was calling to tell you about an exceptionally good employment prospect."

"Mother." Bryant's voice took on a menacing edge. Candice continued, undeterred.

"Do you remember Phil Hopkins?"

"No." Not that Bryant was trying very hard to dredge his memory.

"Phil worked for me about 15 years ago at The Baltimore Sun, when I was supervising new projects in their corporate planning division. He was brilliant, and stayed in touch with me after he moved on. You don't remember him?"

"Nope."

"For heaven's sake, Bryant. His daughter used to babysit you."

"Fiona? Yeah, I remember." Bryant's eyebrows arched in surprised reflex. Fiona Hopkins... that name hadn't rolled around in his head since his teenage years. But man oh man, back when he was 13 that name lingered in his head for a full year. Well, not just her name, it was also her... Bryant smiled and shook the memories of his own budding adolescence away.

"He works in corporate development and strategy now, and is looking to build a long range planning team. It's precisely your area of expertise. He contacted me to see if I had any recommendations."

"Mother, every corporate manager clinging to a middle rung is trying to assemble a team of some sort to heave them up to the next level. I'm not interested in –"

"Phil is a Senior Vice President."

"Oh. Well, in any case, Tribune Company is one of the largest media corporations in the entire –"

"With the New York Times."

Bryant let out a low whistle. Candice, to her credit, didn't let her smile show through the phone.

"I don't understand. I'm pretty in tune with media encroachments in the Chicagoland area, and I didn't realize that the Times was planning to expand in this vicinity."

"Bryant, don't be ridiculous. The opportunity is in New York, obviously. The compensation package would be more than adequate to move your little family into a suitable neighborhood, with money left over to invest and begin building some real wealth. Better late than never. You would finally be able to –"

"Enough!"

"What did you say to me?"

Bryant sighed. "That will be enough, Mother. I love you, and I appreciate your concern, but you aren't listening to me, and you need to. I have a career. My wife has a career. We are building a life together in Chicago. I will not condescend to suggesting to Annie that we pack up and move because it's what you would have done at my age. You and I are different people, Mother."

"Obviously," Candice sniffed. "I was just trying to help."

"I know that." Bryant ran his hand over his face. "I need to get going, to take Josiah so that Annie can get ready for her shift at the lab."

"You don't even have a *nanny* yet?" Candice practically squealed into the phone. Bryant sighed again.

"I love you, Mother. Good Bye."

27 YEARS

"What can I get started for you today?" The barista asked with a smile.

"Medium, nonfat, two-pump peppermint latte, please, and a chocolate cherry scone." Audrey pushed a lock of hair away from her eyes and fished around in an oversized bag for the MasterCard in her wallet.

"That'll be $8.74 please."

Audrey scowled and handed her card to the smiling barista, whose nametag identified her as Kendra. Then Audrey scowled again. It wasn't the fault of the minimum wage earning barista that airport price gouging was so ridiculous. She fished around in her carry-on bag again, this time for a dollar bill to add to the tip jar on the counter.

Audrey stepped down the counter a few feet, toward the raised oval surface where prepared beverages were claimed. She was just slipping a cardboard sleeve onto her cup and looking around for a plastic lid when she heard the intercom announce her flight.

"We will begin pre-boarding Air Portugal flight 8431 with service to Pico Island, continuing to Terceira. First-class passengers, passengers flying with small children, and passengers requiring assistance are invited to step up to the jetway at this time." Strange foreign words followed, which Audrey deduced were the same instructions in Portuguese.

Flushed after hurrying through the crowded terminal from the overpriced coffee stand to her gate, Audrey shoved the little paper bag containing her bakery into the outer pocket of her Kate Spade carry-on, and withdrew both her boarding pass and a small vial. Balancing her coffee cup precariously on the rim of the recycling receptacle against which she stood, she opened the vial and removed two Dramamine capsules. Tossing the vial back into her bag, she swallowed the capsules with her coffee, and stiffened her shoulders against the burning sensation of the hot liquid. Next, she fumbled around in the front pocket of her sand-colored Chinos, and withdrew her black terrycloth Sea-Bands. After more coffee cup acrobatics, she managed to pull the Sea-Bands onto each wrist so that the cone-shaped, white plastic nub of each was pressing firmly into the tendons of the inside of each wrist, precisely three finger widths up from the base of her palm.

Absentmindedly, Audrey reached up to run her fingers over the small palm tree charm that hung around her neck from a thin silver chain. She had purchased the little silver tree on a spring break trip with her best girlfriends, and considered it something of a good luck charm. She wondered briefly if Annie and Madeleine still had theirs. Finally, she confirmed that an empty plastic bag still sat, neatly folded in a readily accessible location in her carry-on, just in case.

The intercom rudely interrupted her own pre-flight boarding ritual.

"We will now continue boarding passengers in the main cabin, beginning with the rear of the aircraft. If you are seated in rows 18 and higher, please step up to the jetway at this time."

Taking a deep breath, Audrey presented her ticket to

the gate agent, walked down the long and gradually descending jetway, closed her eyes for a split second at the threshold of the aircraft, and walked on board to claim seat 30C, an aisle seat near the lavatory. She peered ahead to make sure the unlucky holder of the middle seat hadn't beaten her there and tried to pull a switcheroo. Sometimes that happened, she thought to herself. Her row was empty, much to her relief. She stuffed her bag into the small floor space underneath the seat in front of her, and shimmied into what would be her very own six cubic feet for the next nine hours.

"That's my seat, miss." A balding, modestly overweight, middle age man gestured into Audrey's row. He was clutching a tissue, and judging from his red nose and slightly puffy eyes, was suffering from either bad allergies or a cold.

Audrey stepped out into the aisle to accommodate him, hoping upon hope that he wasn't assigned to the middle seat. He stuffed himself against the window. Before Audrey could sit again, a frazzled looking man with close cropped hair hurried toward the back of the aircraft and, smiling apologetically, pointed at the middle seat. He appeared to be about her age, and had an olive drab canvas bag slung over his shoulder. She waited while he hoisted the bag into an overhead compartment, extracted a paperback book from the side, and slipped rather uncomfortably into the sliver of upholstered and overpriced real estate between Audrey's chair and the man auditioning for the next Sudafed commercial. Audrey perched herself next to him, trying valiantly to shift her weight toward the open aisle.

"Hi there! My name is Dale and I'll be invading your personal space for the next nine hours!" The man in the middle seat thrust out his hand toward Audrey, with a goofy grin. His smile faltered as Audrey simply stared. Finally, Audrey recovered her manners.

"Hi. Audrey." She shook his hand and offered a faint

smile. "Sorry. I'm a bit of a nervous traveler is all. Dale, you said? Nice to meet you, Dale."

In the stilted conversation of strangers, they engaged in small talk about cramped seating, flight delays, and the inevitable, mediocre, mile high meal. Audrey wasn't feeling particularly chatty, but Dale's comments were a welcome diversion from the flight attendant's creepy speech about oxygen masks and floatation devices, so she played along. Quickly, it seemed to Audrey, their conversation took on the natural intonations of two people who were more or less comfortable with each other.

"Are you stopping on Pico, or continuing on to Terceira?" Audrey asked. She studied him for an absent moment, put him at about five foot eleven, noted his athletic build, and observed how he was well groomed in a decidedly no nonsense, closely shaved with no cologne manner. *Nice*, she nodded to herself inside of her head. She noted the small scar along the left side of his jaw.

"Terceira. I'm Air Force, stationed there. Just returning from leave, to see my family in Rockport." Audrey glanced at his left hand and noticed he wasn't wearing a ring. Dale noticed, too.

"My parents and my old dog live in Rockport, and my high strung little sister drove home from Southern Illinois University to round it all out," he clarified. "I'd rather have gone to Lisbon or Madrid for a month, but it would've broken my Mama's heart. And that would have royally ticked off my Dad." Audrey smiled at the image he painted.

"My younger brother thought about military service, almost signed the papers. What do you do in the Air Force?"

"I'm a cook. Why'd your brother change his mind?"

"He hates to exercise, and has a growing affinity for 'herbal' cigarettes. A cook, huh?"

Dale laughed. "Sounds like your brother made a wise career decision. Yeah, being a cook is a pretty good gig.

Twelve years in, eight years to go. Predictable hours, decent working conditions if you don't mind smelling like cheeseburgers at the end of a shift, and a pretty low chance of getting shot. That's more than many people in uniform can say."

Twelve years in. That would put him at 30 years old, she guestimated. "I can't argue with that. How long have you been in Terceira? Do you like it?"

"Just over a year. I have another eleven months to go on this tour, and I'm hoping to extend. The Azores are spectacular. Is this your first visit?"

"Sort of." Audrey fumbled for an explanation.

"Sort of? Is that like being 'a little bit' pregnant?" Dale blushed at his own comment. "Sorry, dumb attempt at humor. But more on point, have you traveled to Azores before?"

"No. I'm here on business, sort of, so it's more like a temporary move than a visit. If I seem awkward, it's just that I'm realizing – at 30,000 feet – how I really have no idea what I'm getting myself into."

"Business?" He was curious, but didn't want to pry.

"I work, or worked, I'm not quite sure how to define it yet, in international public relations. The corporate thing is getting old, so I took a leave of absence and am working on a project for my alma mater. I'm acting as a liaison between Abbott College and *Universidade dos Açores*. My goal is to establish reciprocal semester abroad opportunities for undergraduates at both institutions. It will take a while to learn the cultural topography, if you will, and... this is why I am not the center of attention at parties. You asked the time, I build you a clock, or some other cliché. Sorry."

"No, really, continue. I enjoy hearing about projects that don't involve acronyms." Dale smiled.

"Acronyms?"

"A Crazy Roundup of Nonsense You Must See. BDUs, MREs, TDYs, take your pick. Even on a good day it's

FUBAR, and on a bad day, well, BOHICA."

"What?" Audrey was completely lost.

"I'm sorry," Dale laughed. "I guess I'm a bit apprehensive about getting back to work, and am being crass. Suffice it to say that communicating in the military is like learning a foreign language. Do you speak Portuguese?"

"*Não muito bem*. I'm working on an online crash course right now." She looked embarrassed.

"Ah, don't worry about it. I'm not familiar with the university, but generally speaking the locals are friendly as long as you are respectful. Many of the younger residents speak English."

"I'm counting on that, at least until I immerse myself in the language long enough to become functional. I'd rather not tote around my pocket translator all year!"

"All year? It takes a whole year to arrange a trade of foreign exchange students?" Immediately, Dale regretted what may have come across as a patronizing remark. He had a history of being awkward with small talk, which unfortunately correlated with his history of being awkward on first dates.

"Well, maybe not, but I'm not in much of a hurry." Audrey shrugged in an aloof manner, but her voice suggested that both the question and answer were uncomfortable.

"Excuse me, can I get you something to drink?" Saved by the flight attendant.

"Diet Coke, no ice," sniffed the red nosed man by the window, turning his head away to cough.

"I'd like to purchase a Heineken, please. And one for my seatmate, also, if that's OK?" Dale glanced at Audrey, questioning. Audrey nodded politely.

Dale handed his American Express card to the flight attendant, who returned it along with two cold beers and bagged assortments of peanuts, pretzels, and little biscotti cookies.

"To new adventures?" He raised his bottle tentatively.

"Absolutely!" If the first hour was any indication, Audrey's new adventure would be pleasant enough. As she finished her beer and a tiny handful of twisted sourdough pretzels, the Dramamine kicked in with enough force to lull her into pulling her cardigan sweater tightly around her shoulders and closing her eyes.

When her sleeping tangle of curls found its way onto Dale's shoulder, he motioned for a blanket from the flight attendant, and managed to cover Audrey without disturbing her at all.

"Alright boys, *sopas* on!" Vanessa called to Dale and Miguel as Audrey moved the steaming pot of *Sopas Do Espírito Santo*, or Holy Ghost soup, from the stone kitchen to the rustic wooden table on the small veranda. The aromas of beef and chicken, potatoes and cabbage, all bathing in a heady, garlicky broth thickened with marrow and crusty bread, were more than enough to convince the men to leave their football in the grassy field where they had been blowing off steam and come to the table instead.

"Yes, Mom!" Miguel answered with a laugh and reached between the women to carry a plate of *massa sovada* biscuits and *Ihla* cheese from the narrow countertop to the table. Dale poured generous glasses of locally produced *vinho de cheiro* to round out the meal.

"This is fantastic," Dale announced in between happy slurps of *sopa* and hearty gulp of wine.

"That's because we're awesome. You sure are lucky to be enjoying such a fine dinner with ladies who tolerate your company." Audrey laughed and clinked glasses with Vanessa.

Miguel winked mischievously. "Eh, I'll give the company a 6. But the food sure is better than the shit that passes for dinner in the chow hall."

"Hey, easy there!" Dale scolded. The food jokes got old. The chow hall might not be the epitome of fine dining, but he took pride in his work. When he noticed the sun beginning to set over the beautiful, rolling landscape beyond the veranda, he corrected his mood.

"I would like to make a toast," Dale offered, raising his glass, "to women who cook and give their phone numbers to strange men on airplanes!" Everyone laughed and sipped their delicious Portuguese *vinho*.

"What can I say? You didn't look like an axe murderer, and I was in a gambling mood." Audrey smiled and tipped her head back to watch the sunset, letting her dark curls fall back over her shoulders.

"Will the two of you just hook up and get it over with?" Miguel snorted.

"Go to hell, Torres," Dale snapped, slipping back into his On Duty voice.

Vanessa rolled her eyes and pushed her chair back from the table, intent on procuring another bottle of wine. She wasn't sure if the wine itself was really that good, or if an otherwise mediocre flavor was boosted by this fine Azorean sky, but she didn't really care.

"Oh, baby, you didn't tell him, did you?" Audrey batted her eyes ridiculously at Dale, speaking in an absurd sugarpie voice for comedic effect. "Well, anyway," she continued, leaning forward provocatively and stage whispering, "can I have my panties back?"

Vanessa laughed from the kitchen as both men smiled and shut up. "Down, boys. Keep it in your pants." The women rolled their eyes at each other, refilled their glasses and moved from the table to the canvas patio couch. The women settled in put their feet up on the hassock as they watched Dale and Miguel walk off the veranda to resume their football toss.

"Miguel's right. You really aren't sleeping together, are you?" There was surprise in Vanessa's voice, not because the question might be ill received - she and Audrey had grown close enough over the last six months to ask – but because most of Dale's colleagues just assumed they were an item.

"The friends with benefits thing doesn't work for me, and I'm not looking for a relationship." Audrey sipped her wine.

"Bad experience back home?"

"Bad experiences, plural. The few long-term relationships I've indulged in morphed into disasters, and if I'm brutally honest about it, the only common factor has been me. It's tough, seeing friends from college getting married, who've managed to figure it out. Hell, my friend Annie just had her second baby! But I'm not willing to throw myself out there, trying to rope in a guy because a clock's ticking, or some crap like that." Audrey was starting to feel her *vinho*, which only made her take another sip.

Vanessa watched her carefully for a moment.

"That's too bad," Vanessa said. "Dale's an attractive guy, and housebroken, too. He'd be a good catch, for someone into that sort of thing."

Audrey looked at her quizzically, before Vanessa stood up to refill their glasses.

Half a lifetime seemed to have passed in the six months since landing in Terceira, Audrey mused. Meeting Dale on the plane had been a blessing. Not knowing another soul in Terceira, Audrey was happy to have a willing acquaintance to show her around. Remembering how her hair smelled as she napped against his shoulder, Dale was perfectly agreeable to spending his off duty time as a tour guide and rough interpreter. He also introduced her to Miguel and Vanessa, with the former of whom he shared living quarters and the latter of whom he shared a chow hall kitchen. Audrey worried that Dale resented her obvious 'let's be pals' cloak, but he seemed more or less content to have a friend off base with whom he could forget the responsibilities that came with his rank and simply enjoy his down time.

Dale asked around, and helped her find this adorable

cottage. Mr. and Mrs. Trigueiro, the elderly couple who owned the small dairy farm on roughly ten acres of land near the center of the island were happy to rent the old building to Audrey at a very fair long-term rate. Their singular condition was that she attend Mass every Sunday. They were open minded enough to rent to a foreigner, even a single woman, but drew the line at heathens. Audrey considered the long services laden with interactive rituals to be a fascinating cultural experience and, smiling inwardly at the quaint charm of the sincere requirement, readily agreed. If nothing else, the guaranteed weekly comingling with locals improved her Portuguese.

Audrey's new home, for that is how she considered it, was approximately 600 square feet of open space. The stone walls were exposed on the outside but mortared and whitewashed on the interior, both for aesthetic appeal and to discourage the mildew that favored the damp, salty air. A small generator provided electricity for the two burner stove and mini refrigerator when needed. Audrey purchased her food fresh from a local vendor every morning, and usually left the refrigerator unplugged. Opposite the kitchen wall, a small stone fireplace anchored the sitting area. It was an efficient design, as the cottage was small and the climate mild enough that the fireplace was plenty adequate for both heat and light.

The open space was furnished with a small wooden table flanked by two benches, a comfortable futon couch, and a cane-style rocking chair. Near the door stood a narrow bookcase, sparsely stocked with an odd combination of Readers Digest and Cosmopolitan issues courtesy of the Base Exchange, as well as an imposing looking Portuguese Bible. The stone floor was warmed with a very large, round, rag rug woven in shades of blue and gold. A rather intimidating, painted wooden statue of the Blessed Virgin stood atop the bookshelf when Audrey moved in and, as the owners stopped by to visit from time to time, Audrey thought it best to leave it in place.

Opposite the door and next to the futon couch, a sturdy wooden ladder offered six steps up to the petite loft where Audrey's sleeping area was perched. The smooth wood surface was just large enough to host a very comfortable featherbed topped with a quilt created by Audrey's dear grandmother, one of the only family members with whom she maintained regular contact. A rather rickety shelving unit held Audrey's modest wardrobe and a few creature comforts, including a photo collage and a battery powered satellite radio.

A small vase of blue hyacinths stood in the corner. The color reminded her of Annie's wedding, and made her slightly homesick for her college girlfriends. In one of her weekly phone calls, Audrey's grandmother had mentioned that a birth announcement had arrived in the mail. Annie's a mother now, times two. Audrey rolled the idea around in her head to see where it fit. Then she wondered when Madeleine's inevitable wedding invitation would arrive, and hoped she would be able to swing the airfare to attend.

Audrey's home was neither as modern nor as spacious as the accommodations her friends were afforded on base, but the cottage provided them with a welcome and comfortable escape from their military environment where, even off duty, the rank structure and cliquey politics could be suffocating. She was delighted that her home provided them with such respite, as they certainly provided her with welcome companionship.

Dale came running up the field and onto the veranda where Audrey and Vanessa lounged, football under his arm and perspiration dotting his forehead. "Miguel and I are thinking of going into town for the bullfight. Wanna' come along?"

Tourada à corda, as it was locally called, wasn't bullfighting in the more commonly understood, Spanish sense. The Azorean sport was decidedly more humane, and involved guiding a tethered animal through a crowded square. Observers goaded on by their own *vinho*-fueled bravado occasionally taunted the animals with their coats or other clothing, but injuries were uncommon. Nonetheless, leaving their quiet and airy space for a square that would undoubtedly be crowded with large numbers of men screaming in Portuguese held little appeal for either of the women. Vanessa looked sideways at Audrey to confirm.

"Nah, go on without us, but first build us a fire," Vanessa said. "Who knows, maybe you'll get lucky without us hanging around." Vanessa smiled at her own joke while Dale grimaced.

"I think I speak for both Miguel and myself when I say, with all due respect, that we would rather get lucky with you. Having said that, we'll take what we can get." He walked over to the covered stack of firewood and selected a few large wedges, then reached for a small bucket of kindling. Building a fire was a small price to pay for such a fine dinner.

After a few minutes inside the cottage, Dale peered back outside. "Done, unless my favorite damsels in distress require any other services?" He winked and started to walk toward the road in front of the cottage, where Miguel was waiting.

Dale turned back toward Vanessa. "If I swing by and pick you up around midnight, will that work?" They had all three arrived in Dale's grey Honda Civic. It was an old beater of a car with a broken heater and shoddy upholstery ruined by the previous owner's dog, but the island was small and the car served its purpose efficiently.

Vanessa glanced at Audrey, who waved Dale away. "I don't work until midshift tomorrow – can you pick me up in the morning instead?"

"Sorry. I work at 0400."

"Don't worry about it," Audrey said to Vanessa. Calling to Dale, she added "I'll drive her back." Base was the opposite direction from the university, but again, the island was small.

"OK then. Thanks for dinner, Audrey!" Dale and Miguel drove off, no doubt more interested in finding young Azorean women than in finding a tethered bull.

"Thanks for letting me crash here," Vanessa said.

"I'm happy to have the company, you know that." Audrey replied. She and Vanessa had become good friends and half-roommates of sorts, with Vanessa spending many of her off nights in Audrey's cottage.

"Dale and Miguel are good guys. Most of the guys I work with are good guys. I like my job, usually, but the environment is so…"

"Male?" Audrey filled in the obvious.

"Male, yes," laughed Vanessa, "and guarded. It's cool to joke around, but nobody gets serious, you know? Nobody talks about being homesick because you miss your Mom or your dog, or about not being homesick because maybe your family sucks, or about being lonely, or not knowing your next steps in life, or –" Vanessa shook her head and tipped back her wine glass. "The military is just not that kind of place."

"I miss my Grandma," Audrey stated quietly. "My parents, ah, not so much, and I don't have a dog," she joked weakly.

"It sounds like you have a complicated home life?" Vanessa tentatively questioned.

"You could say that. My parents are fundamentalist Christians. It's hard to talk about. I'm not anti-religion," Audrey quickly clarified, glancing nervously in the direction of the Blessed Virgin statue on her bookshelf. "It's just… they're religious in all the wrong ways. They live narrowly and literally according to scriptures that, to me, seem randomly hand-picked. They are unapologetically judgmental of most people, and particularly of me." Audrey shook her head sadly.

Vanessa frowned. "But not your Grandma?"

Audrey smiled. "No. Gram's awesome. She's a real

blessing – how ironic! She's acknowledged being 70 for about five years now, and volunteers every week at a neighborhood food pantry and a local public school. She's kind and compassionate, beautifully spiritual, but not indoctrinated."

"Then how…" Vanessa let her voice trail off, confused.

"My grandmother divorced her gambling addict husband when my mother was thirteen, and became a single mother back when not having a man in the house was something of a scandal. She joined a church, as she once explained rather bitterly, for the sake of community ties. Grandma thought it would be good for my mother, would provide stability and community, and so on."

"I sense a 'but' in the story somewhere," Vanessa said.

"But this particular church, at least according to my grandmother, turned out to be more than she signed on for. Grandma told me that one of her life's regrets was not leaving the church when she saw my mother being pulled in deeper and deeper. By the time my grandmother tried to actively intervene, my mother was well into her teens and rebelled, interestingly, by sinking deeply into fundamentalism. She married the proverbial Preacher's Son, and devoted her life to her new ideals."

"Her new ideals?"

"Obeying my father and male church elders without question or hesitation. Eschewing science everywhere she thinks it might conflict with scripture. Pulling me out of health class because chastity was the beginning and end of what she wanted me to learn about reproductive health. Pulling me out of PE because locker room immodesty was 'vile.' And on, and on, and on."

"Oh, wow. I'm sorry."

"In some ways, it worked out OK. They sent me to a religious women's college, hoping that it would straighten me out. Instead, it introduced me to a whole world of amazing women who knew they had more to offer than the ability to silently obey. When I realized I was never ever going to live up to my parents' image of a 'good daughter', I gave myself permission to stop trying. It was strangely liberating."

"How'd you end up here?" Vanessa asked, knowing there had to be more to the story than the rather low-level foreign exchange job.

Audrey shrugged. "How do we end up anywhere, I guess. Back in Chicago, I was stuck. I hated my corporate job, so I tried an MBA program thinking I could promote myself out of my misery. I hated the MBA program more than I hated my job. And dating, well, that was a horror all its own."

"Horror, huh?" Vanessa tried to add levity to the conversation. "I've had some lousy dates myself, but most of them would qualify as comedy rather than horror! Take, for instance, my date with Steve. He was polite, a good listener, laughed at my jokes... and answered not one, not two, but three phone calls from his mother during our first and only dinner date."

"Was she dying?" Audrey laughed.

"Yes. Dying an agonizing death over the very idea that her baby boy was alone with someone she hadn't pre-approved."

"Please tell me this was in high school?"

"It was a while ago, before I sorted through everything. But he was older – I think he was 32."

Audrey choked on her wine, and flopped her head on Vanessa's shoulder as they both laughed out loud.

"Oh, there's more," Vanessa continued. "Before Steve there was Brian, who made it his mission to make sure I memorized his weightlifting numbers in several different poses. Then there was Tyler, who concocted an astonishing number of excuses for leering forward and peering right down the neckline of my dress. Oh, and Evan – let's not forget Evan – who asked, with a remarkably straight face, if he could take me lingerie shopping on our first date so that he would have something to look forward to."

"Well, if I needed any further incentive to check out of the dating scene forever, I've found it!"

Vanessa laughed. "In hindsight, I was still deep in denial and was trying too hard. But what about you? Any breast peeping, musclehead panty collectors in your past?"

Audrey smiled. "I almost wish. It's just, never been there, you know? Take Dale, for instance." After an impressive quantity of wine, Audrey was as comfortable talking as Vanessa was with listening. "He's such a sweetheart. He's tall, buff, has a great smile and laughs easily, is a contributing member of society, and would be here in five minutes if either one of us needed anything at all."

"So, why is he at a bullfight with Miguel instead of tangled up there?" Vanessa asked, pointing brazenly at Audrey's loft.

"Because, if I had a big brother, Dale would remind me of him. They all have."

Even through her wine haze, Vanessa paused on her next question. "Are you... have you..."

"No. Yes. Three men, three valiant attempts. Looking back, I'd give them – the attempts, not the men – a 2, a 4, and a 5." The 2 belonged to James, the best man at Annie's wedding, Audrey recalled with a shudder. She sincerely hoped the story never got back to the newlyweds. For her part, Audrey never touched a blue drink again.

"I may not be a sex goddess, but I read Cosmo," Audrey motioned clumsily toward her bookshelf, "and I know for damn sure that it's not supposed to top out at a 5. And I can't believe I'm telling you all of this."

Vanessa shifted uncomfortably, took a long look at Audrey, and a longer sip of her wine.

"You can tell me anything, and you know that." Vanessa gave her a hug and, for a fraction of a second, closed her eyes. "I know what will make you feel better. Be right back."

Audrey watched her dear friend walk into the kitchen area of the cottage, the light breeze catching her long blonde hair as she walked.

"Turtledoves!" Vanessa laughed as she returned with a small plate of confections artfully shaped from a simple recipe of sugar paste, vinegar, and water. Vanessa and Audrey had been turned on to this traditional Azorean delight the first time they stopped at a local market together and were offered a sample as a reward for their failed but charming attempt to communicate with the older gentleman behind the counter in his native Portuguese.

Audrey reached happily for one of the candies, smiling gratefully at her friend. She took a bite, shook her shoulders in honor of its deliciousness, and held out her hand to happily offer the other half.

Vanessa accepted, and caught the tiniest edge of Audrey's index finger in her lips along with the candy. An unreadable expression passed fleetingly over Audrey's face. Vanessa smiled serenely.

As the sun set on Terceira, the mild breeze carried the faint songs of crickets through the familiar, salty air. The fire which Dale had prepared before leaving crackled inside of the cottage, spilled soft light through the open doorway and sent warmly aromatic curls of smoke through the stone chimney into the Azorean night sky. The atmosphere on the veranda became equally thick and bewildering.

With a hand that trembled ever so slightly, Audrey reached for a sip of her wine. Swallowing hard, Vanessa reached over to brush a sugary crumb away from the corner of Audrey's mouth. Audrey shifted almost imperceptibly, so that Vanessa's fingers rested on her lips. Time froze as the women locked eyes earnestly, neither moving nor saying a word.

Vanessa moved her hand to tuck a stray curl away from

Audrey's flushed face and behind her ear. When she lingered there, her fingers dancing across Audrey's neck and sensing her quickening pulse, Audrey leaned over and into the warmest embrace and softest kiss she had ever experienced.

In that singular instant, Audrey understood why she had so desperately sought a fresh start, and why fate had pulled her over three thousand miles away, into the middle of the Pacific Ocean.

As the sun rose on Terceira early the next morning, the women were still tangled in each other's arms, their shoulders draped in long blonde waves and soft chocolate curls. Audrey had never before slept as comfortably or as peacefully as she did that night on the veranda.

Sopas Do Espírito Santo

Place 1 lb of beef bones on the bottom of a large stockpot. Top with 1 lb beef stew meat and 1 bulb chopped garlic. Cover with water and simmer for 1 hour. Add 1 pound cubed chicken and 2 chopped onions. Cover and simmer for another hour. Add ½ head of chopped cabbage and 4 cubed potatoes. Cover and simmer until potatoes are cooked through, approximately 30 minutes.

To serve, place a thick slice of buttered, stale white bread in the bottom of each serving bowl. Sprinkle chopped mint leaves over bread and cover with broth. After the bread has soaked up the broth, cover bread with cabbage and potatoes. Top with beef and chicken. Serve with red wine. Makes 8 hearty servings.

28 YEARS

"Do you remember what this is called?" Madeleine pointed to the symbol near the top of the staff paper.

"G clef?" The little girl hesitantly answered.

"Good! What else can we call it?"

"Treble clef."

"Excellent. And what about this one?" Madeleine asked, pointing to symbol underneath.

"Um, base clef?"

"Good job, MaryBeth. I can see that you've been practicing reading your music, and 'Hot Crossed Buns' is sounding terrific!"

"Thank you! I like your pretty flowers, Miss L." The little girl smiled at the vase of delicate, peach colored tea roses framed with baby's breath and ferns that was sitting on the top of the piano.

"I like them, too." Madeleine smiled.

"Where'd you get them? From a boy? Do you have a boyfriend? Is he nice? What's his name? Are you going to marry him?" MaryBeth looked up expectantly.

Madeleine laughed. "The pretty flowers are from my boyfriend, Andrew. He's very nice and yes, I'm going to marry him. Eventually. Are you ready to play your special song?"

The little girl smiled. She straightened up on the piano bench, scooting forward so that the toes of her pink shoes could reach the pedals. MaryBeth pursed her lips and positioned her hands over the keys exactly as Madeleine had instructed. As MaryBeth began to plunk down individual keys, she whispered the names of the notes quietly.

"C C D C F E." Pause. "C C D C G F!" Pause. "C C highC A Bflat F G, A A Bflat F G F."

Madeleine applauded enthusiastically. "Very, very nice! That's the best 'Happy Birthday' song I've heard in a long time. Your mom will be so surprised!"

The little girl blushed and smiled. "Thank you, Miss L. I want to be a good piano player, just like you!"

"If you keep practicing every day, you'll be famous!"

"Are you famous, Miss L.?" The little girl's blue eyes grew large.

"No," Madeleine replied, smiling. "But I sure love playing piano, just like you!"

MaryBeth gave Madeleine a spontaneous hug. At five years old, the little girl with long pigtails was her most enthusiastic student.

"We're out of time for today, MaryBeth. I'll walk you out to your mom, OK?"

The little girl opened the door to the practice room and darted down the hallway to the seating area at the back of the dusty music store. "Miss L. says I can be famous, Mommy! And she's going to marry Andrew, because he gave her pretty flowers! And I have a surprise for you, on your birthday!"

The mother smiled at Madeleine, handed her an envelope, and confirmed her daughter's next lesson date.

Madeleine glanced around the seating area as MaryBeth's pigtails bounced down the hall and out the door. Spotting a nine year old boy hiding earnestly behind a comic book, Madeleine called out, "Jack! It's your turn!"

The little boy's shoulders sunk. He reluctantly set down his comic book and followed Miss L. into the practice room.

"You said to keep tonight free for dinner, but I didn't know it would be all of this!" Madeleine smiled across the candlelit table as the wine sommelier filled their glasses and gently placed the bottle in a nearby cooler stand.

Andrew laughed. "Where did you think I'd take you, McDonalds?"

"I can down a Big Mac and fries like nobody's business. But seriously, I think this is the only restaurant in Chicago with three Michelin stars. Are we celebrating something?"

Andrew swirled his wineglass. "We are celebrating being back in a town – hell, being back in a state – that even has Michelin starred restaurants."

"Don't be a snob, Andrew. You remember as well as I do how we enjoyed lovely dinner dates back in Iowa."

"Yes. I remember how, by the time we escaped, the staff at all three restaurants with a decent steak and passable wine list knew us by name." Andrew surveyed the room approvingly, comforted by the brisk undertones of the business dinner conversations surrounding them.

Madeleine rolled her eyes and began to fidget with the solitaire diamond on her left ring finger. "I didn't think Iowa was all that bad," she said quietly.

"It was… an experience," Andrew stated sarcastically. "Our rent was practically free; that was a perk. At least the rent was in line with my wages at that damn seed company."

Madeleine stared intently into her wineglass.

"What?" Andrew asked, sensing the shift in his fiancée's mood.

"I get that you disliked Iowa, believe me, I understand. I wish you would understand that my degree program was important to me. Please don't make me feel bad about it."

"Hey, not my intention! I won't quit my day job when I audition for Comedy Central, OK?" Andrew raised his palms in the air in a sign of surrender.

"Deal." Madeleine hated these recurring discussions in which Andrew lambasted Iowa City and extolled the virtues of Chicago. His career took off like a rocket as soon as they returned. Hers, in contrast, more closely resembled a stalled engine. The number of underemployed MFAs in Chicago far exceeded the number of desirable jobs.

"How was your day at the music store?" Andrew asked, trying to change the subject.

"Eh, same old, same old. I had seven students today. Three children practically dragged in by their ears, with overbearing mothers who want me to turn their little darlings into the next Mozart. Three teenagers, two of whom actually have talent, and one of whom can't stop texting long enough to get through a composition. And MaryBeth."

"MaryBeth? Is that the spunky little girl you like?" Andrew divided his attention, eavesdropping on the nearby business dinner as Madeleine discussed her students.

"She's delightful. She likes the flowers you sent me. She thinks they're a good reason to marry you, as a matter of fact."

"Well, I'm glad she approves. I wouldn't want to get on little MaryBeth's bad side!" Andrew chuckled. "I'm glad you found something to keep you busy."

Madeleine opened her mouth and closed it. She swallowed her thought with a long drink of wine. Andrew was too busy surveying the room again to notice.

An unobtrusive, white jacketed waiter came and went. Madeleine and Andrew dined on filet mignon, smashed new potatoes with white truffle oil, and roasted asparagus tips as Andrew explained the intricate details of a project that had occupied most of his workday. His eyes lit up as he talked. His body language conveyed the confidence of a man aggressively driving his career. Madeleine thought of her dusty practice room at the music store and then pulled her attention back to the table, trying to look interested.

As they finished the last bites of their meal, Andrew flagged down a server for their check.

"No dessert?" Madeleine pouted.

Andrew glanced at his watch. "Actually, I have something else planned, and we'll need to pass on the crème brulee. I'll make it up to you." He stood to offer Madeleine his arm, and helped her with her coat at the door. As they waited for the valet to bring their car, Andrew reached into his suit jacket for an envelope. He waved the envelope ceremoniously, and kissed Madeleine on the forehead.

"Tickets?" Madeleine asked.

"To the CSO!" Andrew smiled nervously.

"You bought Chicago Symphony Orchestra tickets?" Madeleine asked incredulously. "For tonight?"

"Yeah. I thought you'd like it. Something Russian." Andrew shrugged.

"Rachmaninov's Piano Concerto No. 3." Madeleine laughed.

"But you haven't even seen the tickets yet – how did you know that?"

Madeleine rolled her eyes. "Really? Do you know which teams are playing on Monday night? I'm a pianist, Andrew."

"Then I guess this beats crème brulee?"

Madeleine offered a light kiss in response, and climbed into the car.

As the usher escorted them to the left center section at the front of the Symphony Center's Fadim lower balcony, Madeleine marveled at the quality of their seats.

She knew Andrew wasn't particularly interested in live orchestra music, and recognized how he must have spent a small fortune on these tickets. Her heart warmed at the gesture.

Midway through the first piano solo, Andrew reached for Madeleine's hand. That's when Madeleine realized that she had been playing along in the air over her thighs, much the way she used to warm up in her little practice room back at the U of I. She smiled sheepishly as she wove her fingers through Andrew's.

With her gaze resting languidly on the concert pianist, Madeleine thought back to her first experience with live orchestra music. She had been six years old and had gone to see *The Nutcracker* with her Girl Scout troop. While the other girls fidgeted in their seats, little Madeleine had sat utterly still, transfixed.

"I want to be a Nutcracker dancer when I get big, because Nutcracker dancers are magical!" Little Madeleine told her troop leader, Mrs. Moldenhauer, during the intermission.

"The correct term is 'ballerina,'" Mrs. Moldenhauer told her, smiling.

"Then I want to be a magical ballerina when I get big!"

Little Madeleine couldn't wait for intermission to end, she was so eager for the magic to resume. The six year-old girls seated around her, unfortunately, were more interested in poking and teasing one another. Frustrated, little Madeleine stuck her fingers in her ears. When they danced in silence, the ballerinas were somehow not as magical for little Madeleine. That's when she experienced the startling revelation that the magic she felt was in the *music*.

Smiling into her memories, Madeleine absentmindedly rubbed the back of Andrew's hand. Mrs. Moldenhauer had chuckled at the innocent suggestion that it must take a "very big radio" to make music in such a large theater. All these years later, Madeleine still appreciated how her troop leader had taken the time to walk her down to the main level of the concert hall and up near the stage, to see the orchestra pit.

Little Madeleine peered down into the pit, which most of the musicians had already vacated. However, a pretty yellow haired lady with dangly earrings was still seated at the great big piano. She waved and smiled up at the wide eyed little girl. Little Madeleine's mouth opened, she was so enchanted. Smiling, the pianist plunked out the first few bars from "Dance of the Sugar Plum Fairy." Just for little Madeleine!

From that moment on, Madeleine knew exactly what she wanted to be when she grew up. She wanted to be magical. Never mind being a ballerina. Little Madeleine wanted to be a "pianorina."

Slowly, Rachmaninov pulled Madeleine back from her memories. At first, Madeleine couldn't understand her seemingly misplaced emotions. She wanted to feel gratitude for Andrew's thoughtfully planned evening. She wanted to feel happiness and contentment, back in her hometown in a world class theatre with the man she loved. She wanted to feel whole, as she studied the look of blissful concentration on the featured pianist's face. But as she watched the woman whose fingers danced across the keys on the Symphony Center stage, Madeleine saw a reflection of her own dreams. When the concerto ended and the pianist stood to take a bow, Madeleine identified her misplaced emotions as the awful sensation of her own heart breaking.

29 YEARS

"I want to come, too. I don't want to stay home with Abby and Danny. They're just babies, but I'm big!" The little boy with soft brown eyes and shaggy hair looked up at his mommy expectantly. Sandy, the family's rotund and drooling beagle pup, whined pitifully in an attempt to help Josiah's cause.

"Josiah, I need you to stay and help Samantha take care of Abby and Danny. She needs your help." Annie kneeled at eye level with the little boy, which was not a comfortable task in a pencil skirt and coordinating, narrow, high-heeled shoes.

"Samantha is mean and not nice. Cocoa says he doesn't like her." The little boy held up Cocoa, his beloved teddy bear, for emphasis. When the teenage girl standing behind Annie smiled and raised an eyebrow, the little boy looked down guiltily.

"OK, Samantha is a little bit nice. But I still want to come, too."

Bryant extended a hand to help his wife straighten up, and scooped the little boy into his arms. "Tell you what, Josiah. How about if you stay home with Samantha, and as a reward for being a big boy, you can have an ice-cream sundae before bed?"

Josiah considered the offer, peering down at the teddy bear for his opinion.

"With chocolate sauce and sprinkles?" Bryant cajoled. Sandy barked.

The beaming smile on his son's face told Bryant that the offer had been accepted, and they would be able to leave the house blessedly tantrum-free.

"Thanks, Champ! You and Abby and Danny get so many of Mommy's hugs and kisses, sometimes I get jealous! So I'm going to take Mommy out for a grown-up dinner, and try to get a few hugs and kisses myself!" Bryant hugged Josiah and winked at his wife.

"Samantha, thank you for keeping your Saturday night free for us, we really appreciate it," Annie said. Samantha was the children's favorite babysitter, and knowing that Samantha's parents were right next door was an added comfort to Annie's new mom hormones.

"There are two bottles of milk in the fridge door for Daniel. He'll need one in about an hour before his bedtime, and the second if he wakes up after 10. To warm them, just set them –"

"In a bowl of hot water for five minutes. I know, Ms. Anderson. Don't worry." Samantha smiled, while Bryant shook his head at the long and familiar routine.

"OK. And Abigail can have a few animal crackers before bed –"

"But not grapes because they are a choking hazard, and Josiah should go potty before he goes to sleep." Bryant finished Annie's sentence for her, with his hands gently on her shoulders, still shaking his head and smiling.

"The cell phone is on, so if you have any concerns just call," he said to the babysitter. "And now, I am going to pry my lovely wife away from her children for a few hours." With that, he placed his palm on the small of Annie's back and guided her out the front door.

As they reached the passenger door of Bryant's black

Nissan Sentra, Bryant's blue eyes glittered mischievously. He abruptly spun Annie around and gave her a long, slow kiss. The setting sun cast a warm glow over Annie's auburn hair, and Bryant took a moment to drink her in. Annie tipped her head slightly back and to the side, examining her husband with a slightly embarrassed smile.

"Well, we both know Mrs. Ednanski is spying out of her living room window. We might as well give her something to look at." Bryant waved in the direction of the tidy blue house across the street and teasingly patted his wife's behind.

"Stop that!" Annie laughed, playfully swatting at his arm.

"Stop what? I love you. Have I told you in the last five minutes that I love you? The neighbors will just have to get used to the crazy idea that Suburban Dad loves Suburban Mom, won't they?" Bryant smiled widely, as Annie laughed again.

As Annie climbed in the open passenger door, she glanced into the backseat. "Bryant! You actually took the car seats out?"

"Of course I did. Just for tonight, let's pretend we're newlyweds again."

Bryant made the reservation for 7:00 which, even allowing for heavy downtown traffic, left them time to stop at Le Bar in the Sofitel Chicago Water Tower. The hotel was only a few blocks from Cice Estiatorio, and even if they were late, Mr. Gianopolous would surely hold their table.

"It's too bad we couldn't stay down here," Annie said absently, admiring the skyline as they completed their gas and brake pedal dance down the Dan Ryan Expressway.

Bryant whistled. "Babe, you do remember that the rent on our one bedroom on Chestnut Street was over two grand a month, yes? All 850 square feet of it?" He smiled tightly while Annie pouted. "Can you even imagine what the rent might run on a place down here," Bryant waved his arm across the dashboard toward the skyline, "that would be large enough to accommodate our three little darlings and their slobbery dog?"

Annie felt bad for bringing up a sore subject on such a lovely evening, and injected a bit of levity. "Well, I do enjoy entertaining Mrs. Ednanski, and I've got to admit, you look sexy pushing a lawnmower."

Bryant tried to keep a straight face, but his wife knew just how to tug the corner of his mouth upward. "Babe, if you think I look sexy pushing a lawnmower, I'd be happy to push one around the house!" He leaned for a quick kiss.

"Keep your eyes on the road, Andretti. I said I missed the loft, not the traffic."

As their car pulled up to the Sofitel, a handsome young doorman appeared quite eager to assist Annie and her very high heels out of the car. *There's something to be said for world class hotels*, Annie thought to herself while offering a flirty smile.

Bryant handed over his keys and a modest tip to the doorman as he offered his arm to his wife and led her inside. "You never fail to turn heads, particularly mine." He smiled and kissed her forehead.

Le Bar was occupied by a pleasant happy hour crowd, and growing more crowded with each passing moment. Bryant and Annie were able to secure the last two remaining seats at the bar. Perched on their high purple velvet chairs, they leaned slightly toward each other over the polished nickel bar. As they waited for their split of champagne, they took in the refined, minimalist atmosphere staged with soft lighting against a black backdrop with violet accents. The upscale, sophisticated room was filled with piped in jazz music just loud enough to attract a young, up-and-coming professional crowd. Bryant felt right at home. Annie's attention drifted to a conversation among three women in their early 20s, sitting further down the bar.

"Tapas and Korean both sound fantastic, so you pick,"

the first young blonde woman said to her friends.

"The tapas bar is closer, so we could save our cab fare for something sweet," the redhead laughed.

"Caramel appletini sweet, or tall dark sexy man sweet?" The second, more petite blonde inquired with a serious face.

"I plan to have both, since you asked," the first blonde joked, "but let's eat first."

"I don't know if I can eat in this," the redhead lamented, running her hand down the black stretch fabric covering her model thin abdomen. Annie grimaced downward at the slight new-mom tummy visible only to her own eyes, and suddenly felt less confident in her Vera Wang wrap dress.

"Honey, I don't think your tall dark dessert is going to notice whether or not you ate a whole side of beef, unless you manage to hook up with the one man in Chicago who can take his eyes off of those come-and-get-me shoes." Both blonde women laughed loudly.

Annie sighed. She remembered similarly ridiculous conversations between herself, Madeleine, and Audrey only a few years ago. The memory only made her sigh again.

"I'm sorry I've been such a mess lately," Annie said. Her clearly surprised husband started to scowl at her choice of conversation topics, so Annie continued hurriedly. "No, really, I'm not trying to bring down the mood, I just want you to know that I'm aware of my... unpleasantries... and I'm really trying hard. I appreciate you. That's all." She took a quick swig of champagne.

Bryant was familiar with exactly what she meant. The difficult birth of their third child, the breastfeeding problems she had experienced, and the post-partum depression that followed. Her physical discomfort and her emotional turmoil had been hard on them both. But Daniel was four months old now, and Annie was turning the corner. Bryant would do everything in his power to help her move forward.

"For better or worse," Bryant said simply, and raised his glass. "I love you, I love the children you delivered into this world for us, I'm thrilled to see you recovering, and I will make it my life's work to show and convince you that you are as beautiful and sexy as the day I pried you out of that lovely white dress."

Annie looked down and blushed, as Bryant quickly but noisily kissed her neck. Annie resolved not to waste any more time on the topic. They finished the split of champagne, and walked back through the hotel lobby on their way to dinner.

A demure hostess ducked into the kitchen just as Bryant and Annie walked through the front door at Cice. Before they had even walked the few steps up to the reservations podium, a finely dressed man in his 60s came sprinting out and captured Annie in what can only be described as a bear hug.

"*Omorfo mou koritsi!* My beautiful girl!"

Annie hugged him back. "Mr. Gianopolous, it's so nice to see you again! I hope you enjoyed your vacation," she said, referring to the week Mr. and Mrs. Gianopolous had recently spent at Annie's parents' resort in Door County.

"It was splendid as always. And how are the *morá*?" He asked, with all the pride of a genuine grandfather.

"The babies are well! They sure keep us busy," Annie smiled.

"And your *sýzygos*?" Mr. Gianopolous inquired with mock seriousness, winking at Bryant. "He treats you well? He makes you happy? He tells you that your eyes are more beautiful than the stars?"

"Well, I don't know about that last part –" At Annie's admission, Mr. Gianopolous put a hand over his heart and looked down his long nose at Bryant, with another fatherly wink.

"But yes, he treats me like a princess and makes me

happy. I think I'll keep him." Annie smiled and squeezed Bryant's arm, relishing the burst of attention from both men.

"Well, if you change your mind, my son Hektor –"

"Mr. Gianopolous, really!" Annie cut him off with a laugh. "I'm a married woman! Why, Bryant and I had a lovely wedding exactly six years ago tonight! You should have seen it," Annie teased, "the reception was lovelier than can be put into words. And the meal, a feast really, well, I'm not sure anything quite like it has ever been prepared before or since."

Mr. Gianopolous's eye's shined. "My beautiful girl, I will never forget."

"OK, ah, I'm sorry to interrupt, but that's enough flirting with my wife." Bryant gave Mr. Gianopolous a one-armed man hug, which Mr. Gianopolous quickly engulfed in his own two large arms.

"Let me escort you to your table," Mr. Gianopolous smiled.

While they knew exactly where they were going, they indulged their gracious host the formality of seating them properly. They returned here every anniversary, always to the same perfect table in the far corner of the magnificent dining room. Every anniversary, Mr. Gianopolous left a small, subtle momento of some sort to adorn their table. This year, Audrey smiled to see a small, clear vase supporting a single stem of blue hydrangea.

Annie and Bryant were each draped with a soft linen napkin and poured fresh glasses of spring water. The pair of tall, ivory candlesticks behind the hydrangea was already lit. A small dish of olives which Annie knew to be from the Gianopolous family groves sat off to the side, surrounded by a few thin wedges of fresh pita. They knew they would not receive menus, nor would they be politely informed of the specials of the evening. For them to inquire would have been insulting. Every year, Mr. Gianopolous lovingly tended to their anniversary dinner himself. And every year, each course was more delicious than the last.

When Mr. Gianopolous reappeared with a bottle of Pommery Summertime Blanc de Blancs, Annie smiled and touched his hand in an appreciative gesture. This time, Mr. Gianopolous did not linger to tease them, but simply filled their glasses, placed the bottle in an ice filled champagne bucket, and declared "Enjoy!" He was ever the gracious host.

Bryant picked up Annie's hand and, turning it over, kissed her palm. "Annie Anderson – Treymont, you are the love of my life. Happy anniversary." Annie wiped a tear from her eye as they toasted their evening, and their life, together..

A server appeared – it was Hektor, Annie realized in a flash of undeserved embarrassment – with a plate of tiny, artfully arranged *Orektikó*. Among the appetizer bites were petite dishes of eggplant *melitzanosalata* and tangy *tzatziki* with thin bell pepper slices for dipping, a pair of slender lamb filled *dolmades*, and two small triangles of *tiropita* bursting with feta and ricotta cheeses. The anniversary couple took their time and savored each bite, knowing that traditional Greek meals were luxuriously long affairs.

"I fired Max yesterday," Annie declared.

Bryant looked surprised. "Really? Why didn't you –"

He cut himself short, remembering his unanticipated late night at work, and the three-against-one bedtime chaos he walked in on when he finally returned home. Bryant quickly changed the direction of his question.

"What finally did it?"

"Lazy stupidness, or stupid laziness, of epic – and I mean epic – proportions. You'd think after having been written up twice and placed on probation, he'd have really committed to working carefully." Annie rolled her eyes.

"Earlier this week, I had Max assigned to a series of SPEPs."

"SPEPs?"

"Serum protein electrophoresis tests. A monkey could perform these tests. All you need to do is place a blood serum sample correctly so that an electric field can carry and separate the albumin and globulins –"

"Annie? Max, not a science lesson." Bryant smiled. It always peeved him when Annie slipped into hematology lingo, as it rarely seemed to make any sense.

"Sorry. All he had to do was put the sample in the correct damn spot and push a button. But apparently – and I swear, I am not making this up – his iPhone game of Angry Birds was competing for his attention, and he jacked up the tests."

"Oh, wow." Bryant shook his head.

"Yeah, 'wow' is one way to put it. The complete inaccuracy of those tests – signed with my name as the supervisor on duty – was largely responsible for one patient being referred on for invasive, expensive, and emotionally devastating tests to search for a rare blood cancer."

"Oh, hell." Bryant took a moment for the enormity to set in. He silently cursed himself for not noticing her distress the night before.

"Skipping a few intermediate details for the sake of our lovely dinner, I got hauled into administration to explain. Approximately ten seconds after presenting me with the details of the incident, Dr. Sabian reminded me through perilously clenched teeth, that the patient may have just cause to sue the hospital."

"I'm sorry, Annie."

Dr. Richard Sabian, the Director and CEO of Northwestern Memorial Hospital, was famous among the local staff at Tribune for being a pompous ass. If he had a new, multimillion dollar grant to wear like a shiny badge on his oversized chest, he couldn't get a reporter to the hospital fast enough. But if Tribune ever caught wind of a story of a different sort involving the hospital, anything within five degrees of impropriety or scandal, Dr. Sabian became as ruthless as he was obnoxious. He would fire Annie the second the mood struck and deal with the legal fallout later, the facts of which Annie and Bryant were both well aware.

"He also reminded me that, if or when the lawsuit is filed, it would – and these are his actual words – 'serve the public interest if someone's head was already on a plate.' Even if I wanted to save Max's skin, which I most certainly did not, it would have been at my own peril." Annie lowered her head for a moment, and rubbed the ridge between her eyes with her thumb and forefinger.

"I'm so sorry I was late last night," Bryant said.

Annie smiled. "If you were home at six sharp, it wouldn't have changed the fact that I have a professional mess on my hands, and have to deal with the fallout. It's over. I have a solid personnel file. I'm proud of the fact that in a span of eight years, I've worked my way from hematology intern to Director of Diagnostic Analytics. And I am not going to let Max or Sabian ruin our anniversary." The arrival of two delicate cups of *avgolemono* encouraged a welcome change of topic.

"This is fantastic!" Annie declared, finishing her first spoonful of the delicate, lemony, egg and rice soup.

"Cice never disappoints," Bryant agreed. "Your hair looks beautiful in the candlelight."

They sat in an intimate silence made comfortable only through years of knowing and loving each other. Their quiet thoughts were politely interrupted by the removal of soup cups and refills of champagne.

Mr. Gianopolous himself proudly served their main course, roast leg of lamb with fragrant yoghurt sauce and crushed potatoes baked with feta. Already approaching contentedly full, Annie and Bryant settled in for the highlight of their amazing and lovingly prepared dinner.

"Oh, this is delightful," Bryant offered after a happy bite of lamb and potato. "How do you think he does this? I mean, does he brine the lamb first, or dry roast really,

really slow, or –"

"Candice called today," Annie said softly.

Bryant paused. "And…" He said slowly, chewing very, very thoughtfully.

"I was directed to tell you that her flight arrives at 4:17 p.m. on Friday and if you can't take off of work to pick her up, you should call and let her know so that she can 'just take a dirty cab' to our house."

Bryant set his fork down with an expression that looked as though a sharp sprig of rosemary from the roast leg of lamb was stuck in between his teeth. He set his right elbow on the table, and massaged his right temple with his fingers.

"And, you were going to tell me this… when?" Annie asked.

"Do you really want to discuss this now, honey?" The question was offered innocently enough, but something flashed in Annie's eyes by the time Bryant's words reached her ears.

"Discuss what?" She asked quietly, with the hint of an edge in her voice. "Discuss the fact that Candice is an incorrigible b… the fact that Candice still treats me like something you scraped off of the sidewalk, or the fact that she will be staying in my home for three days and I seem to be the last person to know?"

"Honey, it's our anniversary, we're supposed to be celebrating."

"And I would like to get back to that, I really would, but between our careers and the children we don't exactly get to talk like this every day." Annie waved a fork back and forth across the table. "I'd like to clear the air on this so that our evening might still end on a high note."

"She's my mother, Annie. With all of her flaws, and I realize she has more than a few, she's still my mother. She wants to attend her granddaughter's birthday party. Is that really so horrible?"

"Do you remember Josiah's birthday party? Let's

recap."

"Annie –"

"First, she asked if I needed help dressing the children in something 'more suitable for guests' after they were clearly already dressed in darling party outfits. Second, she spit her potato salad into her napkin and warned everyone that it was surely spoiled, after having watched me prepare it not an hour earlier. Third, she asked my mother – my own mother – if we needed help with our finances while I continued to look for a 'real' job, and fourth –"

Bryant lowered his forehead into his right hand, still perched above his elbow on the table.

"She patted my stomach and asked right in the middle of opening gifts if we were planning to 'make any big announcements,' then feigned embarrassment and offered an apology in classic Candice form, by suggesting that some women like to retain their baby fat in order to feel close to their babies." Annie had to fight back angry tears.

"I'm sorry. What do you want me to do?"

"I want you to man up and tell your mother that she can either respect your wife and the mother of your children, or she can stay out of my house." Annie looked him straight in the eye as she said it, and he knew she meant every word.

"I need to use the ladies room." Annie stood abruptly and walked quickly down the hallway along the far side of the restaurant. Safely inside, she leaned against the counter, dabbed her eyes, and touched up her makeup. She had said what needed to be said, and was not going to let that evil woman consume any more of her evening.

Taking a deep breath and practicing her smile, Annie walked confidently out of the restroom and toward her table… and stopped cold when she saw Bryant engaged in an animated phone conversation.

Annie instantly began muttering through clenched teeth, and didn't care that the busboy standing near the fire exit could hear every word. "Damnit, damnit! If he's on the phone, tonight of all nights, with his demanding asshat of a boss…" Her rant trailed off as she came close enough to overhear the conversation.

"I am perfectly serious and no, I haven't been drinking. I love you, Mother. But I am a grown man, I have been for some time now, and I am asking – I am insisting, Mother – that you treat Annie with the same courtesy and grace that she has always extended to you. She is the love of my life, and the mother of your grandchildren." He paused, listening to the phone, staring intently at his champagne flute rather than at his still-standing wife.

"That's all I'm asking, Mother. It means a lot to me. No, I'll pick you up so that you don't need to take a cab. I love you. Good night." Bryant rubbed his right temple once more for good measure, and glanced up tentatively at his wife.

Annie leaned over, drew her hand along her husband's tense jawline, and kissed him softly. "Thank you. Really. Thank you."

"Does this mean I'm not bunking in Josiah's room tonight?" Bryant arched an eyebrow in Annie's direction.

Annie smiled, and sampled another forkful of lamb. "I think it's brined *and* slow roasted. And I'm sorry for ambushing you with this tonight."

Bryant shrugged. "She is incorrigible. And thank you for not finishing that sentence, by the way. She became coarse after my Dad left. 'Strike first, lest ye be stricken,' or something like that. She was hard to please when I was growing up, so I can only imagine how she must come across to you. I guess I've tried not to imagine. But I won't let that happen anymore."

Annie didn't quite believe that last part, but at least it was a step in the right direction.

Hektor cleared their entrées from the table, and presented them with small, cordial glasses filled just over halfway with a cloudy mixture of ouzo and water. Annie recalled that she enjoyed the faint aroma of licorice more than the actual taste, but let a small sip pass through her lips to be polite. Bryant found ouzo quite objectionable, but not quite as objectionable as the act of confronting his mother, so he happily obliged Annie in downing both glasses.

Late into the evening, as the crowd in the restaurant was growing thin, Mr. Gianopolous very ceremoniously placed a beautiful plate of desserts on the center of the table. The plate contained a pair of dainty honey and almond metopitta triangles, a pair of petite baklava diamonds, a pair of little kadaifi squares, and a single black box opened to reveal a stunning pair of princess cut, emerald earrings. Annie gasped.

"I'm not sure I can ever convince you of how beautiful you are, Annie. You are more beautiful now, having delivered the miracle of three beautiful children, than even on the day we married. But hopefully I can convince you of how much I love you."

Annie's eyes glistened as she felt the difficulties of the past few months fading away. She reached for her husband's hand across the table, and held on tightly. Annie gently closed her eyes and felt Bryant's familiar, quiet warmth intertwined with her fingers. She traced the lines of his palms and the curves of his knuckles. She ran her index finger lazily back and forth over the curve of the simple gold band on his left ring finger, noting the faint callous at the base of his finger. It was a habit, not a discovery, for Annie knew the strength and comfort of those hands well. For the first time in a long time, Annie felt a sense of peace.

Roast Leg of Lamb with Fragrant Yoghurt Sauce

To brine the lamb, bring 1 gallon water and ¾ cup Greek sea salt to a boil. Remove from heat and cool to room temperature. Add 4 cloves of garlic, chopped, and 3 sprigs of fresh rosemary. Place brine in refrigerator. When brine is cold, pour it over a 6 pound leg of lamb in a shallow pan. Cover and refrigerate for 4 hours.

Remove leg of lamb from brine, wipe with a clean cloth, and allow it to rest in a roasting pan at room temperature for 30 minutes. Place lamb in preheated 450 degree oven for 20 minutes, then reduce oven temperature to 325 degrees (do not open oven). After one hour, check temperature with a meat thermometer. Lamb is done (rare) when the internal temperature reaches 130 degrees. Remove from oven, cover with foil, and let rest for 20 minutes. Carve into thin slices and serve with Fragrant Yoghurt Sauce, below. Serves 12.

Fragrant Yoghurt Sauce: Whisk together 2 tablespoons Greek olive oil, 2 teaspoons white vinegar, 1 teaspoon finely minced fresh rosemary, ½ teaspoon garlic paste, and a dash of salt. Combine with 1 ½ cups plain Greek yoghurt and ½ cup finely minced cucumber (peel and seeds removed). Refrigerate for 1 hour to blend flavors.

Crushed Potatoes Baked with Feta

Boil 3 pounds small new potatoes, scrubbed and poked with a fork, for about 10 minutes or until tender. While potatoes are boiling, whisk together ¼ cup Greek olive oil, juice from 2 lemons, and 2 tablespoons honey. Stir in 12 ounces crumbled feta cheese. Set aside.

Drain potatoes and crush lightly with a potato masher. Transfer potatoes to a large serving platter. Top with feta mixture. Garnish with minced rosemary and coarsely ground black pepper. Serve immediately.

30 YEARS

Audrey was fifteen minutes behind schedule, navigating her way through rush hour traffic on the Dan Ryan Expressway when a taxi cab cut sharply into her lane, inches from her front bumper. Punching her brake pedal and horn with equal ferocity, Audrey wondered who Dan Ryan was, and why anyone hated him enough to plaster this cursed stretch of pavement with his name. Another moment later, still grumbling around bites of the long cold Chicago Dog that would have to serve as dinner, Audrey heard the muffled sound of her phone ringing. Taking her eyes off the road for a few dangerous seconds, Audrey rummaged through her purse.

"I'm sorry, I got caught in traffic. I'm just a few minutes out from —"

"Audrey."

Oh hell. Six weeks without any contact, and they have to call *now*? "Uh, hello, Father. I'm driving, and I'm late for an appointment. Now's not a good time."

"No, it's not a good time," her father barked into the phone. "I realize you've made a sport out of avoiding your mother and me, but you should know that your grandmother is ill."

"Gram?" Audrey asked in a soft voice, drawing a deep breath and signaling in vain for a lane change that would allow her to exit the treacherous freeway and concentrate. She managed to pull off on exit 53C, and stopped her car in a well-lit gas station parking lot on Cermak Road. Looking around, Audrey instinctively locked her doors. The unfamiliar area only added to her sense of growing unease. She vaguely remembered that a theater she used to frequent on discount nights as an undergraduate was somewhere nearby. "Focus," she quietly scolded herself.

"Your grandmother was transferred to Northwestern Memorial last night. Do you think you might fit her in sometime today?"

Audrey ignored the painful jab and pressed for answers. "Transferred? Last night? What are you talking about?"

Her father sighed. "Your grandmother was having trouble breathing and, stubborn woman that she is, took a cab to her local clinic. The physician on duty was concerned that she might be having a myocardial infarction and ordered an ambulance to take her to Northwestern."

"A heart attack? Gram had a heart attack?" Audrey's knuckles were turning white against her steering wheel and her voice was getting higher.

Audrey's father managed to inject kindness into his voice. "We don't know yet, Audrey. I'm on my way back from the hospital now. Your mother is with her. Are you coming?"

Redirecting her flash of anger at the ridiculous question, Audrey asked, "Why didn't you call me last night?"

"I didn't call you last night because I simply cannot bear to imagine how my own daughter, raised in my own home with my own hands, might be spending her evenings these days." Ice returned to his voice.

Oh Lord, Audrey thought to herself. Then she smiled sarcastically at the impromptu figure of speech. "Not that I expect you to believe me, Father, but had you called last night, you would have 'caught' me eating take-out Chinese while watching an I Love Lucy marathon with Felix."

"Felix?"

"Felix is my cat, Father." Audrey smiled and rolled her eyes. Sometimes it was just too easy.

"Hurry up, Audrey. Room 1281. Gram asked for you." He hung up the phone.

Tears stung Audrey's eyes as she tried valiantly to focus on the few tasks at hand. She punched a number on her speed dial.

"Abbott College, International Studies," the receptionist stated crisply.

"Hello, I need to leave a quick message for Dean Riley. It's urgent."

"Certainly. Go ahead."

"Please tell Dean Riley that Audrey Navarro had a family emergency, and will be unable to come to campus today. I will contact her in the next few days."

"I'll let her know. Will there be anything else?"

"No, thank you." Hanging up the phone, Audrey focused her trembling hands on programming her GPS. She was closer to the hospital than she initially realized, and would soon be at Gram's side.

It was somewhere between ten minutes and an hour later, she really couldn't tell, when Audrey came to a cockeyed stop in front of the valet sign near the main entrance of Northwestern Memorial. A lanky, freckled young man wearing a black uniform coat with reflective VALET lettering on the back and sleeves reached for the car door through which Audrey was already exiting.

"Good evening, Ma'am. Valet service is available until nine p.m. After nine, you can request your keys at…"

Audrey was already inside the slowly revolving

entrance doors, trying to nudge them faster as she strained her vision through the long lobby and tried to make out the elevator doors. Her car keys were the last thing on her mind.

Squeezing through the first linear foot of space between the curved glass door and the metal doorframe, Audrey darted toward the bank of elevators, her high heels clacking determinedly on the beige tiled floor.

"Ma'am? I'll either need to see your hospital identification card or have you fill out a quick visitor form." The teenage receptionist offered a bright smile, holding up a carbonless form in one hand and a ballpoint pen in the other. Audrey choked back the string of four-letter word responses that sprang up from her gut, and fished her driver's license out of her handbag.

"I'm here to see my grandmother in room 1281. It's urgent," Audrey bit out.

"The patient's name?" Apparently used to stressed out visitors, the receptionist managed to maintain her glowing smile.

"Bernadette Prescott." Audrey scribbled her way through the visitor form, tearing her guest copy from the hospital copy without waiting for the receptionist to assist. "Is there anything else?"

"One moment please," the receptionist cooed, as she dragged a pink, manicured fingernail down the glass of her computer screen. "Here she is, Mrs. Prescott is in Cardiac ICU, room 1281. Take the second bank of elevators up to the 12th floor, and turn left. The CICU receptionist will assist you."

Audrey's stomach lurched at the mention of Cardiac ICU. Without remembering to offer her characteristically polite "Thank you" to the receptionist, Audrey hurried between the open elevator doors. The doors closed and the floor moved, angering her stomach and making her regret her hasty dinner decision. When the doors opened on the 12th floor, Audrey's eyes were pulled toward the crumpled looking woman rocking rhythmically on a green, vinyl waiting chair. She was clutching a tattered looking Bible between both hands, which were resting on heavy, layered, dark blue ankle length skirts.

"Hello, Mother."

"Audrey." Her mother dredged up a tired smile as her fingers tightened on her Bible.

Audrey noticed, and looked pointedly at her mother's hands. "I'm not going to steal it, Mother."

Mrs. Navarro shook her head sadly. "Don't be difficult, Audrey, please. I know the Lord doesn't give us more than we can handle, but I'm worried about your grandmother. And you... I haven't heard from you in a long while. I'm worried about you, too."

Audrey really didn't want to upset her mother, but she was tired of the Godly-parent-with-the-wayward-daughter routine. "The phone works both ways, Mother. Every time I call home, Father answers the phone. Every time. Without fail, I am rewarded with an earful of his paranoid delusions about my personal life."

"Do not speak of your father that way!" Mrs. Navarro's eyes grew big, and just as quickly she slouched back into the green vinyl. "Your father thinks it best for him to speak to you first, that's all. Your father also thinks it's appropriate for you to call home more often, as a sign of respect."

Audrey tried not to roll her eyes. "And what do you think, Mother?"

"Not now," Mrs. Navarro snapped. "Your grandmother is gravely ill. Now is not the time."

Attempts at getting her mother to speak her own, independent thoughts always ended in "not now," but the words "gravely ill" jarred Audrey out of the impending argument. "I'm going to see Gram now," Audrey said quietly.

"She's resting. Your father went home for a nap, and I'm staying here to pray in case she needs me."

"Then I'll be quiet." Audrey caught the fear on her Mother's face, and softened her tone. "I won't wake her, I promise. I'll be right back."

Audrey focused on the sounds – the periodic, whirring sound of the automatic blood pressure cuff, the sketching sound of the heart monitor, and the faint hum of the IV pump – because the sounds were easier than the smells. The awful, commingled scents of bleached linens, ammonia-based floor cleaner, leftover roast beef and gravy, and lingering perfume made Audrey want to retch. Taking a deep breath through her mouth, Audrey clenched her fingernails into the palms of her hands and stepped inside her grandmother's room. Instantly, her eyes sprang full of hot tears.

Gram looked smaller, and paler, and oh so much older, lying in that hospital bed. Her eyes were closed and she seemed to be sleeping peacefully, probably the result of a cocktail of drugs. As promised, Audrey was quiet. She tiptoed over to the side of the bed, eased herself into an ugly brown vinyl chair, and gingerly placed her hand over her grandmother's.

"Please let her get better, please let her get better," Audrey mumbled under her breath. She steeled herself and tried again. "Dear God, please let her get better. She's a good person. Please?" Audrey reflected upon how long it had been since she directed a request upstairs. Without all of the thees and thys, it actually wasn't too painful.

"Did you bring me a Chicago Dog?" Audrey's grandmother rasped and squeezed her hand.

Audrey nearly jumped out of her skin. "Oh Gram! I'm so sorry I woke you!" Leaning forward, she gave her grandmother a warm hug.

"Relax dear, I'm not dead yet."

Audrey winced. "Please don't talk like that. I won't sneak you a Chicago Dog if you say such awful things." Audrey smiled as she wiped a tear from her eyes.

"I'm supposed to stay 'flat and quiet,' because my heart is weak. Bah. I'd rather meet my end dancing, feather boa around my neck, brandy in my hand, swaying to some blue-eyed young man's best barroom impression of Frank Sinatra." Audrey's grandmother smiled and propped herself up on her elbows.

"Oh, Gram! It sounds like you're going to be just fine!"

"I hope so." Audrey's grandmother became serious. "But someday I won't be. I need to know that you'll be just fine. We all need to find our way in this world. I need to know that you're finding yours."

A few moments passed before Audrey trusted her voice enough to speak. "You're not going anywhere just yet, Gram, but if it makes you feel better, I'm doing fine. I wish my parents saw me differently, that's no secret. But I think I'm finding my way." Audrey nodded. "I know I'm finding my way."

"Are you planning to go back to your old job at that fancy firm, dear?"

"No. I've realized that I hate corporate work, to be honest."

Much to Audrey's surprise, her grandmother offered a wide grin. "Well of course you do. It's about darn time you realized it. Now, what are you going to do about it?"

This time, Audrey let the tear that leaked from the corner of her eye fall where it may. "I'm working on it, Gram. My mentor back at Abbott College has another opportunity that I'm looking into. I promise."

"Is there anyone special in your life, Audrey?"

"The last man I dated was the hot dog man, Gram. It's been a while." It was the truth, sort of, but Audrey's eyes shifted away from the hospital bed nonetheless. Audrey felt the grip on her hand tighten just a bit.

"Audrey, I'm a sick old woman." She raised her hand in the air when Audrey opened her mouth to protest. "That's not exactly what I asked you. I want you to be happy, dear.

Just happy."

Audrey couldn't look up at her grandmother. It took all her strength to breathe in, breathe out. Breathe in, breathe out.

"I'm sorry, dear. I only want you to know – I need you to know – that I love all of you, exactly as God made you, and I want you to be happy."

Audrey looked up, and looked back down.

"I got it all wrong with that Born Again church. All wrong. I meant well, but I goofed. I can live with that, I believe God has forgiven me, but it would be easier if I knew you didn't have to live with it, too. I love you, Audrey. Always know that."

"Her name is Pam." Audrey's words were barely a whisper.

Audrey's grandmother stared off with a bittersweet smile before reaching for Audrey's hand.

"I hope she deserves you, dear."

Audrey let out the breath she didn't realize she'd been holding and silently began to cry tears of relief at her Gram's simple acceptance. Her shoulders shook and tears streamed from her eyes. After a few minutes, she stood up and walked on shaky legs the few feet to the bathroom to gather a few tissues. The one ply paper didn't offer much support, but Audrey pulled herself together and began to talk.

"We met a few months ago, and hit it off right away. She's wonderful, Gram."

Audrey's grandmother squeezed her hand, silently encouraging the bravely offered details.

"She's independent in ways that inspire me, and encourages me to dream big. She makes me laugh, and helps me relax. Her family…" Audrey swallowed deeply before continuing, "knows about us. It's not a big deal to them. It's wonderful. I think you'll like her."

"Does she appreciate a good Chicago Dog?" Gram smiled and winked.

"In her words, she would rather 'eat Felix's kibbles right out of his bowl on the floor rug than eat something as vile as a hotdog from a cart'." Audrey laughed and wiped her eyes.

Gram smiled, and squeezed Audrey's hand again with surprising strength. "Well, I guess you can't have everything but you can be happy. And you deserve to be happy. Do you love her?"

Audrey took a deep breath. "I think I might."

Gram leaned her head back into her pillow, smiled, and closed her eyes. "Stay happy, Audrey. You deserve to be happy. Everybody does."

Audrey leaned over the bed to give her grandmother another hug. As she turned around toward the door, her blood froze. There was her Mother, holding her Bible in front of her chest like a shield, rocking back and forth on her heels, her face frozen in shock and disgust.

"How long have you been standing there, Mother?"

There was a long pause followed by a stony reply. "Long enough to know that I don't even know who you are."

Audrey was determined, absolutely determined, not to fall apart in front of either of her perpetually disapproving parents. She attempted to walk past her mother serenely. Mrs. Navarro flinched and jumped back out of the doorway to avoid touching her own daughter.

Audrey's breath caught in her throat. So, it was going to be like this. Well, it was a long time coming.

"You know what they say, Mother. The Lord doesn't give you more than you can handle." With that, Audrey walked away.

31 YEARS

"Oh! That's fantastic! Of course I'll be there!" *I'll just work around the clock to free up the weekend,* Madeleine thought to herself. "I'll ask him and get back to you tomorrow. Wait, scratch that – I'll surprise him! Two seats, then. OK, bye. And congratulations!"

Madeleine hung up the phone and smiled broadly. Derrick had certainly earned this opportunity. He deserved it more than anyone she knew. Seeing his name listed in the program as the guest pianist with the Chicago Symphony Orchestra would be a thrill, not to mention a welcome reminder that suffering through another degree program with Dr. Fenwick might actually pay off. Eventually.

It had been four years since Derrick had completed his doctorate and escaped Iowa City, and Madeleine's own return to graduate studies had begun to feel more like a long slog than the exhilarating challenge she remembered from years ago. She missed having breakfast pep talks with her dear friend, and felt as if Fenwick had somehow become even more intimidating in Derrick's absence. At least the end of her program was in sight. Weekly meetings on Monday morning with her advisor had begun to set

Madeleine's teeth on edge.

Living apart from Andrew didn't help, she thought to herself as she twirled the diamond solitaire around her ring finger and frowned. He hadn't taken the news very well that she wanted to return for a doctorate, and she supposed she couldn't really blame him. He had been patient about spending a few years in Iowa, but Madeleine knew his position managing the books for a local seed company wasn't exactly fulfilling work. Apparently, she had underestimated just how unhappy he was. She remembered the awful conversation over what should have been a pleasant dinner date as if it were yesterday...

"Damnit Maddie, when did you decide THIS?" Andrew shouted as he slammed his wineglass down onto the table in reaction to her stunning announcement.

"I'm sorry. I've done a lot of research and a lot of thinking, and I realize I'm selling myself short if I don't go for the doctorate."

"You're... selling yourself short... by living up to your half of our agreement to leave Iowa City for someplace with an actual job market?" He had practically sneered at her.

"Andrew, that's not really how I see –"

"So... what exactly would I be doing, then, if I piss away another, what – two years, three years? – of my life tallying seed packets and calculating state sales tax while you play piano? I spent five years and a hundred grand on business school, but that wouldn't be selling myself short?" He glared at her.

Madeleine tried rather unsuccessfully to keep her hands from trembling before speaking quietly. "Andrew, I love you, more than enough to work this out. But if you say 'play piano' again as if I am whiling away my time with Barbie dolls, I will end our engagement and solve both of our problems." She watched him steadily with moist eyes.

It had taken him a long time to answer her. "We'll figure it out," he muttered.

Madeleine tried to shake off the memory of that conversation. After several weeks of reflection and many hours of consideration, they decided very diplomatically to postpone the wedding while she returned to Iowa City to complete her degree. Andrew would keep their new apartment in Chicago where he had begun building his career in earnest, and Madeleine would return when her doctorate was finished. Iowa City and Chicago were only 200 miles apart, they reasoned, and they would take turns driving back and forth for long weekends. That would work.

Except that it didn't. Andrew's new promotion with Bank of America frequently spilled into weekends, limiting his ability to travel. Madeleine had underestimated the increase in repertoire building expectations in the doctoral program, and found herself spending even more time in her practice room. To be fair, Dr. Fenwick never actually said she couldn't take a weekend off. He never said anything. His deafening silence whenever she returned from a trip to Chicago was all the discouragement she needed.

Over the past year, Madeleine and Andrew had done the best they could to maintain their relationship with daily phone conversations and two or three days each month spent together. This made Madeleine even more excited about surprising Andrew with a visit. The concert was late on a Saturday evening, which should be convenient even if Andrew's work week spilled into Saturday morning. Allowing for driving time, she would arrive at the apartment late on Friday. With a smile, she thought of nightwear that might convince him to spend the next morning in bed.

By the time Friday rolled around, Madeleine could hardly contain her excitement. She had packed her clothing and personal items in a very small suitcase, with all the sassiest of intentions. She made sure her gas tank was full, checked the air in her tires, and spent thirty minutes searching for the I-Pass that would allow her to bypass ridiculously long lines on the toll way. Her plan was to spend the day rehearsing and head for the interstate promptly at 5:00 p.m.

"Going somewhere, Ms. LaBlange?"

Fenwick's voice startled Madeleine as she was locking the door to her practice room. *What prompted that question,* she wondered. Glancing down at her suede miniskirt, brown tights, and stacked heel boots, she supposed she was dressed more thoughtfully that usual. She made a mental note to try to spruce up her appearance more often.

"Well, it's five o'clock, and… yes." *I'm a grown woman, for goodness' sake,* Madeleine thought to herself. "I'm driving to Chicago to see Andrew. But I'll be back promptly for our meeting on Monday morning." she added hastily.

Fenwick simply stared at her.

"Have a nice weekend, Dr. Fenwick."

By the time Madeleine got the words out, he had already returned to his office and closed the door.

Madeleine parked her car in front of Andrew's apartment building just after 9:00 p.m. Engrossed in her own thoughts, she didn't notice the noise from the hallway. When she keyed into the apartment, it took her a moment to piece together what she was seeing.

There had been a dinner party, obviously. The aroma of Andrew's familiar bolognese sauce lingered in the air, and the dining room table still held remnants of four place settings, complete with the tablecloth and candles Madeleine had left in the small hall closet next to the guest towels. The atmosphere didn't quite gel with the idea of men hanging out after work, Madeleine thought to herself. Unease began to creep into her lower spine. Then she followed the sound of conversation into the living room.

"What the –?" Madeleine started.

He was giving her a foot rub, or that's what she thought she saw before Andrew practically dumped the woman on the floor in his abrupt, guilty leap off of the couch. Another couple sat in chairs opposite the couch and across from a coffee table littered with half empty wine glasses. Madeleine recognized them as Nicholas, a colleague of Andrew's from the bank, and Nicholas's girlfriend Ellen. They went to a piano bar together the last time Madeleine was in Chicago. When Madeleine had been expected.

As Nicolas and Ellen quietly stood up and walked carefully past Madeleine toward the door, the mysterious woman who had been unceremoniously plopped on her rump look back and forth between the engaged couple, bewildered.

"Maddie, I –" He didn't bother to finish the sentence.

"Who is she?" Madeleine said quietly, her brain having not yet chosen between tears of heartbreak or fits of rage.

"Who are you?" The mysterious woman enquired. She noticed the keys still in Madeleine's shaking hand. "Do you have a key?"

The mysterious woman rapidly turned on Andrew. "Does she have a key? What is going on here? I thought you… we…" and then she saw Madeleine's ring.

As the color drained from her face, the mysterious woman stood up, straightened her shoulders, and smoothed down the fabric of her simple, black cocktail dress. When she walked past Madeleine, she whispered sincerely, "I'm so sorry. I had no idea." She paused and turned her head to give Andrew an icy stare before continuing to explain, "We haven't slept together… but that's not for his lack of interest." With that, the mysterious woman was gone.

"Maddie, please, just let me explain." Andrew stammered.

Madeleine's brain decided at that moment to opt for tears of heartbreak. She removed the diamond from her finger, tossed it on the coffee table, and tried to steady herself by keeping a hand on the wall as she walked out the door.

"Derrick?" She tried to speak clearly into her phone as she locked herself into her car and drove around the corner, pulling over when she realized it was difficult to see through the tears.

"Madeleine! Are you in town already? You know, it means a lot to have you here."

"Derrick, are you... can I... I'm sorry, tomorrow's such a big day for you, I shouldn't have called. I'll see you tomorrow, OK?"

"Maddie, honey, are you alright?"

"I'm OK, yes, I'm just... no." and with that she completely fell apart.

"Are you at Andrew's place? Maddie?" Derrick asked, very tentatively.

Madeleine took a drink from the water bottle still perched in the cup holder from her road trip, which had suddenly turned into a nightmare. "I'm outside the building, in my car. I can't go back in, Derrick. I can't, it's just – ."

Piecing together the approximate details of the situation didn't take her dear friend very long. "Stay where you are, honey. Please don't drive. I have a two bedroom suite at the Drake Hotel. Ethan is on his way here. I'll call him and ask him to bring you along. Maddie? Whatever it is, you're going to be OK."

Sitting in the third row of section 1M in the Melk Main Floor at the Chicago Symphony Center was a luxury that Madeleine did not anticipate. She sat between Ethan and an elderly, season ticket holding gentleman who was delighted to have been able to upgrade to a rarely available single seat in such a prime location. Madeleine was thankful for not having to sit next to an empty seat.

"The two of you make a lovely couple," the gentleman said politely to Madeleine and Ethan, who smiled at each other, enjoying the easily mistaken absurdity of the comment.

"She's a lovely woman, isn't she?" Ethan said to the gentleman, offering a reassuring hand squeeze and a sympathetic smile to Madeleine.

Listening to Derrick's masterful execution of Ravel's Piano Concerto in G Major was just what her heart needed. It might not be enough tomorrow, but for the moment it served to remind her that she would always have music and her love of the piano, even if her other love had fallen apart. She wasn't going to dwell on that tonight.

There was comedic irony in Derrick performing this particular work by early twentieth-century composer Maurice Ravel. Popular lore, at least as Madeleine remembered, was that Ravel intended to publicly debut his Concerto himself but ended up bestowing the honor upon another pianist because he had become so exhausted performing a variety of works by Liszt. Reflexively, Madeleine massaged her hands at the thought of the hulk handed composer who continued to haunt her.

Despite the connection, or perhaps because of it, Madeleine adored this composition. Ravel's Concerto followed the conventional three movement form, but that is where Ravel's obedience to convention came to an end. His expansive, opening Allegramente movement was infused with a curious blend of native Basque and American jazz notes, the latter of which Ravel fell in love with during travels late in his life. Madeleine began to quietly contemplate the possibility of travel. Adventures abroad had provided inspiration for myriad composers; perhaps they could provide inspiration for a heartsick piano student as well. The reality that her future was no longer tied to Chicago was jarring, but not entirely unappealing.

While Allegramente was reminiscent of more fanciful pieces by Gershwin, the second Adagio Assai movement conjured memories of the melodramatic works of Mozart. Ravel wrote the first theme of this movement to spotlight the piano, which Derrick played as though he, Ravel, and the Boesendorfer Model 290 Venetian-made grand piano, were organically connected. As high notes of wind instruments signaled the end of Derrick's solo, Ethan and Madeleine exchanged proud smiles.

What the third, Presto movement lacked in length it made up for in technical complexity. This, Madeleine observed, is where echoes of Liszt challenged the rapid transitional finesse of any pianist. This is where the fruits of Derrick's difficult apprenticeship under Reynold Fenwick were revealed. Listening to Derrick's masterful skill throughout the rapid sonata gave Madeleine a faint hope that her own studies under the same advisor would mold her into the concert pianist she once envisioned herself capable of becoming. Fenwick shook her confidence, but to be fair, he hadn't fired her as an advisee, and he had a grim reputation for doing so when less than satisfied with a student. As Fenwick wasn't one to offer compliments – ever – Madeleine had to hold onto whatever unspoken acknowledgement of her progress she could find.

The concert ended in exuberant applause, with the curtains closing and reopening to a second rendition of Presto as an encore. Dr. Derrick Haughton offered the audience a deep bow and waved regally as the curtains closed for the second time. His performance had been technically flawless, and he hoped the review that would follow in the Chicago Tribune would praise his artistic interpretation equally highly. The publicity afforded him by this performance could go a long way toward furthering his career. Or hindering it. He shook the thought from his mind, and looked forward instead to an evening with both his partner and his dear friend.

"Coffee, honey?"

"Yes. And orange juice, and an aspirin if you have one," Madeleine said wearily, wandering out of the room Derrick had graciously offered her for the weekend. Man, her head was rocking, and the sunlight streaming into the sitting room certainly didn't help. She curled herself into the upholstered chair situated in a corner shielded from the sun, wearing a posh white bathrobe supplied by the hotel.

Derrick laughed as he strolled toward the coffeepot in the kitchenette. He was a vision of contrasts, his hair perfectly styled as though he had been awake for hours, even as the clash of grey lounge pants and a faded, multicolored Pink Floyd T-shirt suggested otherwise. He knew from his grad school days that Madeleine was an early riser, and he wanted to be available if she needed to talk. Ethan, he was sure, would remain racked out in the opposite bedroom for at least another hour.

"Orange juice is on its way up, along with fruit, cheese, and sinfully wonderful chocolate croissants. I'll call the desk and ask for the aspirin." He smiled at her, wanting to be available, but not wanting to pry.

"I think I had two glasses of wine too many last night." Madeleine massaged her forehead. "Or three."

"Ah, it was a night for celebrating." Oh, that came out very wrong, Derrick quickly decided. The awkward look on his face made Madeleine smile.

"It was a night for celebrating! You were amazing, Derrick. Just amazing."

"I've never heard that from a woman before," he said as he smiled fiendishly.

Madeleine threw one of her slippers at him and laughed. Then her face drew into a resigned sigh.

"It's over, Derrick, between Andrew and I."

"So I gathered. Do you want to –"

"He wasn't expecting me, and when I arrived…" Madeleine paused, rubbing her forehead again.

"He was either an ass in the general male sense, or…"

Derrick had a feeling about this, "the apartment was a little too crowded for your taste?"

"That. Both, actually. He didn't even have the balls to follow me out."

"Has he called?"

"A few times," Madeleine said, waving her arm in what Derrick assumed to be the general direction of her cell phone.

"And?"

"Generic groveling. I'm so done." There was a surprising note of confidence in her voice. Even Derrick looked surprised.

A knock at the door signaled the arrival of their breakfast. Derrick signed the slip as a large round platter was placed on the coffee table. He busied himself by arranging breakfast plates, politely avoiding eye contact as Madeleine gathered her painful thoughts.

"The thing is, it's become clear over the past few years, and especially over the past few months, that Andrew's idea of balancing our respective careers over the course of a lifetime began and ended with his willingness to spend a few years in Iowa."

Derrick nodded. He and Ethan had several conversations about Andrew's obvious distaste for Iowa, and his laser-like focus on getting back to Chicago. In all of their dinners and game nights together, neither Derrick nor Ethan had ever heard Andrew even consider the possibility that Madeleine's opportunities might beckon her elsewhere. Ethan, a businessman himself, pointed out that Andrew could land a job anywhere, but didn't seem inclined to be flexible.

"Good riddance," had been Ethan's quiet comment when he arrived at the suite two days earlier with a tear-stained Madeleine in tow.

"And you realized this long ago, didn't you?" Madeleine followed her question with an assessing stare. It wasn't an admonishment, but a candid statement pointed at her dear friend. Derrick handed her a plate, and she selected a plump raspberry for her first bite of the day.

"It's hard to get your eyes in focus when you're in love, Maddie. Don't be so hard on yourself."

"I don't know what I'd do without you, Derrick." Suddenly, Madeleine smiled. "You know, before I introduced him to you and Ethan, Andrew felt pretty threatened by you. And now look, he's driven me away and into your hotel room."

Derrick laughed heartily as he bit into a chocolate croissant. Madeleine followed his lead, and actually groaned with pleasure as the buttery, flaky, chocolaty combination rolled around in her mouth.

"Oh. My God. This is so good. This is better than sex good." Madeleine drank a gulp of coffee, devoured another bite of croissant, and suddenly didn't feel as though she would need the aspirin.

At this, Derrick almost choked on his breakfast. "If that's how you feel about a pastry, you have a lot of catching up to do. Adios, Andrew!" He lifted his glass of orange juice in a mock toast.

"I wish I could help, Maddie, but Ethan might take it the wrong way. Rumor has it that last night's sexy first trombone player is both single and straight. I could see what I can arrange?" He grinned at Madeleine and dodged to the left as she chucked her other slipper at him.

Back in Iowa City, Madeleine surveyed the vestiges of the broken relationship which littered her apartment. She would pack up Andrew's fancy espresso machine and his two drawers of clothing and personal items, and send them back cash-on-delivery. On second thought, she would just take the high road and pay the damn shipping. No loose ends that way. The framed engagement photo on her bookshelf made her pause, but she was determined not to waste any more tears on what could (she tried desperately to reassure herself) turn out to be the best thing for her career and her happiness. She stashed the frame in the back of the short file cabinet under the dining table in her tiny apartment, unpacked her weekend bag, and settled in for a fitful night of broken sleep.

Earlier than usual on Monday morning, she headed across campus to her practice room. Unceremonious as the space may have appeared to anyone else, room 121A was her safe place. She could be alone with her coffee, her thoughts, and the keys of her comfortably plain practice piano. With reassuring familiarity, Madeleine settled herself onto her piano bench, hovered her fingers in the air above the keys, and performed as the sun rose until her heart seemed to beat to the tempo of the music. As always, the first sounds were heard only in her head. Only after the sun was fully present, when the arrival of other students and their professors dragged the unpleasant background sounds of typical morning commotion through the tiny space under the door and into her safe place, did Madeleine actually touch the keys.

Earlier than usual on Monday morning, he saw her turn her key in the lock and enter. A devout insomniac, he found inspiration for his personal compositions while sitting in the well-worn, honey colored couch as the moonlight streamed through the tall, narrow window and across his piano onto the walnut table. Soon enough, the moonlight would give way to the first faint rays of the sun, and his safe place would be polluted with the unpleasant background sounds of typical morning commotion. Only then did he start his first pot of coffee, condescend to a sport coat, and affix his esteemed professor mask for the tedious duration of the day.

She didn't realize that, as he sat on the well-worn, honey colored couch sipping a warm mug of cardamom tea, he could see a reflection in his oblong, antique mirror through the glass window in her practice room door and right to the bench of her piano. It had been an incidental observation at first, as neither professor nor student had any reason to suspect that the other would enter the building at such an early hour. For a long time, consumed by his compositions, he hardly gave it a thought.

He honestly couldn't remember when the awareness of her, a lowly MFA student for God's sake, had crept in and solidified within his consciousness. He became aware of her peculiar habit of traveling all the way across campus every early morning to lock herself in her practice room and sit silently at her piano. He noticed with idle curiosity the way her hair caught the first faint rays of sunlight as she moved almost imperceptibly to what he assumed was the music in her mind. Sometimes she turned her head enough so that he was offered a fleeting glimpse of her profile. He became abruptly and angrily aware of danger when he caught her working through a melody with her eyes closed and her lips slightly parted, and he realized that he was holding his breath. That was a long time ago, he seethingly recalled. It had been right before she became the first and only graduate student (a lowly MFA student at that!) to blow up in his office.

No, never, and absolutely not, he had admonished himself that very same day. He had never before been distracted by a student. Hell, for years he had barely even noticed beautiful women even when they did not pose a grievous threat to his reputation and career. Not that he thought Madeleine was beautiful. That's not what he meant. And why were his hands so unsteady over the familiar staff paper? Because he needed a cup of coffee. Yes, that was the only plausible reason.

She was supposed to leave. She should have been gone months ago. She should have taken her MFA and left on her merry way with her yuppie fiancé to wherever it was that he planned to drag the two of them. Chicago, he thought she had mentioned. The husband would nurse a career, she would manage the family, and maybe she would teach a few piano lessons on the side to yuppie neighborhood children for a few extra dollars. They would become a modern day, completely uninteresting Ward and June. That's how it was supposed to go, and how he intended to think of her.

Except that's not what happened. She was more driven than he anticipated. When she approached him the year prior to inquire about the possibility of returning for doctoral studies, she had been as nervous as he was stunned. He recalled how the strange stirring of nameless emotions had coiled dangerously inside of his gut like a snake. On a visceral level, he sensed danger, but he couldn't turn her away. Madeleine had talent. He wondered if she knew? God, she had a natural gift for the piano for which scores of aspiring composers and performers would have dropped to their knees and wept with gratitude. He remembered dismissing her tersely, telling her he would consider bringing her request to committee, knowing on the spot that he would of course grant her request, even as the snake coiled and tensed mercurially inside of him.

A long year had passed since Madeleine had begun her doctoral studies, and thus began spending more time with Dr. Fenwick in his office, at his piano. She had no way of knowing he had never let another living soul touch that instrument before. He had simply never deemed anyone worthy.

She was always uncomfortable in his office, he knew this very well. Although it displeased him to see her so nervous in his presence, he understood that the distance both personal space and public authority provided were helping to keep the turmoil inside of his belly at bay. Hence, he put forth no effort to make her feel at ease. That harsh and unyielding decision was strangely easy for him, until this morning.

Earlier than usual this morning, he could see that something was terribly amiss in room 121A. He observed rather curiously how, even as she sat at her piano, Madeleine's head hung slightly back in meditation rather than slightly forward in song. Her skin looked a bit pale as if she hadn't slept well. He almost smiled, as he could well relate to that particular curse. What raised his curiosity to alarm, however, were her hands. They weren't hovering in the air, poised to play notes in her mind and eventually spill music into the air. They were still.

Madeleine's hands had such grace and such beauty. Her magnificent hands had a soul unto themselves and, Fenwick acknowledged in the farthest, deepest corners of his mind, he craved the early morning trance brought about by watching her hands glide through the air as her hair caught the faint light. But this morning they were still. The snake coiled and uncoiled. Suddenly, she raised both hands in despair, her palms touching, her thumbs resting under her chin and her index fingers grazing her eyebrows. It was at that instant Fenwick noticed the absence of the diamond. The ring was gone. The snake recoiled and hissed as the mug slipped from Fenwick's grasp and crashed to the floor.

Across the hall, Madeleine screamed.

"Damn, damn, damndamndamn," Fenwick seethed as he kicked his heel against the couch for good measure before rising to clean up the mess. He closed his eyes briefly as he heard the sturdy knock on his office door.

"Come in, Ms. LaBlange," he offered through slightly clenched teeth.

"Is… are you… is everything OK?" Madeleine noticed he was wearing dress slacks and a white linen shirt, but with the sleeves rolled, and minus a tie and jacket. It was, she mused, the most casually dressed she had ever seen him. The look suited him, she determined. It suited him very well.

"Apparently not," Fenwick said sarcastically, without so much as glancing in Madeleine's direction. He busied himself by sweeping up shards of glass with a small hand broom from his closet.

"It's just, well, it's five in the morning." Madeleine was

still too rattled from the sharp noise and the realization that she wasn't alone to put together a coherent sentence.

"So it is." He turned his head and scowled at her.

"I'm sorry for interrupting. It's just, I like to come in early to practice, and the noise from your office startled me. I thought I was alone up here."

"Likewise. Do you make a habit of coming in so early, Ms. LaBlange?" Fenwick stood to his full height and stared down his nose at her.

"Well, sometimes," Madeleine stammered. "That's not a problem, is it?"

"Not at all, Ms. LaBlange, though I do need to finish my work now."

"Yes, of course," Madeleine nodded her head and retreated through the door.

"I'll see you at nine, yes? You've been practicing Chopin, as I requested?"

"Of course. Good morning, Dr. Fenwick."

"Good morning, Madeleine." He watched as she closed the door softly behind her and took a deep, cleansing breath.

Reynold Fenwick decided he would, for the first time ever, attend the university sponsored Foundation Ball next weekend. He knew such retched events were laden with glittery cliques of young wannabe socialite women who happily availed themselves to tenured professors, and that was exactly what he needed. Yes, he simply needed an evening with an attractive woman who might provide... companionship... without endangering his career.

Fenwick pushed aside his distaste for such pageantry, grasping onto the hope that the diversion would keep the snake at bay. The snake that had been coiling and uncoiling in his belly, since the moment he laid eyes on the now naked ring finger of Madeleine's enchanting hands.

32 YEARS

"Buenas noches! Bienvenidos a la Isla Turística Azul. Good evening, and welcome to the Blue Island Resort!" The slender, raven haired concierge smiled warmly at the new arrivals as a waiter appeared, right on cue.

"A margarita for the *senora?* For you as well, *senor?*" Upon receiving their fully anticipated agreement, the young man handed dangerously full, jumbo sized margarita glasses to each of the tourists. Annie smiled when, with the glass still at half an arm's length away, she could smell the strength of the tequila.

"I can't believe we're actually here." Annie looked around wide-eyed, taking in the palm trees, the pale blonde sand, and the turquoise water visible from the massive, white marble foyer where they stood.

"I can. I had to move heaven and earth to escape for a full week, remember? It's high damn time we took a vacation." Bryant rolled his eyes at the memory of haggling with his boss about taking time off during an election season. Never mind that he hadn't taken a day of vacation time in the past two years, and it was always election season in Chicago. Frowning, he tried to banish his boss from his mind.

"Let him go," Annie warned through a sweet smile, reading Bryant's mind. "You didn't bring –"

"No, darling, I didn't bring the iPhone."

Annie looked at him skeptically, certain the darn thing was lurking in a suitcase somewhere, waiting to be checked during stolen moments.

Bryant laughed and put up the hand that was not holding the stem of a margarita glass in the air, in a gesture of surrender. "I swear, I left it in my office. I told him that if he insisted I bring the iPhone along, I would take the evil intruder scuba diving and feed it to a tropical fish. That was the end of the discussion."

Annie smiled triumphantly, locking arms with her husband to follow the concierge outside and across the resort to the villa that would be their home for seven glorious nights.

"Have you had dinner?" The concierge asked, her heavily accented English making the simple question sound exotic.

"No. We've been traveling since this morning." Bryant looked beyond the woman at the darkening blue water lapping against the sandy beach. "So far, the view alone is worth the travel."

"Novela is open until nine tonight, and features a 200 item continental style buffet. Novela offers an outdoor dining option perfect for a night such as this," the concierge stated as she waved her hand through the mild, salty air in the approximate direction of the slowly setting sun.

"You'll find Novela by following the lighted walkway past the infinity pool. Bailar, on the south end of the beach, is open until midnight, and offers authentic *Mexicano* street food. Sirena, located in the building we just left, is available by reservation only. I would be happy to arrange a reservation for you, perhaps tomorrow night? Sirena offers the freshest seafood entrees in all of Cabo San Lucas. Please enjoy."

Annie suddenly felt famished upon hearing the restaurant descriptions, and considered the wisdom of drinking such a potent margarita on an empty stomach. She smiled at Bryant and placed her hand over her belly to signal her intent.

Bryant purposely misunderstood, raising and lowering his eyes above and below his wife's hand before smiling mischievously into her eyes. He was hungry, too, but not for dinner.

"Do you offer room service?" Bryant tipped his head politely toward the concierge as Annie blushed right down to her toes.

"Yes, of course. Private dining is always an option. A full menu is located on the coffee table. To order, simply dial 0 on your room phone." The concierge paused in front of a high, dome topped wooden door and reached for her keys. She pushed open the heavy door and stepped aside. "Your villa."

Annie stepped inside and breathed in the heady floral aroma from a bouquet of tropical flowers in shades of yellow, orange, and red sitting in a pottery vase on a white side table. Her eyes caught the brightly colored braided rug which anchored the white wicker furniture of the sitting room and softened the terracotta-tiled floor. Her eyes drifted to where the floor met the white stucco wall and climbed up past a beautiful tapestry woven in all of the colors of the sunset to the cathedral ceiling above.

Two doors were open to her right. The nearest revealed a luxurious bathroom framed in the same terracotta and stucco. Larger than many bedrooms, Annie mused, the bathroom was complete with a sunken Jacuzzi tub for two, a marble surfaced double shower with soft recessed lighting, a warming shelf stocked with lush cotton bath sheets, two fluffy white robes, two pairs of slippers, small bottles of every bath product imaginable, and a champagne bucket already stocked with bubbly and ice. Annie smiled, thinking to herself how she could be perfectly happy spending the entire week in the bathroom.

Curious, she walked softly toward the second door, in awe of her surroundings. Bryant wordlessly exchanged gratuity and room keys with the concierge, who excused herself with a polite but knowing smile. Annie's breath caught when she saw the bedroom. It must have been the size of her and Bryant's first apartment, and as grand as anything she had ever seen in an upscale magazine. A wide, low stone fireplace spanned the right wall, framed by short stacks of split wood and a pale blue fainting couch. The bed, perpendicular to the door, dominated the left wall. It was a study in contrasts, the dark mahogany frame lightened and softened by a sheer silk canopy. The pale blue pillowy comforter appeared to be as soft as a cloud, and was accented with square white pillows of antique lace and silk shantung.

The wall opposite the door wasn't really a wall as much as a frame for two wide pairs of French doors which opened to a breathtaking view of the ocean. The doors were propped open, flooding the room with late afternoon sunlight, salty air, and the hypnotic sounds of the surf colliding gently against the sandy shore.

Annie approached the bed, leaning forward to run her fingers over the silk pillows, as Bryant stepped quietly behind her and kissed her shoulder. She turned her head slightly to offer him a smile, and he grazed her lips with the tips of his fingers. Annie closed her eyes.

Bryant wrapped one arm gently around her waist and ran his other hand through Annie's hair. When he slowly pulled out the beaded combs holding the sides of her long, dark hair carefully in place and tossed them aside, Annie realized they wouldn't be dining out soon. Hungry though she was, the realization made her shiver with delight.

"Oh, my goodness. I can't believe how famished I am!" Annie smiled at the server as chips and salsa, guacamole, *carne asada*, roasted peppers, and fresh tortillas were placed on the wicker patio table before them. While taking a long siesta with her husband certainly had its perks, Annie realized that she hadn't had a bite to eat since arriving at the resort hours earlier. Who knew street food could smell so wonderful?

"We must have worked up an appetite," Bryant suggested mischievously, winking at his wife. Annie blushed. What a thing to say in front of a complete stranger!

"I don't mean to rush you, but the kitchen closes in 30 minutes. Can I bring you anything else?" The young woman smiled politely, waiting.

"Two more margaritas, *por favor*," Annie answered.

They dined quietly under the night sky for a little while, replenished, thoroughly relaxed and sated. When their margaritas arrived, Bryant lifted his glass in a toast. "Happy early anniversary, Annie!"

Annie sighed nostalgically. They clinked glasses. "I really can't believe it's been ten years already. Well, nine and a half years, technically."

"Remember, my warranty expires in June so if you plan to trade up, you better decide quickly."

"Nah. Do you have any idea how long it takes to house train a husband?"

"I guess a deal's a deal. To us!"

"Do you hear that? The ocean sounds enchanting. And just look at all of the stars! Thank you so much for this, Bryant."

"What are you thanking me for?"

"For bringing us here, for planning this. It was a wonderful idea."

Bryant didn't say anything, and focused his attention on meticulously rolling steak and peppers into a tortilla.

"Is something wrong?" Annie asked.

Bryant hesitated. "No. Well –"

"What is it?" Annie pressed. She was smiling, but her eyes looked concerned.

Bryant rubbed his forehead. "Look, I'm risking serious brownie points by telling you this, and I hope it doesn't cost me a single second of seeing you naked on a Mexican beach, but this was, ah, actually your mother's idea. She contacted me and suggested I take you somewhere 'warm and wonderful' for our anniversary. She reminded me that it would be easiest for her and your dad to watch the children over the winter, during the off season at the Inn."

Annie laughed. "Oh Bryant. A helpful idea does not a guilty man make. Thank you for taking off of work to fulfill my mother's idea. There, do you feel better now?"

Bryant laughed weakly. "Yeah, I suppose I do. Sorry."

"I'm glad we're celebrating a few months early, rather than a few months late. I've never been good at waiting for anything!"

Bryant sipped his margarita thoughtfully, to avoid having to respond. Planning this vacation quickly was also Mrs. Anderson's idea. Bryant reminded himself that Annie's mother had always been exceptionally thoughtful and must have noticed the combined job stress they were experiencing lately. Smiling at his wife, he desperately hoped that this vacation had nothing to do with the information pamphlets he had accidentally spotted on Mrs. Anderson's desk.

Bailar Margaritas

Shake together ½ cup of pure agave tequila, ¼ cup triple sec, juice from 1 large lime, and 2 teaspoons simple syrup. Pour over ice into two salt rimmed margarita glasses. Garnish with lime wedges and enjoy!

33 YEARS

Audrey made herself comfortable in a sturdy, worn armchair upholstered in a scratchy, burnt orange fabric. "This pattern must be older than I am," she murmured to herself. As her supervisor fielded an unanticipated but apparently important phone call behind her simple oak desk, Audrey scanned the room. She had of course been in Dean Riley's office many times, but the details always intrigued her. The office was quite large but decidedly unpretentious and desperately begged for the attention of an interior designer, not that it would ever get its wish. The room was almost accidentally color coordinated in the sense that all of the furnishings seemed to hail from the 1970s when everything, at least in Audrey's limited understanding, had been festooned in awful but coordinating shades of brown, orange, and yellow.

At least the room had been freshly painted since her last visit. The brown wallpaper, Audrey shuddered to remember, had not been removed (for that would have been expensive) but had been painted a creamy ivory shade. Two watercolor paintings adorned the largest wall.

One depicted the main entrance of Abbott College and the other depicted an impressive stained-glass window from the chapel of Abbott Convent where Dean Riley lived. The frames were new and looked expensive. Gifts, Audrey concluded.

Dean Riley's bookshelves had always fascinated Audrey, particularly back when Audrey was a young student. In addition to a wide selection of predictable authors representing Western, Christian-oriented history, philosophy, and art, Audrey's eyes took note of the ancient words of Eastern minds like Tao and Confucius right alongside more modern words of controversial Western authors like Foucault and Marx. Annie remembered stumbling across Mein Kampf in Dean Riley's shelves years ago, and also remembered the Dean's candid response.

"Human nature is complex, Audrey. If we only study the easy parts, the safe beauty and the accepted wisdom, and avoid the complex, ugly interpretations and the challenges to accepted boundaries of good and evil, we fail to try to live up to our divine potential."

"What do you mean, 'we fail to try'?" Audrey had asked all those years ago. She remembered how Dean Riley had smiled at the question.

"Anyone who pretends to have cornered the market on divine potential is selling you a crock of boloney, Audrey. And 'boloney' was not the first word choice to pop into my head." Young Audrey had simply stared, agape.

"All any of us can do, Audrey, is live the life we believe we have been called to live, and to live it as correctly as we understand 'correctly' to mean. That," she motioned to the offending book in Audrey's hand, "represents an extreme, outlying interpretation which history demands we confront rather than ignore."

"Also," Dean Riley concluded her very wise lesson by saying with a wry smile, "censoring books is just dumb."

Audrey snapped out of the memory as Dean Riley

hung up the phone.

"I'm sorry to have kept you waiting." Dean Riley extracted a file from a drawer behind her and quickly turned her full attention to Audrey. "Before I forget, Maria Bettencourt Silva was awarded a Trustee's Scholarship for next year. I thought you'd be pleased." Dean Riley smiled at Audrey.

"That's fantastic! She was beside herself, worrying that she might need to return home without a degree." Audrey shook her head.

"Ordinarily a two year reciprocity agreement is enough. We were hoping that *Universidade dos Açores* would take into account Maria's unanticipated struggles with American English that first year, but –"

"But Chancellor de Pimentel, with the blessing of a legion of administrators, is still upset about having to provide Portuguese language tutoring for our 'embarrassingly monolingual students', and uses that as leverage for scholarship funding for his own students at every opportunity." Audrey scowled. "Believe me, after five years in Terceira kowtowing to that man, I know the drill."

Dean Riley smiled patiently. "In any case, the scholarship committee came through, and Ms. Bettencourt Silva will be able to complete her nursing studies."

"How are our girls doing over there?" Audrey asked.

"Aside from the incident with Ms. Parker," Dean Riley raised an eyebrow, "they are doing well."

Audrey cringed inwardly. Despite her own carefully crafted and delivered pre-placement seminars covering cultural norms, mores, and behavioral expectations of foreign female students on the conservative, highly religious island, there was no accounting for the dangerous mix of local young men and visiting hormones. Outwardly, Audrey tried an attempt at humor.

"Oh, c'mon. How many girls right here in our own residence hall do you think could manage to adhere to a 'door open and two feet on the floor' policy against a backdrop of flirty foreign men if such a ridiculous protocol were ever implemented at Abbott College?" Audrey smiled mischievously.

Dean Riley ran her fingers nervously over the Franciscan cross that hung from her neck and gave Audrey a stern look. "I'd prefer not to contemplate that actually."

Katharine Riley, Ph.D., Dean of International Studies at Abbott College, softened her stare. "What I would like to do is thank you, Audrey, for your hard work establishing the international exchange program between Abbott College and *Universidade dos Açores*. In the five years since your tenuous first meetings with Chancellor de Pimentel, 42 Abbott College women have been afforded the opportunity to live and study in Terceira."

"I'm almost more proud of the fact that 17 Azorean girls managed to convince their parents that studying at a private women's college in the Midwestern United States really does fall short of selling one's soul to the Devil."

The last few years had been more than an adventure, Audrey mused. Professionally, she had woefully underestimated the effort and finesse required to establish a robust foreign exchange program between Abbott College and *Universidade dos Açores*. Her limited Portuguese proficiency that first year had been viewed offensively by the Chancellor with whom she had the misfortune of coordinating most of her efforts. His opinion of her declined sharply when he realized after peppering her with blunt questions, that while Abbott College was affiliated with the Roman Catholic Church, Audrey herself was not. At least not in the sort of born and bred fashion that he was expecting.

"*Façade*," the Chancellor had sneered under his breath more than once.

When Audrey realized she was in real danger of being dismissed outright by the Chancellor, she shared her concern with Mrs. Trigueiro. She had nothing to lose.

When Mrs. Trigueiro suggested that her husband would invite the Chancellor over for a Sunday meal, Audrey's eyes nearly bugged out of her head. This, Mrs. Trigueiro assured her, was the way to accomplish things in Terceira.

As a community leader, the Chancellor had been socially obligated to accept the invitation from the local farmer to enjoy a humble Sunday meal. Audrey smiled as she recalled the look of utter astonishment on the Chancellor's face when he entered the Trigueiro's modest stone home and found Audrey, apron clad, toiling away in the kitchen under the tutelage of the farmer's wife.

"Well I have to live somewhere, don't I?" Audrey recalled muttering to herself as she chopped and stirred.

Throughout the dinner, the Trigueiros and the Chancellor spoke in rapid Portuguese. Audrey could understand less than half of what was said, but caught several references to her own supposed desire to improve upon her poor cooking skills, and the fact that she kept a very clean and proper cottage. Audrey found this to be irritating drivel, but dared not interrupt.

The Chancellor offered a considering glance in Audrey's direction after Mrs. Trigueiro emphasized how Audrey joined her and her husband for High Mass every Sunday, and Mr. Trigueiro followed with a blunt observation that the girl never flirts with the local men. Mrs. Trigueiro made sure that the Chancellor did not escape before he clearly understood that Audrey was a good girl, modest, and welcome to stay in their farm cottage for as long as her work kept her in Terceira. The following week, Audrey received permission from the Chancellor to meet with a select group of faculty and administrators to begin building an exchange program.

Personally, well that was a less linear experience. Audrey returned from her time abroad with a surprising penchant for cooking and a critical self-awareness she hadn't possessed before. For that alone the experience had been worthwhile. Audrey had also come out of the experience with a solid, reliable friend in Dale. He had tacitly understood Vanessa's orientation for a long while, and really never thought about it in reference to Audrey. He did, however, press Audrey for information when Vanessa stopped driving out with him and Miguel to the cottage.

"We had a sleepover." Chew on that for a while, Audrey thought to herself, highly annoyed with his slew of questions.

"You – huh?"

"Had a sleepover."

Audrey locked him with her most patronizing stare for several seconds, waiting for it to sink in. "Jesus, Dale, do you need me to spell it out for you?" She sincerely hoped not, because she wasn't sure she would have been capable of explaining. The evening lived in her mind as a long series of wordless, verbally indescribable images and emotions.

"Oh. You mean, well… damn." Dale had ran his fingers through his hair, buying himself a moment to think. None of the smartass comments he may have offered in a room full of men seemed quite appropriate. He pieced together that this was a new development for Audrey. He ventured it wasn't for Vanessa.

"She didn't, I mean –" Audrey recalled how embarrassed Dale was by his own question.

"No, no, it wasn't like that. Not at all. Please don't think that about her. I don't know if I can explain it, because I don't understand it well myself, but she gave me the opportunity to learn who I am. To learn why I've felt emotionally adrift. She gave me hope that I will, at some point, feel completely fulfilled. And that, Dale, is a cliché you can wrap with a big red bow!" Audrey remembered reaching over to swipe Dale's baseball cap and place it on her own head, before pouring them each a much needed glass of wine. It was all she could have done to make an awkward conversation with her best guy friend slightly less weird.

In the weeks that followed that fateful evening, Audrey had long talks with Vanessa. The women shared a few dizzying intimate moments, but in the end they agreed it wouldn't be healthy to try to build anything beyond a friendship. This was all so new to Audrey and it was sometimes painful. Vanessa was long past self-discovery and it wouldn't be fair to her, Audrey reasoned, to have to deal with the baggage brought into a relationship by someone with so many questions. In hindsight, she still believed it was the correct decision. Vanessa had opened a door, for which Audrey was grateful, but the next steps needed to be taken inside of her own head.

Audrey quickly tried to bring herself back when Dean Riley interrupted her thoughts. "As we discussed, the program is firmly established now, and Abbott College no longer feels the need to keep your full attention on the Azores exchange. Instead, we would like to shift your talents elsewhere –"

"To Jamaica," Audrey finished the thought. She was as prepared for this discussion as she was ever going to be.

"Yes, to Jamaica. However, you answered my brief email inquiry with a veritable dissertation on why we should focus on Aruba instead. Your... thorough response... admittedly surprised me. I thought it only fair to meet with you personally to discuss the possibility, however remote it may be."

Dean Riley's voice suggested curiosity with a hint of caution. Audrey knew her well, not only as a supervisor, but as a faculty member a lifetime ago when Audrey was an undergraduate student at Abbott College herself. Audrey knew how to approach this.

"Dean Riley,"

"Katharine, please."

"Katharine, I did a fair amount of background reading related to your concept of expanding Abbott's international exchange program into Jamaica."

"Yes, it's just a concept right now, but our exploratory surveys show a high level of student interest in traveling to Jamaica. Northern Caribbean University is reasonably comparable with Abbott College in terms of size and scope, and the cost of living is reasonable."

"All of that is true, yes."

"But…" Dean Riley prompted.

"The University of Aruba has a more modern pulse which I think will appeal to our traditional age, undergraduate students. Keeping in mind that students in the 18 – 24 age group are statistically most likely to apply for international learning opportunities." Audrey measured Dean Riley's nod before continuing.

"As a constituent country within the Kingdom of the Netherlands, Aruba offers a slightly Scandinavian, slightly European flair. That cosmopolitan edge extends into the student body at U of Aruba, which boasts a population that includes not only native Aruban and mainland Dutch students but also visiting Latin American and Asian students."

"Why not just send our students to New York for a semester?" Dean Riley countered.

"We could do that," Audrey said, "but our students are already keenly aware of how New York represents the 'melting pot' notion of America. If our students wanted New York, they would visit on spring break. Or they would be SUNY students rather than Abbott College students at all." Audrey gathered her thoughts and kept pressing.

"Sending Abbott College students to the University of Aruba would provide our students with the opportunity to see 'melting pot' ideals played out in other parts of the world. The diversity inherent even in their small class sizes, led by international faculty, may be a perfect environment for our American students to experience democratic, civil discourse in a place that does not have a history of militaristic empire building."

Without really intending to, Audrey raised her voice to an impassioned pitch. "Isn't it important for our students to realize that the United States may be diverse, but may not set the bar where civil discourse is concerned? Aren't those realizations an important part, or shouldn't they be an important part, of the international experience?"

"And you don't feel that our students would gain this experience at Northern Caribbean University?" Dean Riley asked pointedly.

"No."

Almost thirty years of experience as an administrator in higher education had taught Katharine that the most important issue to untangle was often not the first issue presented. And so, she waited.

Audrey found the silence unbearable, but clearly Dean Riley intended for her to explain. "No, I don't. Northern Caribbean University is approximately the same size as Abbott College, but that's really where the similarity ends."

Dean Riley turned a palm upward in mild disagreement. "They're both private colleges with a Christian heritage as well. Isn't that relevant?"

"Actually, it illustrates a fundamental difference. Abbott College has a proud Catholic heritage, true, but is currently run by a lay Board of Trustees. We do not impose doctrine upon our students. Even if the Board for whatever reason decided to go that route, the extent to which religious doctrine could be imposed upon the student body," *or visiting employees*, Audrey silently thought, "would be theoretically limited in that religious interpretations cannot supersede civil rights in this country."

Dean Riley arched an eyebrow sharply. "I imagine you're going somewhere interesting with this, Audrey?"

Audrey inhaled and steeled herself. No guts, no glory. Her job and her principles were both at stake, and she desperately hoped they weren't in conflict.

"Abbott College has a proud history of providing, or at the very least consciously striving to provide, a welcoming environment for all students. Valuing diversity with respect to characteristics such as economic status, immigration status, ethnic heritage, religious beliefs or a lack thereof, political beliefs, and – sexual orientation has been the norm for at least as long as I have been acquainted with this institution."

Dean Riley occasionally taught a communications course aptly titled, "Communication, Verbal and Nonverbal." Audrey may not have noticed it herself, she certainly hadn't intended it, but her half beat pause before that last thought did not escape her supervisor. Dean Riley decided not to interrupt, and instead contributed a meaningful pause to the conversation.

Clearing her throat, Audrey continued. "Surely students hailing from such an inclusive environment as ours will expect to find the same at a foreign university engaged in a formal student exchange relationship with Abbott College. I've made a few contacts, and I feel confident that the University of Aruba is such a place."

"Have you made similar contacts at Northern Caribbean University?" Dean Riley asked.

"No, I have not. Regardless of what the administrators and faculty at Northern Caribbean might say," Audrey tried to hide her distaste, "Jamaica as a whole is widely recognized as being the most homophobic island nation in the Caribbean, and one of the most homophobic nations on earth."

"That's quite an accusation."

"It's not so much an accusation as a transparent but little known fact. Americans are enchanted with Jamaica's waterfront resorts, which ironically aren't even owned by Jamaican people. I don't doubt that the 'idea' of a semester or two in Jamaica might be appealing to some of our more spray tanned undergraduates, but –"

Dean Riley arched her eyebrow again, reminding

Audrey to keep it professional. In truth, the Dean was listening carefully, and waiting for Audrey to lay out a case for Aruba that they could use to successfully convince both the Abbott College President and the Chairwoman of the Board of Trustees to move forward with Audrey's plan.

"But these same undergraduates may have no idea that the country to which they are traveling is culturally intolerant of gays and lesbians, and has a laundry list of homophobic laws including, for example, a law which dictates that male homosexuality is a crime punishable by up to ten years of hard labor."

"I see." Suddenly, Katharine saw very clearly and was irritated with herself for taking so darn long to get there.

"How important is this change in focus, from Northern Caribbean to the University of Aruba, to you personally?" Dean Riley held her voice as casual as possible, but felt her expertise in interpersonal communications momentarily floundering.

No guts, no glory. She could always return to the corporate ladder, and maybe even start a rung or two higher this time. "If Abbott College moves forward with plans to establish a foreign exchange program with Northern Caribbean University, I'm sorry, but I will be unable to assist." Audrey tried to keep her hands natural and her teeth unclenched.

"And if we change direction slightly and work to establish an agreement with the University of Aruba?"

Audrey smiled hopefully. "I would do everything in my power to make the program even more successful than our pilot program with *Universidade dos Açores!*"

Katharine Riley leaned back in her chair to think for a moment. There was more on the line here, she realized, than the direction of an exchange program. She had known Audrey for fifteen years, knew her relationship with her family was tenuous at best, and had enjoyed watching the transformation from silly 18-year old Audrey to confident, career driven Audrey. Katharine recognized that it was important, personally, to get this right.

"Social justice issues are important to me, Audrey, as they are to the President Severson and Dr. Aguilera. You may recall that after Dr. Aguilera was appointed Chairwoman of the Board, an annual series of very well-designed internship opportunities opened exclusively for Abbott College students at the North Chicago LGBT Outreach Center." Katharine eyed Audrey evenly.

Surprised, Audrey wondered if all of this had transpired during her time in Terceira. She never made the connection.

"I will expect a succinct proposal, no more than five pages in length, outlining the specifics of your intentions with the University of Aruba by Thursday afternoon. Let's plan to meet for 30 minutes on Friday morning, so that we can clarify any lingering details before I bring your plan to my meeting with the President at the end of the day on Friday." Dean Riley smiled at Audrey, who in turn released the breath she didn't realize she was holding.

"Thank you. Really, thank you Dean… Katharine. I'll work hard to make the program in Aruba successful. Our students will love it."

"I know you will, and I'm sure that's true." Katharine paused. "Audrey, will Pam be joining you? During your time abroad?"

Audrey tried not to let her head swivel around as she realized that of course Dean Riley remembered how Pam had joined her in attending a few minor college functions. A basketball game, a student theater production, an employee picnic – those sorts of events. The sorts of things to which someone might bring a roommate or maybe their mom.

Audrey recalled with a faint twinge of guilt how she had discarded last year's invitation to the annual Abbott College Graduation Gala. Part of her would have loved to dress extravagantly and spend the evening wishing the new graduates well. But a Gala event… it wouldn't have been equivalent to bringing Pam to a basketball game and she wasn't ready to field questions. Another twinge of guilt. For goodness' sake, her own parents were still trying desperately to convince themselves that Pam's presence meant nothing more than sensible rent sharing. More guilt.

"Well, I don't, I haven't…" Audrey stammered and glanced up at Dean Riley, who was watching her curiously. Instantly, Audrey's temperament changed from one of awkward discomfort to one of confidence and clarity. It was the unexplainable *'Eureka!'* moment she had needed for a long while.

"Yes. She will have a few details to work out with her employer as far as telecommuting is concerned, but the details don't seem insurmountable. So yes, Pam will be joining me for at least a few months. A year would be a long time for us to be apart."

Dean Riley smiled. "I imagine it would. You're young, and from the little I know of Pam, she compliments you well."

"Thank you, Katharine." Audrey did her level best to keep the tears behind her eyes even as her vision clouded.

"Human nature is complex, Audrey. Always remember that."

34 YEARS

Madeleine fumbled around in her messenger bag, glanced down at a crisply folded piece of paper, and carefully punched the numbers 2 – 4 – 5 – 3 – 1 into the keypad on the battered steel door. The tiny red light did not turn green. She pulled on the door anyway, but it was locked tight. Shrugging, she tried again. 2 – 4 – 5 – 3 – 1. The lock tumbler didn't make a sound, the green light did not glow, and the door surely did not open. After a third unsuccessful attempt, Madeleine tucked a stray lock of hair behind her ear, refolded the paper, and took a deep breath. First her flight into Logan International had been delayed, then the taxi driver got lost in the labyrinth of downtown Boston road construction, and now this. It was Murphy's Law.

Knock, knock, knock. No answer.

Knock, knock, knock, knock, knock. Nothing.

Knock, knock, bang, bang, bang. BANG, BANG, BANG. Madeleine shook her sore hand ruefully. It wouldn't do her any good to injure her hands. She leaned against the door, fumbling around in her messenger bag again, this time for a map of the premises. If she walked around the corner and down what promised to be a creepy service alley, she would find the loading docks of the Boston Symphony Orchestra's Symphony Hall. Maybe luck would be on her side, and she would find an unlocked door.

"Oaf!" As the door flew open behind her, Madeleine grabbed the doorjamb to keep from falling unceremoniously onto her derriere. She scowled over her shoulder as an annoyed looking security guard scowled back.

"That you, poundin' on the door?" He demanded briskly.

"Yes, sir. The one and only." She smiled radiantly, delighted to find such a small blessing as an unlocked door. Her smile was not returned.

"Miss, I don't know you from the Mother of Jesus. Now what you need?"

"I'm, ah, I'm Madeleine LaBlange. The understudy, er, the Baltimore understudy. They sent me here to rehearse?" Madeleine knew she sounded ridiculous, but after glancing at her wristwatch, she was starting to panic.

"Oh, I see," the security guard drawled suspiciously, not really seeing at all. "You one of them, huh? You got some identification?"

Madeleine fished around in her bag yet again and offered her Maryland driver's license.

"Good Lord, now what I supposed to do with this? You got some staff identification?"

Madeleine was determined not to cry. "No, sir. I'm new. I don't have anything other than this letter," she looked down to find the folded paper and pushed it into his hand, "which tells me to come to this door and enter this code. The code doesn't work."

"That's 'cause you is at the wrong door. This here's the security door. Different code. You lookin' for the performers' door." He leaned outside and pointed. "It's just down the block there, see?"

"Sir? Can I just use this door? I'm supposed to be in

room –" Madeleine glanced back at her folded piece of paper – "Room 4A at 11:00 a.m." Her voice was desperate.

The security guard let out a hearty laugh. "11:00 huh? Well, then you is late." He shook his head, considering her. "C'mon. I like you. I'll walk you in. There won't be anyone in Room 4A, though, they already on stage."

All of the color drained from Madeleine's face.

Perhaps he was simply surprised that someone with such a fair complexion could become even more pale, but as he ushered her through the steel door and down the service corridor, the security guard gave Madeleine a sideways look of pure pity.

"You new, huh? What you play?"

"Piano, Sir. I'm filling in as the pianist for tonight's performance."

"Tonight? And you late?"

"Apparently."

The security guard stopped in front of a door marked "Stage Left". After pausing for a second, he patted her on the arm. "You better buck up, girl, or they will eat you alive."

With that he left her standing in the doorway, terrified.

Madeleine squared her shoulders and opened the door, taking in the familiar din of chairs being shuffled, music stands being adjusted, and instruments being tuned. She approached the conductor purposefully, stopping a respectful six feet away to avoid interrupting a conversation between the Maestro and a harried looking cellist. After several seconds the cellist stalked away, clearly unhappy with the outcome of the discussion. It was a bad omen.

"And you are?" The conductor looked down from his riser at Madeleine, waiting.

"Good morning, Maestro Sandburg. I am Madeleine LaBlange, your pianist for this evening's performance."

"Miss LaBlanc, you are late."

"LaBlange. Madeleine LaBlange, and I do apologize for that. My flight was – "

"With all due respect, Miss LaBlanc, the curtain rises at 7:00 p.m. for 2,625 classical music aficionados who have paid dearly for their tickets, regardless of what happened on your flight."

"I understand, Maestro."

"May we begin?" Maestro Sandburg's voice dripped with sarcasm. The first violinist, a prim looking woman in her 40s, wearing her glossy black hair in a severe twist, snickered upon overhearing the chastising remark.

"Oh, grow up." Madeleine muttered under her breath as she made her way to the piano, hoping for a reprieve that never came.

"Attention, everyone!" Maestro Sandburg tapped his polished walnut conductor's baton on the top of his podium stand. "The understudy from the Baltimore Symphony Orchestra is finally here. With any luck, we will be able to pull this off tonight. Miss LaBlanc, I'm sure you won't mind if we skip the perfunctory introductions, considering the time?"

Madeleine gritted her teeth. "No, Maestro."

Situating herself on the edge of the piano bench, Madeleine felt her sour mood lift as she studied the impeccably maintained Steinway piano before her. It's not that she was particularly impressed. With much amusement, Madeleine noted that not even the piano used by the globally renowned Boston Symphony Orchestra was as magnificent as the piano in Dr. Fenwick's office.

Good heavens, why Fenwick would cross her mind today of all days, Madeleine had no idea. It must be that he always made her nervous, and she was plenty nervous now. She survived those nerve wracking years though, and escaped with her coveted doctorate in music. Fenwick deigned to congratulate her and even offered an awkward compliment about her potential just before her graduation ceremony. His rare awkwardness, Madeleine smiled to remember, was how she knew he was being sincere.

In the seconds before Maestro Sandburg lowered his baton to begin the concerto, Madeleine gave herself an emergency pep talk. "If I could survive Fenwick, I can surely survive this. Today is the opportunity I have been waiting for. This is my moment. *Carpe diem!*" The voice in her head quieted as the baton came down and Madeleine spent the next 47 minutes offering her carefully rehearsed rendition of Chopin's Piano Concerto No.1. Her performance was exemplary.

"Ms. LaBlange, I believe we just might get through this evening's performance unscathed." Maestro Sandburg stalked off the stage in the opposite direction before Madeleine could pick up her chin, having received a most unexpected compliment.

The musicians began to scatter, grateful for a few hours of freedom before the big performance. Still seated herself, Madeleine endured a pointed, withering look from the first violinist before she turned on her heel and marched away. Madeleine's confusion at such rudeness was interrupted by a soft, heavily accented voice.

"Welcome to Boston, Ms. LaBlange. I'm Aleksi, first viola."

Madeleine smiled broadly, relieved that someone, anyone, was actually treating her with kindness today. "Thank you, Aleksi. I'm Madeleine, pleased to meet you."

"I don't mean to be indecorous, but would you care to join me for a quiet lunch? I understand you just arrived and you have a long evening ahead of you." He smiled, appearing genuinely concerned for how she was holding up.

Madeleine hesitated for only a second. "Lunch would be lovely. I'm embarrassed to admit, I simply tossed my suitcase and garment bag by the door. I was so late in arriving!" She motioned toward the luggage sitting near the stage door. "Do you happen to know where I can leave those for tonight?"

Aleksi thought for a moment. "I suppose you could use Dominica's dressing room. I'll go see if –"

"No, no, that's alright," Madeleine hastily interrupted. She knew enough of Dominica Rafaele's reputation to know that the BSO's contracted pianist was a diva to the nth degree. Madeleine believed in karma, and had no intention of crossing Ms. Rafaele. "Is there just a spare room or something, a place I might duck in for a few minutes before the curtain call?"

"Duck in?" Aleksi laughed. "I apologize. American figures of speech are just so peculiar to me. Yes, there is a small, unassigned dressing room where you might 'duck in,' as you say. I'll show you, come with me." He reached for her suitcase as she gathered her bag, and they walked down the service corridor to a tiny, drab room nearly devoid of furniture.

"Well, at least the door locks!" Madeleine tried to sound cheerful.

Thirty minutes later, the two musicians were sharing antipasto and linguini with clam sauce at a small, unassuming bistro several miles away from the Symphony Hall. Madeleine was sure she would be eternally grateful for Aleksi's help in getting through this bewildering day.

"Can I ask you a question?"

"I haven't been in Boston much longer than you," Aleksi joked, "but I'll try."

"The first violinist... I, ah, get the sense that she is less than pleased with my presence?"

"That's Lillian. Don't worry. She wouldn't hurt a bee." He looked so earnest. Madeleine coughed into her napkin, trying to disguise her laugh.

"What is it?" Aleksi asked, alarmed.

"I'm so sorry. You're being so kind, and here I am, acting like a child!"

"I don't understand?" Aleksi tipped his head sideways, waiting.

"A fly." Madeleine giggled. "You mean, 'she wouldn't

hurt a fly.'"

"Oh – ha! A fly! Ok, Lillian wouldn't hurt a fly."

"Well, you wouldn't know from the way she was staring me down for the last few hours. Is there anything I need to know?"

"Her fiancé is an understudy pianist in Cleveland. When BSO was left without a pianist at a most inopportune time, Lillian assumed he would be asked to fill in. He's been here before, from what I understand."

"I don't understand. How did the Boston Symphony Orchestra find itself without a pianist, mere days before a scheduled piano concerto performance?"

"Maestro didn't explain?" Now Aleksi looked confused.

Madeleine smiled. "When you're an understudy with a lesser orchestra and opportunity knocks on your door, you don't ask a lot of questions beyond 'what time' and 'where'."

"I see. Well, Dominica had minor surgery a few weeks ago. At least, it was supposed to be minor – a few days off, then back to work. There were complications and a rather serious infection. She'll be fine, but she's still under observation, and will likely be away for two more weeks."

"And the understudy?"

"Broke her right index finger playing baseball with her nephew, just last week."

Madeleine gasped. "Isn't that a contract violation?"

"Absolutely," Aleksi conceded solemnly. "She must love that boy, because that baseball game cost her a cast on her hand and a dent in her career."

Madeleine shook her head. "It's all so surreal. I mean, if the violinist's – if Lillian's – fiancé performs in Cleveland and has performed in Boston, he clearly has more experience than me. I'm not complaining, just baffled."

"Well, I'm happy you're here," Aleksi stated, selecting a few olives and a thin slice of pancetta from the antipasto plate, "but it is a bit surprising, yes." He chewed carefully,

148

considering how much to tell her.

"The truth is, Jamison – Lillian's fiancé – was expected to join us. Maestro Sandburg was traveling earlier this week, delivering a guest lecture for an old friend of his who went the academic route, and when he returned we were abruptly told to expect you."

"When was this?" Madeleine asked.

"At Monday's rehearsal."

"But I wasn't even called until Monday evening!" As far as Madeleine was concerned, this was getting weirder and weirder.

"Do you happen to know where Maestro traveled?"

"Hmm… I'm not sure. Ohio? Iowa? It all sounds the same to me."

Madeleine was stunned silent.

"We should get back." Aleksi smiled. "Thank you for joining me. I hope I didn't bore you. Now, let's go get ready for your big night!"

One hour prior to curtain call, Madeleine stopped pacing her dreary dressing room long enough to slip into an elegantly simple, long black gown. She fumbled with the hidden side zipper, no thanks to her trembling hands. After twisting her hair into a simple updo, Madeleine searched for a paper towel to blot her perspiring hairline. Breathing a silent prayer of thanks for clear prescription-strength deodorant, she rummaged through her bag for a sleeve of Rolaids. Finding them, she chewed three tablets greedily and pressed a hand to her stomach to fight a wave of nausea.

Madeleine knew that if she were unable to pull herself together in the next few minutes, her career would be over. There wasn't an orchestra in the world willing to take a chance on an emerging pianist with crippling stage fright. The thought made her want to vomit.

"Madeleine? Do you have a moment?"

It was Aleksi's voice. Madeleine took a deep breath and

forced herself to open the door.

"A package arrived for you. Is everything OK?" He was dressed in his formalwear, annoyingly relaxed, and looking at her quizzically.

"Yes, thank you." Madeleine forced a smile and reached for the small FedEx box in Alexi's hand.

Returning to the lone chair in her makeshift dressing room, Madeleine examined the box. It had been sent from New York late the previous night. Curious about the sender and wondering what would justify the expense of such expedited shipping, she began to tug at the cardboard tear strip to access the contents.

The tear strip gave way unexpectedly, causing two objects and a note to tumble onto her lap. After a few seconds of confusion, Madeleine burst into unrestrained laughter. She picked up the small, plastic dollhouse piano and set it on the rickety table beside her. Then she picked up the tiny piano bench, to which Derrick had glued a plastic ballerina figurine.

Madeleine was still chuckling as she read the enclosed note, clutched it to her chest, and realized her evening would be fine.

"To my favorite pianorina. Knock 'em dead."

Linguini with Clam Sauce

Boil 1 lb dry linguini in salted water for approximately 6 minutes (leave slightly undercooked). While linguini boils, add 3 tablespoons olive oil, 4 diced anchovy filets, 2 diced garlic cloves, and ¼ cup finely diced onion to a hot pan and sauté for 3 minutes. Add 1 tablespoon crushed *herbes de provence*, ½ cup chardonnay, and a 15oz can of baby clams (undrained). Add linguini and cook an additional 2 minutes until liquid is absorbed. Garnish with coarse ground sea salt, crushed herbs and diced red peppers.

35 YEARS

Annie pushed the heavy cart down the concrete walkway to the next unit, trying not to spill the basket of shampoos, conditioners, miniature soaps, and pillow mints that she had balanced precariously atop a larger basket of coffee pods, sugar packets, and fresh creamers. The little cylinders of fresh cream were at the root of the impending avalanche but at least, as Annie mused, she had worn down her father and convinced him not to stock those horrid little packets of powdered artificial creamer any longer. She shuddered at the thought, keeping a hand balanced on the stack of toiletries.

She unlocked suite #14, the Rosebud Suite, and efficiently set into her work. In no time she had stripped the high, king sized canopy bed, carefully folding the antique quilt adored with hand stitched applique roses and setting it out of the way on an antique wingback chair. She stripped the bed quickly, an act which required a surprising amount of arm strength to accomplish without moving back and forth around the large ebony frame. Carrying the soiled linens outside, she deposited them into the large, canvas bag attached to the front of the housekeeping cart and removed a stack of 1000-threadcount, Egyptian cotton ivory sheets and coordinating, embroidered pillowcases from the second shelf on the side of the cart. After inhaling suspiciously, Annie smiled. Apparently her father had taken her other suggestion and changed the laundry additives, as well.

In less than five minutes Annie remade the bed with crisp hospital corners, fluffed pillows, and smart looking, individually wrapped pillow mints. She moved on toward the bathroom area with the same efficiency, using the towels lying on the floor to catch the water collected near the drains in the sink and the tub before depositing the heap in the same canvas bag as the sheets. The bathroom demanded careful attention because nothing was a more marked turnoff to a guest than a less than spotless bathroom. Annie carefully set to work with her nonabrasive, biodegradable cleaners to make the oversized Jacuzzi tub, the large marble sink, and the Kohler Whisper Flush toilet gleam. She remembered to place the toiletries in the bathroom basket before mopping the floor this time, reflecting ruefully upon the slip she had taken a few days earlier. She had been more annoyed about needing to mop the floor a second time than she had been about twisting her ankle in her haste to dance across the wet floor to deposit more shampoo in its assigned place.

After the bed and the bathroom were tended, Annie set about completing the lesser tasks: the dusting, the vacuuming, the window cleaning, and spot polishing of key areas such as light switches, phone receivers, TV remote controls, drawer handles, and doorknobs. As she spot polished, she checked drawers and closet shelves to make sure nothing had been left behind and set the thermostat at a comfortable temperature. Finally, Annie carefully checked to make sure that all of the light bulbs, remote control batteries, Kleenex boxes, and the nightstand Gideons Bible hadn't been stolen. After only a few weeks of cleaning rooms, nothing surprised her anymore.

"Mom, is the cart ready?" The tall, thin, pre-adolescent

boy asked, eager for the responsibility of delivering the laundry back up to the house.

"Not quite, Josiah. But while you wait, you could refill the box of firewood outside of #13."

"OK Mom, got it!" The boy yelled back and took off in the direction of his grandpa's stacks of tarp-covered split pine logs. Annie watched him run, knowing his easy, little boy gait would all too soon be replaced by the profile and movements of a teenager, and then a young man. She tried not to think about it.

Josiah had sure been a good kid these past few months; Annie couldn't possibly have been more proud. Sure, knowing his allowance would double in recognition of his help with the Inn on Sunday afternoons helped, but he was a thoughtful child with or without incentive.

A few minutes later, Josiah returned with a small cart stocked with wood, which he dutifully placed in the box outside of suite #13, the Sugar Maple Suite. Then, leaving the empty cart where it sat, he ran over to Annie with a bottle of water.

"Grandpa says you're working too hard, and if you don't take a break and come eat some lunch, he's gonna' feel bad."

"Tell Grandpa I have two more suites to clean and I'll be finished in another hour."

Josiah smiled. "Grandpa said to tell you, after you tell me that you aren't coming, how he's going to let Abby and Danny eat as much candy as they want until you come eat some lunch. And he said they can have soda pop, too – in five minutes!"

Annie groaned, but left the housekeeping cart where it sat and walked back to the main house with her gloating child. She knew when to surrender and her father knew exactly how to make that happen.

"Annie, what a surprise! And here I thought you'd be too busy for lunch." Mr. Anderson winked at his daughter, who shook her head but otherwise pretended not to notice the cola-colored reside on the bottoms of three, clear plastic cups sitting on the countertop.

When her father kissed her on the cheek and motioned for her to take a seat at the kitchen table, Annie protested. She started to reach for bowls and a soup ladle to help serve lunch for the five of them.

"Annie, sweetheart, I know you mean well, but this was the deal. You have to let me keep my end of the bargain." He looked at her with clear blue eyes, his grey hair slightly rumpled from a morning of corralling boisterous grandchildren, as though his pride was at stake. Annie gave up and flumped into the nearest kitchen chair in a rather unladylike manner. Pushing a few damp curls away from her face and behind her ears, she silently acknowledged that perhaps it was time for a quick break.

"Ok, you're the boss! I'm starving. What's for lunch?" She smiled lovingly at her father while her children giggled. He looked better, younger, when the children were around.

"*Ma belle fille,* you are in luck!" Mr. Anderson exclaimed in a fantastically bad French accent that drew peals of laughter from his eight year-old granddaughter.

"Monsieur Josiah has prepared for you a delectable bowl of chicken noodle soup, complete –" her father paused for dramatic effect "– with oyster crackers!" Josiah carried a bowl of soup to his mom with a grin and a deep bow.

"Mademoiselle Abigail has prepared for you a fabulous, fruity, funny face!" Mr. Anderson cued Abby, who carried a salad plate to her Mom in two hands as she had practiced. The plate featured a roughly cut strawberry nose, orange and blueberry eyes, and a smile created from a halved banana. Annie hugged her daughter.

"And for the grand finale, mini-Monsieur Daniel has prepared for you a batch of chocolate chip cookies!" At his grandpa's signal, Danny came charging forward with telltale chocolate streaks along his chin, clutching a chocolate chip cookie in each hand.

Danny extended his offerings to his mother, exclaiming proudly, "I was the official taster!"

"I can see that," Annie smiled. "Did you thank Grandpa for helping you?"

"I did, and Grandpa thanked me for being here to play with him!" Danny smiled up with all the innocence of a six year-old as the lump caught in Annie's throat.

The last two years had been difficult for the entire family, but they had been particularly brutal for Annie's father. Her mother's diagnosis had been a complete shock, unearthed after routine tests at an annual physical suggested something was amiss. Annie's parents tried everything the doctors suggested, but despite aggressive treatments, her mother's health had declined rapidly. In less than a year the illness transformed Annie's mother from a vibrant, glowing woman into a mere shadow of herself, sleeping in the medically transformed sunroom of the main house at the Inn almost 24 hours per day. Annie's father clung to that shadow with everything he had, both before and after she passed.

While Mrs. Anderson was still fully cognizant and mobile, the family had spent their time wisely. They recorded old family stories, sorted stacks of photos, lovingly arranged scrapbooks, and reminisced. Under her mother's expert guidance, Annie finally learned to make her maternal grandmother's perfect pecan pie. Annie and Bryant arranged to take her parents and their children to Disneyworld for a full week. The children built wonderful memories with Bryant recording as many video cameos and snapping as many thousands of pictures as he could without crossing into the morbid. Annie and Bryant made sure to have wonderful things planned for the children for several hours before their own bedtime every evening, so that Annie's parents could return to their own room to rest.

Near the end, Mrs. Anderson would spend her waking hours talking to Annie about her father and the love they had shared for thirty-nine years. She had asked Annie to help her father with the Inn however she was able and to help her father let the Inn go when it was time. Annie promised both, without considering which of the two might be more difficult.

Annie and her father closed the Inn temporarily before Mrs. Anderson died, and left it closed through the winter months. However, when Memorial Day loomed near, Annie understood what her father would never say. The tourist season in Door County, Wisconsin, was robust – but it was short. The Inn had been able to absorb the financial aftershocks of closing prior to last year's lucrative October season when, in an ironic twist, the warm, dry weather had held long enough to bring leaf peeping tourists up the peninsula almost until Thanksgiving. The financial reality remained, however, that the Inn would need to open for the summer high season. Somehow.

Annie's amazing mother had done the work of several normal people during the high seasons every year at the Inn. While Annie's father and a local teenage boy handled the firewood, the repairs, the maintenance, and outdoor upkeep of the Inn, Annie's mother handled most of the rest. She reluctantly acquiesced to hiring Marjorie, a full time housekeeper, and worked as a part time housekeeper herself on the weekends. Mrs. Anderson handled the reservations, the accounting, the shopping and stocking, and woke up at 4 a.m. every morning to prepare the breakfast baskets herself. She never allowed another cook into her kitchen, not even when the Inn began booking all 30 suites on many weekends.

In short, there was simply no way her father could operate the Inn without significant changes. For about five minutes, Annie wished he would sell the expansive property and retire. Maybe to Chicago, she mused. By minute six, however, she remembered that the Inn wasn't a property in his eyes. It was the life he had built with his wife and it was one of the most important parts of her that still remained. Annie remembered her promise.

As it turned out, Bryant had been expecting the conversation for several months. He wasn't looking forward to it, but he had certainly had enough time to consider the many directions in which the inevitable discussion might proceed.

"Will things settle down at work after the merger?" Annie had asked him one night as he rubbed her feet.

"In theory. That's the plan, anyway." A low fire crackled in the fireplace which Annie studied as Bryant refilled their glasses of chardonnay.

"Do you think you might be able to take a little time off?" She asked casually. The fire popped.

"Sure. I've taken a grand total of two hours of vacation time, for Abby's dance recital, since your -" Bryant caught himself. He stared mightily into his lightly aged, oak barreled wine.

"Since my mother passed. Yes, I know you've been working hard. So, we might be able to head up to the Inn this coming May?" Annie took a long sip to steel herself for his answer. He had done enough already, she knew that. This wasn't his mess. At least, it shouldn't be his mess.

"I was kind of hoping for an actual vacation, but sure, we can venture up. How long are we talking?" At Annie's half panicked expression, he realized that they had indeed ventured into 'the Talk'.

"I don't know what to do, Bryant. I don't know what my dad is going to do." Annie looked down at her wringing hands, and when her shoulders started to bunch and contract, Bryant knew she was fighting a losing battle to hold back tears.

"After losing her, he still has… what they built together. It's all he has left. If he can't operate the Inn, he'll need to…" Annie inhaled, and kept inhaling as her eyes grew wide and white, without fully expelling the air she was violently pulling in.

Bryant wrapped his familiar arms around her and held his wife solidly as the second wave of grief washed over her. He didn't have a magic answer, but tonight he could be strong enough for them both.

In the end, a temporary solution had proved less problematic than either of them anticipated. They started, as they almost always did, with their children. Josiah, Abby, and Danny loved their Grandpa Anderson dearly and they adored the Inn with a fervor only adventurous young children are capable of shamelessly displaying for any length of time. Annie and Bryant had built a wonderful life for their children in Chicago, but it was in the Northern backwoods – along the quiet lakeshore, in the meadow alive with wild daisies and lupines, and in the low cherry orchards for which Door County was so famous, where the children simply blossomed.

Annie took a leave of absence from the hematology lab, which coincided unfortunately well with the loss of a rather large NIH grant. She was able to negotiate a six month leave, with a written guarantee holding her seniority. A reasonably experienced but less credentialed, less expensive employee would be hired to temporarily fill her role. Annie and Bryant talked with their children's three teachers, as well as a retired schoolteacher turned educational consultant in Sturgeon Bay, and arranged for the children to transition into a small, Door County elementary school for the final six weeks of the school year. As the children were doing well academically, this was thankfully not an enormous concern. If anything, it might help them to make a few friends to play with over the summer months.

Annie and the children moved into the main house at the Inn during the first week in May. The transition, from their point of view, had been remarkably easy. Dover Park Elementary School welcomed the three Anderson children warmly, and even shy little Danny made a new friend the very first day. Annie's father doted on the children at every opportunity. Every day, Annie could see the lines on her father's face soften, his hands loosen, and his posture relax just a little bit more toward normal. She suspected he was sleeping more soundly now that he was no longer alone in the house.

While the children were in school, Annie worked with her father at whirlwind speed to bring the Inn back to its full charm and as close to complete efficiency as possible. While Annie updated the inventory lists and completed purchase orders, her father edged the lawns and mulched the flowerbeds. While Annie renewed advertising contracts and confirmed reservations, her father repainted the porch swings and cleaned the koi pond. In the evenings, they worked through a long list of short tasks and enjoyed the company of the children. Annie cherished the time with her father, but missed her husband deeply.

Back in Chicago, Bryant arranged his work schedule so that he could work twelve hour days, Monday through Thursday, allowing him three day weekends to spend up north. In theory, it was a sound idea. In practice, it flat out sucked. Three weeks into the arrangement, Bryant realized he had yet to escape his office inside of twelve hours. He was lucky to get home early enough once or twice each week to actually get eight hours of fitful sleep before heading back downtown.

As Bryant set out into the driveway for his fourth straight Friday-evening road trip, a stray can of Red Bull slipped out of the side pouch of his travel bag. The can hit the concrete at just the wrong angle and exploded spectacularly all over the driveway, the car, and Bryant's denim jeans. He cursed in an equally spectacular fashion – loud enough to provide plenty of free entertainment for old Mrs. Ednanski across the street. The four and a half hour drive from Chicago to Cherry Harbor had rarely been a problem in years past because it had usually been associated with family road trips and long, relaxing vacations. Everything was different now. Piggybacked onto stressful, compact workweeks and knowing that his assistance with heavy maintenance was needed throughout the weekend, the drive was hell.

Bryant never shared this with Annie, for he knew she was trying desperately to stay upbeat and cheerful for the sake of everyone. He would take care of this. Bryant had made a few calls, cashed in a few favors, and would explain everything to Annie soon enough. He was responsible for his share of screw-ups, no doubt, but he had never hidden anything so substantial from Annie during their twelve year marriage. An angry gulp of Red Bull from the spare can in the glove box helped Bryant wash down a few ibuprofen tablets and some of the guilt he felt.

Annie carefully dabbed a bit of gloss over her pale pink lipstick and double checked that the backs on her favorite emerald earrings were secure. She frowned at the pleats of her floral print, knee-length sundress and considered quickly changing back into her blue, A-line crepe skirt while Bryant read stories with the children.   Muttering under her breath, Annie rolled her eyes. For goodness' sake, she was acting like a teenager going on a first date rather than a grown woman joining her husband for dinner.

The truth was she felt the importance of this rare dinner date, as things hadn't really been normal between them since Annie and the children left Chicago eight weeks earlier. Left Chicago… it sounded so sinister, but they both knew it was temporary and necessary. Annie suspected how difficult the separation, the dual commitments, and the long drives were for her husband though he never complained. Sometimes, she thought, it would have been easier if he did complain.

Annie curled up on the front seat of the Nissan for the leisurely, winding drive up Highway 5 from the Anderson Inn to the Three Pines Supper Club, so that her head rested comfortably against Bryant's shoulder. He leaned his head slightly to the right, so that his cheek grazed her soft curls.

"You smell wonderful," Bryant complimented, before quietly kissing the top of his wife's head.

"I miss this," Annie whispered. "I'm glad your Mom is here to spend time with the children. They've been looking forward to seeing their Grandma Candice all week."

Bryant tried unsuccessfully to disguise his laugh as a cough and became momentarily interested in the mirror on the driver's side door.

"What?" Annie huffed rather indignantly.

This time Bryant didn't bother attempting to hide his amusement. "If somebody would have told me five years ago that you would be glad to see my mother, I would have recommended them for substance abuse counseling. That's 'what'." He looked down at her chidingly.

"A fair point well made. Can we agree that your mother has changed rather dramatically in the last year or so?" Annie asked with a wry smile.

Bryant wondered how much to tell her. A man didn't have to be a brain surgeon to know that discussing one's mother on a date was a surefire mood killer, married or not - especially when married. Then he caught a glimpse of Annie catching a glimpse of him thinking. Spill it, her expression clearly demanded.

"My mother and I talked a lot after…" Oh hell. The only thing worse than discussing his mother was discussing the funeral. He wondered sarcastically if Annie's father has a spare pair of flannel pajamas that he could wear to stay warm when Annie kicked him to the couch.

"It's OK," Annie said softly, patting his leg. "Even as shelled as I was I could see that your mother's demeanor took a turn for the better after that hellish week. I appreciated all of her help with the children. I'm sure you had your hands full with just me."

"She was really taken by how much of the funeral – the photos, the side conversations, the eulogies, all of it –

centered on the children and included me." Annie looked up quizzically. Bryant cleared his throat and continued,

"She expected to see and hear plenty about you, the daughter and the only child. I think she was... stunned... to see that your father, your extended family, and your parents' wide circle of friends discussed the five of us as all having been important to your mother."

"But that's completely —"

"Crazy? Yes. Did you expect otherwise?" Bryant looked at his wife with an arched eyebrow.

Annie snorted. "Are you telling me that she was surprised to learn that the rest of the world views our family as, um, a family and not as 'Bryant and His Collection of Unworthy Dependents'?"

Bryant took one hand off of the steering wheel to pinch the bridge of his nose. He sent up a quick prayer to the gods of marital harmony to please keep this evening from spiraling downward.

"I'm sorry," Annie offered, seeing the stress on his face. "That was a cheap shot. Continue."

"The short of it is, she realized what she's been missing. She realized how close your mother was to the children and how much the children loved her. It hit her that her relationship with her grandchildren was lacking."

"Yes. It was." Annie stated evenly.

"And it hit her that the reason for her rather shallow relationship with the children was her guarded attitude toward you."

"She said that? Candice actually said that?" Annie was incredulous.

"She did. She called me to apologize, Annie. She told me she regretted how long it took, and the circumstances required, for her to realize that I was a grown man and lucky to have such a wonderful family."

"And you never told me?" Annie's stare warned Bryant that he was venturing into rocky territory again.

"It was right after the funeral, Annie. I figured the last

thing you needed was drama from my mother." He looked at her. He was right. An emotional revelation from Candice would not have been well received, and Annie silently acknowledged as much.

He continued, "She wanted to talk to you. She wanted to call, or fly back and —"

Annie groaned. "Yes, exactly," Bryant continued. "I told her that I wanted nothing more than peace between the two women who have held all of the power over my sanity for the last twelve years, but her revelation would need to wait until everything settled down."

"Thank you, I think." Annie replied.

"I also told her that, better than telling you how she felt, would be showing you how she felt."

"You said that? I'm impressed." Annie kissed his cheek.

"Remember our first night out after your mom passed?" Bryant asked.

As if Annie could ever forget. She remembered how exasperated she felt when Bryant told her that his mother was in town for a business conference and asked if she could stop and see the children. Annie had been so upset by the intrusion that Bryant suggested they leave for dinner together when Candice arrived. Annie hadn't even worn make-up, but made the Herculean effort to leave the house.

"We had hot dogs and popcorn on the beach. I remember."

He wondered if she remembered walking for miles along the shore, wordless, clutching his hand as if he were the last safe harbor in the world. His heart hurt with the memory of how shattered she had been.

"She didn't actually have a conference to attend, Annie."

"What?" She heard Bryant, but didn't quite register what he actually said.

"She came to see the children. That's all. She came to

bake cookies."

"She flew to Chicago to bake cookies? I don't really know what to say to that."

"There's nothing to say. Just try to believe that she's trying. Late in the game, but she's finally trying."

"Candice, the cookie baking grandma. Huh." Annie shook her head, but Bryant could see that she was smiling. He eased the car off the highway and onto the gravel parking lot of the Three Pines.

Bryant was halfway through his king cut prime rib and jumbo baked potato before he realized that he was eating at a rather ungracious speed. Annie noticed, but sadly reflected on how he must be in the habit of eating many dinners alone these days. As she refilled their wine glasses, Bryant looked up from his steak and sheepishly set down his fork.

"Dry cherry wine," he stated with amusement after glancing at the label.

"Yes, it's local. You know that. Why are you grinning like a Cheshire cat?" Annie asked, with a trace of annoyance.

"Let's just say, years ago, I loved you enough to pretend that I liked this." Bryant swirled his glass with a glimmer of mischief in his eyes.

"Years ago you loved me?" Annie screeched.

Bryant's amusement turned into a full laugh. "Oh c'mon, Annie, that's not what I meant! This –" he motioned to the wine bottle "– has grown on me, much like you have." he stated with a grin.

"What do you mean?" Annie asked defensively. "Everybody likes cherry wine."

"No, everybody definitely does not. It is, shall we say, an acquired taste." He kept his lips serious, but his blue eyes twinkled.

"What a weird evening," Annie observed. "First you spring a revelation about your cookie-baking mother, and now you insult my local wine." She rolled her eyes at

Bryant.

"Our local wine," he countered evenly, before settling into an awkward silence. After a few seconds, he lowered his voice. "I need to talk to you about something, Annie."

"Nothing along the lines of 'we need to talk' ever ends well." Annie laughed.

But Bryant's face was deadly serious. He was clutching his linen napkin as if he needed something solid to hold onto. This was the face of a man with a secret, Annie decoded. Her stomach clenched.

"You're scaring me, Bryant. What is it?"

Bryant took a long drink of wine and slowly exhaled. "I've always been honest with you, Annie, every second of our marriage. I've always believed honesty includes transparency, which is why I feel nervous and guilty right now." He kept his eyes on his plate as he talked. Annie placed a hand over her churning stomach as her husband haltingly continued.

"I haven't been very transparent lately, but I need you to know that it's only because I haven't wanted to make you worry. Or get your hopes up. Or make you angry because maybe it's not what you want at all, in which case I've just nominated myself for the Stupid Husband of the Year Award."

"Transparent? My hopes up? What on earth are you talking about, Bryant?"

"I've arranged for a job transfer, Annie."

Annie choked on her wine. Not a cough, or a brief sputter from awkwardly breathing in a drop of liquid, but a full-fledged choke, beginning with a loud hacking sound and ending with Annie spitting cherry wine all over the white tablecloth as other diners stare in rapt amazement sort of choke.

Bryant jumped out of his chair and darted around behind Annie to pat on her back and wipe up the mess. "Jesus, Annie, are you OK?"

Annie took a moment to regain both her breath and

her composure, staring down a nosy stranger until he returned his attention to his own table. The distance between Chicago and Door County was hard enough. If he was transferring somewhere else... if he had arranged for it... She fixed her gaze on Bryant and simply said, "You did *what*?"

"I should have talked to you sooner. I'm sorry. Obviously," he motioned down at the table, which vaguely resembled a crime scene, "it was a mistake to wait to tell you. I thought you were juggling enough lately, and I wanted to be sure, so I waited until -"

"Are you leaving me?" Annie asked quietly.

Bryant stopped in midsentence. He closed his mouth, opened it, and closed it again as all of the color drained from his face. He rubbed the bridge of his nose with one hand, rubbed his temples with both hands, and let his forehead slide silently into one of his palms. When his hand started to shake, he slowly straightened up, pushed back his chair, and stood. Without a word, he turned from the table and walked through the small, dark paneled dining room and out the front door.

In utter shock, Annie focused on the precise moment before her. She willed the tears to stay behind her eyes as she waved her Visa card to catch the attention of the teenaged waiter. After signing the check, she stood on wobbly legs with as much dignity as the situation afforded and walked stiffly outside.

Bryant was leaning against the hood of the car facing the highway, waiting, which startled her. Then Annie remembered that they weren't in Chicago, and she couldn't exactly call a cab if he left her stranded here. She walked toward him, at a complete loss for words.

"What the fuck was that?" He growled at her in a low, snarling voice.

"You're scaring me," Annie said softly, which was the literal truth. In all the years she had known Bryant, most of them intimately, she had never, ever heard that voice.

"You think I'm… leaving you?" He sputtered, kicking the gravel to emphasize his fury.

Annie was bewildered. She stopped about ten feet short of the car, afraid to get any closer to the man whose level of anger was unfamiliar to her. "A job transfer?"

"To Sturgeon Bay. Damn it, Annie. It's a hell of a pay cut, but the cost of living is lower, and…" his words ground to a halt, a silence for which Bryant compensated by kicking the gravel again with added rage.

Annie was silent for a long, long while. Bryant wouldn't even look at her, so he didn't know when the tears started. They streamed out of the corners of her eyes silently, rolling gently down her cheeks and under her chin before dropping onto her chest and finding a home in the soft confines of her cotton dress. When her breath became jagged, he finally glanced in her direction. After a moment or two, he offered her a handkerchief. He was fiercely angry, Annie knew, but she didn't see hate in his eyes. Her tears started with fresh vigor when she realized Bryant's anger was dissipating, allowing his eyes to reveal a wounded, raw hurt.

"You think I would leave you? What have I ever done to make you think for a second that I could ever leave you?"

Annie's eyes were clouded, and she lurched toward the car for balance as she felt her knees begin to give way. Bryant caught her, strong and solid as he had been in her presence every second since her mother's hideous illness and death. He pulled her against him, muttering "Damn it, Annie." softly into her hair.

There was nothing to say. There was no apology for this type of misunderstanding. Annie simply looked at her husband, silently asking if he would forgive her.

"If I knew keeping it from you was going to cause so much fucking drama, I would have told you earlier." He wasn't looking directly at her, but the change in his tone told her that they would, eventually, be OK.

"When did you.. why didn't you…" Annie silently cursed herself. She could spit wine in spectacular fashion, but couldn't manage to spit out a question to her own husband.

"I didn't think it would work, so I didn't think it was worth mentioning at first. It's not like Door County is a big market, so I knew there wouldn't be many transfer opportunities within Tribune Company. But Tribune has ever-growing tentacles, so I took a long shot."

"When?"

"I contacted a few people, sent a few letters about three months ago. Just to see if I would get a bite." At this revelation, Annie's eyes grew wide. Bryant continued, "I did, a small one. As it turns out, Tribune executives were looking for a new district liaison up here, but the money they were willing to shell out for it was a joke. We negotiated."

"When?" Annie asked again.

"Just a few days after you left. I knew you were maxed out, adjusting to the workload of the Inn, helping the children acclimate, spending time with your Dad, and I honestly didn't think anything solid would come of it. So I didn't say anything."

"You should have."

"Apparently. After we hammered out a salary and job description, there was still the matter of whether your dad would even want us hanging around all of the time." Bryant eyed his wife nervously.

"Did you talk to my dad about this before you talked to me?"

The dead evenness of her question made his spine prickle. He tried to ignore the narrowing of Annie's eyes.

"When he and I were painting a few weeks ago, I mentioned offhand that Tribune might be expanding operations into his corner of Wisconsin. He stopped working for a moment, Annie, and looked away from me. Then he joked that he wouldn't dare to dream of having his family move back to 'these old Northern hillbilly woods', but if I got sent here by mistake there would be plenty of room in the main house."

Annie tried to remain indignant at having been overstepped in such a blatantly old fashioned way, but the image in her head was softening her heart.

"I knew... I knew, Annie, that this would mean everything to him."

"And what about me? What about my job? The house? The kids?" They sounded like fair questions in her head, but the anger that flashed again in Bryant's eyes made Annie rapidly second guess herself.

"Seriously? OK. I'll call them back and turn it down. Never mind." Bryant started to walk toward the driver's side door.

"Wait." Annie hurried over to him, and placed her hands on his hips. "I'm just... stunned."

"I gathered," Bryant said sarcastically.

"I need a minute. I'll never be able to convey how sorry, how very, very sorry I am for jumping to the wrong conclusion."

"You think?"

"Let me finish, please. I'm sorry. And I will be sorry for a long while. But this is quite a bit of news to just drop on me, considering that our marriage has been one of open communication and honesty, always. I've never bought an expensive pair of shoes without letting you know, Bryant, and you just dropped on me the fact that you applied for and accepted a job transfer without even running it by your wife. Grant me that small detail, at least."

"Would you rather stay in Chicago?" Bryant asked pointedly.

"No, but that's not the point."

"That's exactly the point. If I would have asked you earlier, you would have been torn between your desire to live here, to help your dad, to keep the Inn as a family legacy, and between what you perceive as my career goals and our family's financial autonomy. Am I correct? Grant me that small detail in return."

Annie's silence was all the acknowledgement he needed.

"I want this too, Annie. Maybe that's hard for you to understand, and to be honest that's hard for me to accept, but I want this life for our children. I want the stability and the fresh air. I want to stop driving two thousand miles a month to see my wife. I want to share a life and a bed with you every day. I want you to be happy."

"I'm sorry, Bryant. I love you more right now than ever, if that's possible."

"I would never leave you, Annie. Damn it." He pulled her in close and kissed the top of her head. It wasn't exactly the romantic dinner he had planned, but he knew by now that marriage was full of odd twists and turns, and through it all, he loved this complicated woman.

When they returned to the Inn after a somewhat awkward drive, Annie gave Bryant a quizzical look. At the fork in the drive, Bryant turned left toward the suites, while the main house was off to the right.

"Got something to say?" Bryant arched an eyebrow at his wife.

"I think I've said enough for this evening," Annie conceded.

Bryant parked the car in the guest lot and looking tired but smiling faintly, walked around the car to assist his wife. He wordlessly dangled a guest key and guided Annie to the front door of the Birch Suite. It was Annie's favorite. He unlocked the door and motioned for Annie to enter.

It had been almost twelve years since Annie had felt such delighted surprise upon entering a room and her thoughts momentarily drifted back to their wedding reception. Bringing herself back to the present, she took in the images of the room she considered to be quite familiar. Wood was stacked, waiting, in the natural fireplace. Bryant stepped quietly around his wife, lit one of the long matches from the tin on the hearth, and soon the room was aglow with soft light. She heard a faint noise and realized it was ice settling in the bucket on the side of the Jacuzzi tub, allowing a bottle of champagne to sink a bit deeper. Two glasses and a box of Annie's favorite chocolates, Godiva champagne truffles, also adorned the tub.

Annie heard music playing softly, wordless notes of jazz and blues, and then her eyes went to the hyacinths. Heavy blue stems stood proudly in clear vases on each of the nightstands on either side of the bed. The quilt had been turned down, and Annie's breath caught when she noticed the sheets had been sprinkled with pink and white rose petals. She stared in utter, bewildered amazement at her husband.

"My mother will be here for three more days, keeping the children on a well-supervised sugar high. Your father called Marjorie, whose daughter Jane is home from college for the summer. Jane will be helping her mother with housekeeping for the next few days. Reservations are at a brief lull, and your father made clear to me that he can handle them. In fact, he made clear to me that any interference on your part will be considered a vote of 'no confidence'."

"Do they know Josiah has -"

"A violin lesson tomorrow morning," Bryant finished her sentence. "Yes. Now stop mothering and daughtering and inn-keeping for a few breaths."

Annie let it all sink in as a stunned smile tugged at the corners of her mouth.

"This means, my love, that we are officially on vacation for three glorious days." Bryant removed his tie, and started to work on the champagne cork. He almost dropped the bottle when Annie leapt at him with a joyful hug. Their dinner disaster was no match for the love they felt for each other and the life they were steadfastly building together.

"We can talk about everything, I promise. I will warn

you though," he tilted his head toward his suddenly alarmed wife and flashed her a wicked grin, "I'd rather talk while you're naked."

Annie threw her head back in her first carefree laugh of the weekend, and hung the Do Not Disturb sign on the outside door.

Danny's Chocolate Chip Cookies

In a large mixing bowl cream together 1 cup softened butter, ½ cup white sugar, and ½ cup brown sugar. Add 1 egg and 2 teaspoons pure vanilla extract; combine well.

In a separate bowl, blend together 1 ½ cups flour, ¾ cup rolled oats, 1 teaspoon baking powder, ½ teaspoon baking soda, and ¼ teaspoon ground cardamom. Add dry ingredients to wet ingredients and stir. Fold in 1 cup semisweet chocolate chips and 1 cup dark chocolate chunks.

Drop by rounded teaspoons onto cookie sheets lined with parchment paper. Bake for 10 minutes in a preheated, 375 degree oven. Makes 4 dozen cookies.

36 YEARS

"Wake up, sleepyhead."

Audrey tentatively lifted one eyelid, glanced around the classically appointed hotel room, then abruptly turned her head into her synthetic down pillow to shield against the aggravatingly bright morning sunshine. "Why are you so happy?" Audrey grumbled. "Come back to bed."

Unwinding the large white bath towel from her damp hair and tossing it over a nearby desk chair, Pam cinched her fluffy, purple, terrycloth bathrobe and jumped onto the empty side of the queen sized bed. Wrapping her arm around the sullen, blanketed lump that was Audrey, she planted a kiss in the disheveled curly brown hair that poked out angrily from the top of the thick white comforter. "Your cheerful disposition in the morning is just one of the many things I love about you."

"You're killing me, Pam. You. Are. Killing. Me." Audrey picked her head up long enough to glare at the alarm clock before continuing. The clock read 7:15 a.m. "It's 3:15 in Fiji. That means it's 3:15 inside my head. I've only been back a few days."

"Well, you're not in Fiji anymore. We have a full day planned, Audrey. I'll order breakfast!"

"Slave driver." Even as she said it, the bite left her voice and Audrey grudgingly convinced herself that spending time with Pam was more important than sleeping in. She tried to ignore the fact that her pillow was exceptionally comfortable.

After getting the program in Aruba off the ground, Audrey's latest exchange student project for Abbott College had taken her to Fiji, alone. Pam could only arrange for a two-week vacation, and the airfare for so short a trip was exorbitant. As it turned out, Audrey left early and the project failed. When political chaos erupted and the Constitution of Fiji was abruptly abolished, the rights of gay and lesbian residents of the island nation became unclear. Audrey made the final decision to leave when a legally planned gay rights march was ominously cancelled by police. It was not a decision she made lightly, but Audrey had made clear during candid discussions with Katharine Riley, Dean of International Studies and her direct supervisor, how she was unwilling to live and work in a hostile political climate, no matter how warm the weather or how pristine the beaches.

"I missed you, Audrey. I don't want to squander our time together away from my family. God knows we'll see enough of them this week. For that, I apologize in advance." Pam collapsed backward onto the bed, her towel-dried hair flicking against Audrey's cheek. She used her arm to shield her eyes. Whether Pam was shielding against the sun or the possibility that something could go wrong in the close quarters of her family was unclear.

Ah, yes, Audrey reflected. The 20th Annual Marquardt Family Reunion. It was the reason they were in Denver, and the main reason Pam was so damn perky this morning. Audrey knew Pam was eager to see her cousins as well as her far-away sister's new baby. She had laughingly warned of crazy uncles and a gossipy, overdressed great aunt. Audrey, however, couldn't shake her uneasy feelings. On the one hand, it was wonderful to know that the

Marquardts were so welcoming of their relationship; Audrey and Pam certainly weren't feeling the love from Audrey's own family. On the other hand, she didn't know how to respond or how to react. The dynamics of large families were unfamiliar to Audrey, and the idea of a nonjudgmental family such as the one Pam promised, well, that sounded like fiction.

Audrey crawled out from under the covers. "Don't order breakfast, let's go out. Somewhere we can sit outside and see the mountains. Give me fifteen minutes, OK?"

"Got it. I'll warn you all about Aunt Betty over eggs benedict." Pam flashed a mischievous smile as Audrey groaned and headed for the shower.

By 8:30 a.m. in Denver, or 4:30 a.m. in Audrey's head, Audrey and Pam were seated in comfortable wicker chairs at a small round table outside of Maxie's Café in the picturesque Red Rocks area.

"Can I bring you ladies something to drink while you look over the menu?" The young, blonde haired waiter asked.

"Coffee, please, cream no sugar, and a glass of water." Audrey said. She knew from her travels that staying well hydrated would help her adjust to the altitude.

"A Bloody Mary, spicy, with a red beer chaser." Pam requested.

"Coming right up!" The waiter promised and scurried away.

"I don't know how you can drink that," Audrey grimaced. "Pepper and celery salt aside, the thought of drinking beer in the morning makes my stomach roil."

Pam laughed. "I'm celebrating. Are you really taking some time off, Aud?"

Audrey stared out the steep rocky face dominating the view from the quiet pedestrian street. If one could overlook the expensive wardrobes à la Brooks Brothers decorating the young professionals on their way to Denver's high rise office district, the street would feel like something right out of the Wild West.

"Yeah, I think so. I can't complain about traveling from one island to another for a living."

"No, you can't." Pam interrupted with a smile.

"But I'm tired of living in cottages, apartments, and guest rooms that never quite feel like home. I'm tired of being away from you more than I'm with you. It's time for a change, and since I don't really know what that change should be, taking some time off feels like the best approach."

Brad, the blond haired waiter, returned with their drinks and took their breakfast order.

"Cheers to that," Pam said, clinking her tall, garishly decorated red glass against Audrey's coffee mug.

Audrey delved into her bananas foster French toast, following a big bite of vanilla flavored brioche, bananas, and walnuts with a greasy slice of bacon. "So, tell me again what I'm getting myself into this afternoon."

"Sure thing. You've already met my parents, so you know Debbie and Larry are harmless. They like you. A lot. My sister Kate, well, it's nothing you haven't seen before. Her new baby will be a welcome distraction from the unspoken 'I'm sorry God made you this way, but I love you despite your unavoidable flaw' vibe she gives off."

Audrey groaned. "And your brother?"

"Donald won't be here. Between his cigarette smoking and his devotion to bachelorhood, Kate finds needling him in public to be absolutely irresistible. He told mom that it would be better for all involved if he feigned a work obligation."

"And your mom agreed? To his missing the reunion?"

Pam just shrugged. "He wasn't asking permission. Uncle Dan will try to kiss you, so watch out for that. It's sort of a rite of passage." Pam chuckled when Audrey winced.

"And crazy Great Aunt Betty," Pam continued, "well, she's the life of the party. She has absolutely no social filter whatsoever. She thinks it, she says it, and she doesn't care who is around to overhear."

"You say that fondly?" Audrey asked.

"I love her to pieces," Pam laughed. "You'll see."

Audrey and Pam spent a lovely afternoon sightseeing and window shopping in Denver and stopped for margaritas before trekking out to the park pavilion reserved for the 20th Annual Marquardt Family Reunion picnic kick-off event. Despite Audrey's anxiety over attending such a function, she was enjoying the excitement Pam exuded over seeing her family again. Audrey tried mightily to push her feelings about her own family's lack of welcoming aside.

"Uncle Dan!" Pam called, with more volume than was really necessary, to the balding older man lumbering toward her with outstretched arms. Pam shot Audrey a reminder smile.

"Baby girl! Pam! How are you, baby girl!" Uncle Dan practically lifted her off the ground with his big bear hug, and planted a ridiculously generous kiss on her left cheek.

"Oh, Uncle Dan. Only you could manage to call a 40 year-old woman 'baby girl' and actually mean it."

"40, bah. You were in pigtails just last year, I think. And who is this, baby girl?" He asked, smiling toward Audrey.

"This is my partner, Audrey. We've been together for a long time now, but this is the first time I've been able to drag her to a reunion." Pam smiled.

"Audrey! Welcome!" He let go of Pam and stretched out his bear paws in Audrey's direction.

Audrey was ready for him, and quickly turned her head to the side as she was swallowed up in a giant hug. When he let go and she started to step aside, she realized that nobody truly escapes the kiss. Pam coughed in a feeble attempt to disguise her laugh as Uncle Dan planted a wet kiss right on Audrey's forehead, already arched upward in surprise.

When he walked away, Pam wiped off Audrey's head with the napkin surrounding her beer bottle. "Well, at least you got that out of the way early."

"Gee, thanks." Audrey grumbled as Pam smirked.

"Food's on!" They heard a woman's voice yell from the kitchen of the pavilion.

"We'd better hurry," Pam said, already turning in the direction of the voice. "This clan is ruthless when it comes to lunch. If you want anything good, you need to get in line early!"

Audrey followed her to the buffet, collecting a Styrofoam tray, napkin, and plastic utensils from a side table. They loaded up their plates with standard picnic fare including pulled pork sandwiches, fruit salad, baked goods, and what looked like a thousand delicious - if starchy - side dishes.

"Darlene brought her potato salad!" Pam was clearly enthusiastic. Audrey glanced over and cringed. She always thought potato salad, heavy with eggs and mayonnaise, was gross – and hazardous at warm, outdoor picnics such as this. She shook her head as discreetly as possible when Pam offered a scoop.

"This is different, Aud. It's German potato salad, my cousin's recipe from her German mother-in-law. Not a speck of mayonnaise in the whole bowl, and a little bit of bacon for flavor. Delish!"

"When in Rome," Audrey acquiesced to a level tablespoon deposited suspiciously on her plate. Pam was right, it was darn good. Pam was also right about the bowl being empty long before anyone went up for seconds.

When Pam went to throw their empty plates away and got sidetracked by a relative, Audrey walked away from the picnic table to watch a volleyball game in progress. She didn't notice the septuagenarian woman walking toward her wearing a bright purple shirt and a green baseball cap over her shoulder length grey hair.

"So you're the woman who makes Pam happy. What is your name, dear?" Audrey was a bit thrown off balance by the sudden comment but recovered quickly enough.

"Audrey. I'm Audrey Navarro. It's a pleasure to meet you, Ms. -" She waited for the older woman to add a name.

"Betty. I'm Aunt Betty!" The woman smiled, and thankfully did not try to kiss her.

"Pam has always been one of my favorites," the old woman continued. "Her mother isn't flaky like some of my nieces and nephews, so it stands to reason that Pam turned out just fine." Audrey noticed that there were many family members within earshot, and apparently Aunt Betty couldn't have cared any less.

"Uh, well…" Audrey couldn't think of a suitable reply.

"How long have the two of you been together, dear?"

"Pam and I met about six years ago. I suppose we've been together nearly that long." Six years. It was hard to believe so much time had passed, and Audrey's own parents didn't even want to meet her. Audrey tried to dismiss the thought.

"Do you plan to get married?"

A familiar arm came across Audrey's shoulder, rescuing her with a gentle squeeze. Pam answered. "We'd love to get married, Aunt Betty, but it's a little more complicated than that."

"I may be up in years, Pam, but I'm not a crazy old bat. I know all about the ridiculous antics of uptight politicians but isn't it possible, sort of, in a few states?"

"Well, yes, but…" Pam faltered.

"But what? If you love her, than marry her, it's not that complicated. In that regard, I do harbor old-fashioned sensibilities." Aunt Betty stared at Pam, exasperated.

Pam started to get frazzled. "I'm not sure now is the best time to talk about this, Aunt Betty."

"Nonsense. Why is that? Because you love a woman? I just had this same conversation with your cousin Steve, who is still stringing along the same poor girl I've been seeing at this family circus for years. So don't think you're special. Love is love, and commitment is commitment, and that is that."

Audrey placed a calming hand over Pam's forearm and smiled at the infamous Aunt Betty. "I think you're right, actually. I respect that mindset."

"I believe Iowa is one of the states that doesn't have a penis counting problem. I saw it on the news, right after Wheel of Fortune. You could get married there, I think. Or leave the country all together. Straight people elope all the time!"

Neither Pam nor Audrey heard the second half of Aunt Betty's statement because Pam was too busy yelling "Aunt Betty!" and Audrey was coughing from the water that she accidentally breathed in.

"Oh, for goodness' sake, girls! Don't act like you're 17. This country has a penis counting problem. I'm just telling it like it is." She stood straighter and adjusted her baseball cap for effect.

"You always do, Aunt Betty, but I'm afraid you're not making any sense right now." Pam gave Audrey a look that suggested perhaps Aunt Betty's age was affecting her faculties.

"I'm making perfect sense. The way I see it, any two idiots can get married in this country as long as the penis count is correct – one per marriage, no more, no less. You don't need to have a job, a high school diploma, a driver's license, a clean criminal record, or a letter of reference. You don't need to demonstrate any capacity for problem solving, compassion, common sense, or love. You for darn sure don't have to have mutual respect, honesty, cooperation, or even faithfulness within a marriage. The government doesn't care.

"But you could have all of these things," Aunt Betty continued, "and be denied the right to marry if the penis count is incorrect. And because I'm willing to tell it like it is, people think I'm the crazy one." Aunt Betty tipped back a bottle that looked more like hard lemonade than a soft drink, and arched a white eyebrow daring either of the women to disagree with her.

"Aunt Betty, I do believe you're the wisest woman I know." Pam smiled at her fondly and gave her a warm hug.

"If you decide to get married, please tell me. I'd love to be there!" Aunt Betty looked as though she had a follow up thought, but a young relative with a beer in his hand spotted her and walked past a little too quickly for an innocent man.

"Jason, come back here. I need to talk to you. What's this I hear about you spending your car insurance money on a tattoo? Have a seat, young man."

Bananas Foster French Toast

Whisk together 3 eggs and ¾ cup cream in a shallow bowl. Use a paring knife to cut a vanilla bean in half lengthwise, and scrape the seeds from the center. Whisk seeds into the egg mixture.

Dip 8 thick slices of day old brioche into the egg mixture. Flip bread to moisten both sides. Cook on a hot, buttered griddle for 3 minutes per side.

While French toast is cooking, melt ¼ cup butter in a sauté pan. Add ¼ cup brown sugar, 2 sliced bananas, and ¼ cup chopped walnuts. Cook over medium heat for 2 minutes, or until bananas are lightly caramelized. Spoon mixture over French toast. Serves 4.

37 YEARS

"*Jó estét*, Madam LaBlange," the young man greeted her with a deep bow.

"Good Evening, János, and thank you for making me so comfortable already," she replied sincerely, enjoying the sound of the eager intern's flawless English laced with a rich Hungarian accent. She followed his quick, lanky frame through a set of heavy, dark wood doors and down a long, rich, burgundy carpeted hallway.

János stopped in front of a tall door exquisitely inlaid with exotic woods. Madeleine smiled to see that the nameplate greeted her personally, if formally. János held the door open and gestured with his arm and another smile for her to enter. Madeleine stepped into the tastefully furnished performer's suite, her very own for the next three days.

"You will find the personal items you've requested in the dressing room to your right. If anything does not meet with your satisfaction, please let me know. The remainder of your belongings have been transferred to the Corinthia Hotel Budapest on your behalf. The entire hotel has been recently remodeled; I trust you will find the accommodations to your liking. Did you encounter any difficulties with your travel that you wish for me to report, Madam?" János watched her expectantly.

"No, thank you. Everything from New York to Budapest has gone perfectly smoothly so far!" Madeleine laughed and knocked three times on the nearest wood object, an ornately carved end table. The curious look on the intern's face made it clear that the act of superstition was lost in translation. Madeleine started to explain, then simply smiled.

"If you please, I would be happy to give you a tour of the Hall. Perhaps you would prefer to dine first?" János waited eagerly for her response.

The Hall. He said it so casually. Madeleine still found her very presence in an outer corridor of the world renowned Béla Bártok National Concert Hall to be surreal. As excited as she was to take a tour, Madeleine couldn't deny that she was astonishingly hungry.

"Dinner would be wonderful, actually. It feels like days have passed since leaving New York and airline food leaves a bit to be desired! Where do you recommend I – "

"Our concierge has already been updated on your food preferences, Madam. I can have dinner delivered right here for you in 15 minutes."

Madeleine was momentarily confused, before remembering answering an exhaustive list of questions a week earlier, related to the comfort of her stay.

"Are you a performer yourself, János?" It might be perceived as an insulting question, insinuating that his work at the Hall wasn't enough, but his overt joy in assisting her made Madeleine wonder at his background.

János blushed. "I am a student, Madam. I play the *cselló*." He paused awkwardly, looking even younger than his actual years. "It is truly a pleasure to meet you, Madam."

"Would you like to join me for dinner, János? I have a dear friend joining me tomorrow, but this evening – I would love to learn about your repertoire." She smiled at him, the faintest whispers of the lines of wisdom crinkling in the corners of her eyes. It wasn't all that long ago, Madeleine mused, when she was the doe-eyed student admiring concert performers. She intended to be gracious about the role change.

János blinked. His face alternately blushed, then went pale. "It would be an honor, Madam LaBlange."

They enjoyed a lovely meal together. It was, Madeleine reflected with utter amusement, the first time she had been asked for an autograph.

As the early morning sun peeked in through the drapes, the warm chocolate, soft almond, and muted olive hues of Madeleine's bedroom suite at the Corinthia Hotel danced to life. The glow was a positive sign, Madeleine decided, refusing to acknowledge the slow churning in her stomach. She glanced at the clock. 6:52 a.m. In twelve hours, eight minutes time, 1,433 people would be sitting in silence waiting for her piano performance in one of the most magnificent concert halls in all of Europe. What could go wrong?

Madeleine extracted herself from the plush bed linens, using all of her will to convince her stomach that today was just another day. She focused on seeing Derrick after the… in the evening. The thought made her smile. It had been almost a year since she had seen him last in Prague, where he had a seasonal contract. She and Derrick had made a pact to visit in person at least annually, no matter where their work took them. Or maybe, especially where their work took them, as their respective careers had led to some interesting visits.

She remembered their time together in Prague and started to laugh. Derrick was pleased to hear that she was dating, so she brought Vittorio along. He was a little known opera singer she had met a few months earlier, and Madeleine found she enjoyed his company in a comfortable but noncommittal way. He wanted to make contacts in Prague anyway, and offered to tag along with Madeleine. After Prague, she reflected on how their time together had rarely been in the company of others. She still couldn't believe how poorly she had misgauged Vittorio's ability to make civil conversation in small groups.

"You are an opera performer, Madeleine tells me." Derrick had said by way of opening, offering his hand.

"I am an opera artist," he sniffed in return, and gave Derrick's hand a single shake.

Madeleine laughed again to remember how Derrick had arched an eyebrow in her direction, the corner of his mouth already curling into a subtle smile.

"Oh I apologize," Derrick replied, baiting him. "I'm just not clear on the difference."

"The difference," Vittorio huffed, "is that performing requires skill, and skill can be taught. Artistry in innate, and can be brought to the fore and polished, but not simply taught from nothing." He actually tipped his head back an inch or two as he said it.

"Well, you must be proud of how well taught your girlfriend has managed to become," Derrick offered with a mixture of sarcasm and distaste.

"We are companions, and yes, she is a fine performer. Very fine." At this, Vittorio reached over to pet Madeleine's hair. Madeleine coughed over her glass of chardonnay.

"You don't mind if I speak with your... companion... for a moment, do you?" Derrick asked. He didn't wait for a reply, but walked over to the terrace doors of his apartment rental and stepped outside.

When Madeleine followed, Derrick looked at her, eyes smiling, and shook his head. "Honey, why are you killing calendar squares with him? Please tell me you didn't pay his airfare to follow you here."

"DERRICK!" Madeleine chastised. "Of course I didn't pay to bring him along, what do you take me for?"

"Sorry. Had to ask. Do you love him?"

Madeleine only glared at him.

"Again, had to ask. Because I love you. After all these years, even Ethan loves you. You're like our little sister, Maddie. Whether or not you want a 'performer' and his partner as brothers, you're stuck with us. Do you love him?"

"Of course not." Madeleine stated simply. "He's company. We enjoy each other's company."

"Is he good company?"

Madeleine tried her best to pretend that she didn't understand the question. This only drew a wicked smile from Derrick, which made her cringe.

"Is he toe curling, lips parting, gasping his name while desperately clutching the bed sheets with your nails good company, or is he just company?"

"I don't think that's a question many big brothers ask their little sisters, do you?" She replied evenly.

Derrick chuckled. "Maddie, it's your life and your company. But in case legions of straight men haven't brought it to your attention, you're all grown up now. Enjoy your company, but don't settle. That's all." He kissed her cheek and walked back into the sitting room.

"Vittorio, forgive me for keeping Madeleine. It's been a while and we had some catching up to do. May I refill your wine?"

Vittorio was just about to hold his glass up to Derrick when Madeleine interrupted.

"Vittorio, I'm not feeling my best tonight. I think it was the long flight. Would you mind terribly if I stay here and nap? Would you be able to call a car back to the hotel?"

Vittorio flared his nostrils briefly at being dismissed by his performer, but he had more important things to do and people to see in Prague. "No problem, darling. You have a key?"

"Yes, thank you. Good evening, Vittorio."

Derrick closed the door behind him and spent a long, late night laughing and drinking with Madeleine. By morning, Vittorio's belongings were gone from their hotel room and Madeleine never heard from him again.

Still laughing at the memory, Madeleine showered and prepared for the first half of her day. Even though she had stayed in some very fine hotels, Madeleine couldn't help but be impressed by the facilities in her suite at the Corinthia Hotel. Her deep massage tub and separate shower were solid marble, gently warmed, as were her fluffy towels. The rain shower, she observed giddily, featured filtered water and precision temperature control. Adjustable lighting and music were nice touches. She wished she could spend all day in this bathroom, but she was disciplined. By 7:45 a.m. she was downstairs in the lobby of the Corinthia, coffee in hand, waiting for the car to take her to the National Concert Hall.

She asked the driver to wait for her to enter, because the employee entrance to which János had directed her the night before did not look promising. Also, truth be told, the entire passageway behind the building was barely wide enough for the car and looked rather creepy even in the morning light. There was no need to worry. Exactly as János had promised, a morning custodian greeted her at the door and, after checking her identification, ushered her inside. After a wave to the driver, the black car drifted away.

The next few minutes were spent twisting through the cavernous outer hallways of the National Concert Hall in a fog, as Madeleine was already drifting to room 121A in her mind. This simple performance trick had calmed her nerves and allowed her to maintain a sense of clarity through every performance she had given since leaving the University of Iowa for the second time, four years earlier. No matter how far she had traveled, or how overwhelming the venue, Madeleine had an uncanny ability to transform her immediate surroundings into her humble practice room.

To a casual observer, Madeleine was obviously seated

at a Concert Grand piano on the main stage of the Hall. Had she glanced straight over the piano and actually focused her eyes, she would have seen ornate acoustical carvings in shades of red, blue, and yellow spanning the second and third levels, but she never noticed. Had she glanced to the left, she would have seen the 92 towering pipes of the Béla Bartók National Concert Hall's organ, an instrument so magnificent that its creation required collaboration between the German *Orgelbau-Mühlhausen* and the Hungarian *Orgonaépítő Manufaktúra*, but it never caught her eye. Had she glanced to the right, and astonishingly enough she did not, Madeleine would have noticed four majestic levels of gleaming, pale wood seating, in crisp view close up, but swallowed into darkness halfway back. If the house lights were on, she would have been able to see how every seat was arranged so that patrons could align their ears and their eyes with Madeleine's position. She would notice all of these details when the concert ended, of course. Madeleine would drink in the marvel of it all, just as she had in every other concert hall in which she was afforded the honor to play. But until it was over, she was simply in room 121A, wearing comfortable jeans and a simple knit sweater, coffee by her side.

She closed her eyes and hovered her hands above the keys, but did not touch them. There was no need. As her hands glided through the air, she heard every note of tonight's movements from Liszt's *Années de Pèlerinage* in her mind. She would not allow herself to become overwhelmed by the enormity of performing Liszt's music in his home country, so she simply confined herself to room 121A.

After spending months perfecting every movement, Madeleine had worked painstakingly to divide the expansive composition, a trio of compositions, really, into two sensible concert length blocks. She paired each block with complementing pieces by Chopin, and would perform two full length performances on two consecutive nights. If history held true, she would have an almost identical audience both nights. Both concerts had sold out together, months in advance.

Hours later, Madeleine was again offering forward Liszt with flawless execution. This time, her coffee was offstage, and her jeans and sweater were replaced with a stunningly simple, floor length black Armani gown. Her pale hair was coiled just above the nape of her neck into an elegant chignon held in place with a silver clasp adorned with a diamond accent.

She was so breathtakingly beautiful, he had to close his eyes to avoid distraction and truly hear her bring Liszt to life.

Madeleine savored the somber low notes and allegro tempo of the first movement, recognized in English as The Chapel of William Tell. She would have been able to feel the massive audience settle collectively inward, away from their lives outside of the Hall and onto the first chords of music, if she had been so inclined. Madeleine, however, was settled inward on room 121A, where she never attracted an audience.

Or so she had thought.

With seamless transitions, the first movement gave way to the lyrical melodies of the second, At the Lake of Wallenstadt, and then the transitioning tenor of the third, Pastoral. In the fourth movement, Beside a Spring, Liszt had Madeleine's fingers dancing along almost the full length of the piano. Only fifteen minutes into *Années de Pèlerinage*, most of the audience had successfully cast aside reality, and lost complete awareness of the daily hummings of their minds outside of the Hall. Such transcendental experiences were why many aficionados of classical piano were willing to pay so dearly for their tickets.

For one audience member, the tormented daily hummings had finally conjoined with reality. When Madeleine played the fifth movement, aptly translated as Storm, his hands knotted with sympathetic tension.

After the intermission, the music shifted into the movements written by Liszt during the second year of the three years he had devoted to the composition. On average, the movements were dramatic yet comfortable, vaguely reminiscent of Mozart, as if Liszt himself had matured to the point of acknowledging the influence of other composers. Madeleine concluded the evening with the sixth movement of the second year, Sonnet 123 of Petrarch. Applause quickly evolved into a standing ovation as Madeleine stood and bowed deeply to the approving audience.

The blinding stage lights made it impossible for her to notice the tall gentleman in the impeccable tuxedo who abruptly returned to his seat in the third row of the main floor. In the happy commotion of the concert finale, nobody noticed how the color had drained from his face or how his hands trembled. Nobody gave it a thought when he excused himself ahead of other patrons in the row to hunt down a stiff drink as quickly as possible.

Then again, nobody else had noticed when Madeleine stood to face the audience that her left ring finger was still bare.

After the curtains were drawn, János immediately handed Madeleine a bottle of spring water, congratulated her profusely, and escorted her back to her Performer's Suite. At the door, he sheepishly handed her a typed message and explained that while the message was received in the morning, János had strict orders to wait until after the performance to share it with her.

Madeleine assured János that she wouldn't need anything else before the next day, and closed the door to offer her attention to the folded piece of paper. Her shoulders fell and her face shrouded with utter, childlike disappointment when she learned that Ethan had broken his ankle the day prior and Derrick needed to return home to care for him. Madeleine's much anticipated and always relaxing evening with Derrick was gone, and she was so sorry for it she almost could have cried. At least the hotel is comfortable, Madeleine muttered to herself ruefully. She poured herself a glass of wine from the iced bottle in the sitting room and was packing up the few personal items she wished to bring with her to the Corinthia when she heard the somewhat hesitant knock at the door.

Gritting her teeth, Madeleine stared at the heavy wood door and briefly considered ignoring the offending sound. Her mood had deteriorated since receiving Derrick's message and she wanted nothing more than to return to her hotel suite and soak in the big marble tub. However gracious she may have felt about dining with an intern the night before, she was in no mood to mentor anyone just now. She plastered a smile to her face and opened the door to greet János.

He was clearly mortified to interrupt her after a concert, having no doubt taken abuse from other performers for committing the same offense. Madeleine softened her smile.

"Yes?" She quietly inquired.

"I am so sorry, Madam LaBlange, so sorry to interrupt you after your magnificent performance, but –"

"What is it, János?"

"There is a gentleman here to see you, Madam. I explained that he would need to leave a message with the concierge, but he was rather insistent that you would be willing to grant him a few minutes."

Madeleine was at a loss. Derrick wasn't coming, she wasn't dating anyone seriously, and she didn't know anyone in Hungary. She was tired and growing increasingly annoyed.

"His name, János?"

"Reynold Fenwick, Madam." He waited for a reply, as Madeleine quickly sorted through layers of bewilderment and intimidation. Fenwick, in Budapest? She was startled, but had no reason to be intimidated by the man now, she supposed.

Madeleine dismissed the loose knot in her stomach as hunger and shrugged. "Show him in, please."

János glanced nervously down the hall and motioned forward. As a shadow approached the doorway, the intern said goodnight and stepped aside.

"Madeleine." He forced himself to smile as casually as he could manage, and offered a polite bow from the doorway.

"Dr. Fenwick!" Madeleine tried not to appear as flustered as she felt. After four years away, the man still intimidated her. "Please, come in."

He grimaced at her formal greeting, but then again, he had never done anything to encourage informality. Unwavering professional decorum allowed him to mentor Madeleine toward her doctorate without… incident.

When he stepped into the sitting area, Madeleine remembered his large presence with a start. Maybe it was his formalwear, or maybe it was the singular influence he held over her years as a student. Probably it was a combination of both. In any event, Madeleine felt disoriented, unable to decipher whether she was thrilled or terrified to see him.

"You played splendidly." It was a simple statement, but Madeleine nervously noted that his eyes were sincere. She was frustrated with herself for feeling so disjointed around him after studying for so long under his direction.

"Thank you, Dr. Fenwick," she said.

"You're welcome, Dr. LaBlange," he replied with hint of a smirk. "May we dispense with the titles now?"

"I'm sorry, it's just – you're in Budapest?"

"It appears that way, yes." Fenwick's eyes shifted awkwardly around the Performer's Suite. Madeleine noted that this was an environment where he should feel right at home, but she had never seen him look so uncomfortable. She also noted that this was the first time she had ever seen him outside of the university.

"It's nice to see you." Lame, but she really didn't know what else to say. Reynold Fenwick was simply the last person on earth she expected to pop into her sitting room after a concert in the center of Europe.

"Let me take you to dinner. I know how exhausting these events always are. You must be famished, and Budapest is a very fine place to seek out a meal." He didn't smile exactly, but his offer felt genuine.

"Unless of course, you are meeting someone?" Fenwick tried to mask his horror at the thought.

She had her escape. All she needed to do was claim prior plans, and "That sounds wonderful, Dr…"

This time he laughed softly. "Reynold, please. It's been a long time since your student days, Madeleine. If you can't address me by the name my mother gave me, I'll have no choice but to feel that the idea of sharing a simple meal together is unseemly to you."

There was irony in how he paired his words with an arched eyebrow Madeleine remembered very well from her student days, but Madeleine let it pass.

"I'll need just a moment, Reynold," she replied, accentuating his name, "and I'll be happy to join you."

"I'll wait outside." With that, Fenwick stepped out into the hallway. He paced the luxuriously carpeted hallway and ran his fingers through his hair, wondering what in the hell he was doing. His perfectly tailored tuxedo suddenly felt slightly too tight along every seam.

Madeleine hurried from her sitting room to the dressing area, to study herself in the mirror. She dusted a bit of mineral powder over her cheeks, in a vain attempt to disguise her flushed appearance. She tried not to think about how her old advisor unnerved her, because the thought only made her angry with herself, which ratcheted her heart rate even higher. He was her former advisor, not her 'old' advisor, she self-corrected. He hadn't seemed to age at all, save for a few streaks of grey along his hairline which were very becoming.

The blessedly fleeting thought made Madeleine set down her dusting brush with a little too much emphasis, causing the slightly concave dusting bowl to skip and clatter along the countertop.

Dinner with Fenwick. What could go wrong?

"*Első Pesti Rétesház*" Fenwick instructed his driver, and they were on their way.

"Where are we going?" Madeleine asked.

"A new favorite of mine, which translates as 'First Strudel House of Pest'. The restaurant itself has only been open for a few years but the building in which it is housed was built in 1812."

"Fitting," Madeleine smiled, meaning that the year 1812 reminded her of Tchaikovsky's 1812 Overture, which is often mistaken as the William Tell Overture, and she had played The Chapel of William Tell earlier today. Oh, hell. *Will the hamster in my head please get off of the damn wheel for a few minutes,* Madeleine silently chastised herself. But the hamster was the only thing keeping her mind off of Fenwick and his well-tailored tuxedo.

Fenwick looked at her curiously. "Have you been to Hungary before?"

"No, this is my first trip. I arrived yesterday morning. It's all a bit surreal."

"I enjoy Budapest. It's something of a juxtaposition of new European money and old European mores, with the old maintaining an impressively firm grip on the culture."

"Do you travel here often?"

"No, unfortunately. The university occupies most of my time. I spent part of a sabbatical year here – I believe that was in between your programs." He said it nonchalantly, knowing full well that his time abroad was during her absence.

"What brings you here now?" Inexplicably, Madeleine was almost reluctant to ask.

"I was invited to give a lecture and performance demonstration at the Academy of Music. I'm only here for a few days and had the evening free." His tone was nonchalant, but his eyes slid reluctantly from hers as he spoke.

The car slowed to a stop and the driver looked over his shoulder. "We have arrived, Sir," the driver stated.

"Thank you. I'll get the door for the lady." In a flash, Fenwick was outside of her door and offering a hand as Madeleine gathered the hem of her dress to step out of the low and spacious town car. As he assisted her out and up, Madeleine's attention was again pulled to her center, and she reflected on how hungry she really was.

Warm ambiance and decadent aromas greeted the well-dressed pair immediately upon their arrival at *Első Pesti Rétesház*. Madeleine and Fenwick were ushered graciously into what appeared to be the well-appointed dining room of a large private home. The plaster walls were painted a warm gold color and were accented with gilded mirrors, while the small antique wood tables were set with embroidered ivory linens.

"*Valami inni?*" Their waiter inquired. Madeleine looked at Fenwick, who mimed the question by lifting his water glass.

"Mineral water, please."

"Yes," replied the waiter, indicating that he followed her English.

"*Arran tokaji* and water," Fenwick requested. He knew Madeleine was performing again tomorrow and understood her abstinence, but wagered he would be better company with a drink in hand than without. The waiter nodded and disappeared.

"What do you recommend?" Madeleine asked, glancing at a menu she couldn't read. It was a practical question, given the circumstances, but also a comfortable topic of conversation.

"I haven't tried anything here that was not to my liking, but the spicy chicken strudel with paprika cream sauce is one of my favorite starters."

"When in Rome," Madeleine laughed.

"Roast duck legs with letscho potatoes and red cabbage is also good, if memory serves."

"I'll let you order. I think I'm too jet lagged and overwhelmed from the performance to make any clear decisions right now."

Fenwick sipped his whiskey and studied her for as long as he dared. "Your performance was exemplary tonight, Madeleine."

Madeleine felt herself blush from head to toe under the weight of his compliment. "Thank you," she replied nervously. "I hesitated a bit on the third -"

"Nonsense." Fenwick cut her off abruptly. Despite being admonished, Madeleine smiled at the familiar tone in her former advisor's voice. "You were extraordinary."

Grateful for the interruption of the waiter, Madeleine welcomed her plate of strudel and tasted it a bit over studiously. "Now this is extraordinary!" Madeleine declared. They ate in contemplative silence for a few moments.

"Thank you for coming to see me, Reynold. It was quite a surprise, and a pleasant one."

Reynold was silent for a moment, his face unreadable. "The very eager intern assigned to take care of you was under the impression that you may have had plans this evening?"

Madeleine grimaced. "Yes, Derrick was planning to be here. A personal matter kept him home at the last minute. We try to see each other at least once a year, when our schedules allow."

"I didn't realize the two of you kept in touch so closely. I suppose commiserating while suffering under the same advisor helped you forge a tight friendship." Fenwick sipped his whiskey with a straight face. When Madeleine looked suitably uncomfortable, Fenwick broke out into a laugh.

"Oh come on now, I was once a graduate student

myself. My advisor was a bastard. By the time I graduated, I hated his guts. But I could probably suffer through a dinner with him now that enough years have gone by." Madeleine laughed when Fenwick actually winked at her.

"We didn't hate you, exactly." Fenwick arched an eyebrow at Madeleine's candor. "You were hard to please. I think Derrick and I both appreciate that now."

"You've both done very well for yourselves," Fenwick said simply.

"I suspect you've had a hand in that from time to time," Madeleine said, remembering her Boston debut.

Fenwick waved his hand dismissively. "'Oh, what a tangled web we weave,' or something like that. My Shakespeare is rusty."

"Scott."

"Come again?"

"Shakespeare didn't actually write that. It was Sir Walter Scott." Madeleine smiled smugly. Fenwick found her facial expression strangely refreshing.

"You were harder on me than on Derrick." Madeleine let her smug smile fade as absentmindedly ran her fingers across her linen napkin.

Fenwick sipped his whiskey and glanced out the window, silent.

"Why?"

Reynold Fenwick let the question linger in the air for a moment, tasting the duck course which had just arrived. He didn't remember the bits of plum cooked into the red cabbage from his last visit, but in any case it was divine.

"The years have been good to you, Madeleine."

"What? You make it sound as though I'm 100 years-old!"

Fenwick blanched noticeably. "That's not what I meant at all, forgive me. I mean that you have clearly found yourself as a pianist. You've developed a repertoire and – more importantly – a persona after whom the world's most magnificent concert halls will clamor."

"A repertoire?"

Fenwick looked self-conscious. "I follow the performance world closely, Madeleine. I follow my former students, all of them, even more closely. I'm impressed by what you've done in the last few years. New York, Boston, London, Madrid, Venice… there were others, I think. You've done well."

He knew the others, but cut himself off when he caught the incredulous look on Madeleine's face. "I must say, I'm surprised you stayed with Liszt. Surprised, but pleased."

"With all due respect, Dr… Reynold, you rather drilled him into my head!" In her laughter, she didn't see him grimace at her slip back into using titles.

"You had the talent for Liszt, so we played Liszt. We could have played Beethoven, I suppose, but anyone over the age of twelve can play Beethoven. Se we played Liszt."

Madeleine found herself exasperated with how flippantly he described what to her was a decision resulting in years of torment. She was reluctantly grateful for the experience, so let her exasperation pass. "Nobody will ever accuse you of being unable to offer an opinion, Reynold." Her eyes twinkled when she said it, and Fenwick thought his cheeks might have colored for a fleeting second. He took a sip of whiskey, just in case.

They engaged in small talk about the university, the National Concert Hall, places to see in Budapest, and compositions Madeleine was contemplating for future performances. Madeleine mentioned, with humor and hardly an afterthought, how she didn't realize the life of a concert pianist allowed little room for socializing, let alone dating. Reynold Fenwick laughed along in a carefree sounding way, while torturously wringing his large hands under the table. They finished their meal and much to Madeleine's surprise, talked until the candles on their table extinguished themselves and she realized they were the only diners left in the room.

"I really am glad you came to see me, Reynold. It's not as if you've never heard me play before. It means a lot to me that you would choose to spend one of your evenings in Budapest with me." She placed her hand on his forearm in the back of the town car and stilled in surprise as a current of energy coursed through her.

Reynold cleared his throat as Madeleine continued, "You may think this is funny, but I was nervous to see you. I suppose a student – advisor relationship looms rather large, even when one is much closer to 40 than 21!"

"I'm glad that approaching 40 is helping you move past your college years," Fenwick replied dryly. When the town car pulled up to the Corinthia Hotel, Fenwick asked the driver to wait. He escorted Madeleine into the lobby.

Reynold Fenwick reached for Madeleine's hands, and held their arms between them in a friendly, chaste pose. "It was a pleasure to see you, Madeleine. I hope you don't mind if I stay in touch."

"I would enjoy that. If I may be candid, it's a pleasure to see you outside of Iowa. Good night, Reynold." In a spontaneous gesture of gratitude for his mentorship, or that is what she told herself, she reached out and up to kiss his cheek. With a flushed complexion, she turned toward the elevator.

"Madeleine?"

Madeleine was already stepping into the elevator but tried to calm her breathing as she looked back over her shoulder.

"I was harder on you because you were better. You remain the most talented pianist I've ever seen." The elevator doors closed, and he was gone.

Madeleine struggled to unlock the door to her suite, because her hands were shaking. Walking dazedly through her sitting room, she unzipped her long gown and stepped slowly out of her evening wear. In moments, she was curled up in bed with flannel pajamas and a freshly washed face, ready to rest up for the next day's performance. First, she had a phone call to make.

"Derrick? It's Maddie. I'm sorry to hear about Ethan. Are you sitting down? Have I got a story for you."

The second evening's performance began with After Reading Dante, the longest of the movements in all of *Années de Pèlerinage*. Madeleine leaned directly into the dark and dramatic composition, conjuring intense meaning from every chord. Music continued to bleed from her fingers, through the piano and over the audience, as Madeleine worked her way through movements named after prayers offered to guardian angels, trees and fountains surrounding villas, crying, grieving, and healing. In music and in life, Liszt was nothing if not complex.

As Madeleine swayed between the highest and lowest octaves of the piano, appreciative gasps and astonished murmurs confirmed the collective amazement of the audience. That an American, and a woman, could capture the essence of Hungary's beloved Liszt was almost unbelievable. But 1,433 people were seeing and hearing the unbelievable with their own eyes and ears.

Madeleine's subtle movements had the effect of making the stage lighting appear to dance across the gold metallic embroidery of her Badgley Mischka gown. The sleeveless sheath exposed her fair, admirably toned arms and back, while the modest V neck added a touch of demure. Madeleine's hair was again pulled back in a simple chignon, this time locked into a gold filigree clasp.

Years of study and intense self-discipline allowed Madeleine to once again visit room 121A inside of her mind. The audience members were the least of her concern. She kept her mind firmly planted in her practice room, to avoid revisiting the previous night's startling conversation with Derrick. As long as her mind stayed in room 121A, she could delay replaying the dream that woke her, breathless, just before dawn.

She ended her second performance in Budapest with

Sursum Corda, translated as Lift up Your Hearts, and relaxed a bit as she breathed in the ambiance of The National Hall. When the curtain closed, she began to walk offstage, but was drawn back to the piano for a moment of reflection. Madeleine's typical laser-like focus was tempered with a carefully guarded sentimental streak. As she sat, poised to perform but lost in a daydream, she had the eerie sensation of a strong, commanding presence behind her. Before she could collect her thoughts, she could smell his faint, musky cologne. Madeleine inhaled sharply and turned around.

Reynold Fenwick stood several feet behind her, speechless, as though he didn't quite understand how he ended up in precisely the spot where he stood. His eyes were soft but his mouth was tense, and he held a single, long stemmed rose. Cautiously, he stepped forward and laid the rose on the bench next to Madeleine.

"I'm sorry to startle you. I meant what I said."

"About being the best, or about giving a lecture at the Academy of Music?" There was no malice in the question, only bewildered curiosity.

Fenwick's eyes widened for a fraction of a second. He looked almost relieved. "I'm not in the habit of intruding, but while I realize I am about to do exactly that, will you have dinner with me again?"

Madeleine could think of a thousand reasons to say "No," beginning with Fenwick's drill sergeant demeanor during her graduate school years and ending with her phone conversation last night. "I don't know," she stated honestly. "Why don't you join me for a glass of wine backstage and we can talk."

Fenwick tipped his head in silent agreement and held out his hand to assist Madeleine. When she placed her hand in his, Fenwick feathered his thumb across her knuckles and ever so briefly closed his eyes. Madeleine tried to ignore the catch in her breath.

Back in her Performer's Suite, Madeleine slipped out of

her shoes and sat on the couch while Fenwick poured two glasses of lightly oaked chardonnay from the chilled bottle left by János on the side table. Fenwick surveyed the rather lavish refreshments and the charming congratulatory card. "It appears you have more than one admirer, Madeleine."

She smiled. "János, the intern who has been tasked with taking care of me, is a cellist. He is a student at the Academy of Music." Madeleine emphasized this last point while eyeing Fenwick levelly.

"Ah, I see." He dipped his head down acknowledging his error, and raised his palms slightly in an apologetic stance.

"I don't understand. What is there to lie about? Why are you really in Budapest?"

"I came to hear you play."

Madeleine started to grow exasperated with the ridiculousness of the conversation, and her voice took on a slight edge. "I live in New York, Reynold. You must know that. You said yourself that I play in New York, Boston – if you wanted to hear me play, you certainly wouldn't need to fly halfway around the world. What is going on?"

"Please don't be alarmed, Madeleine." The softness in his voice countered the edge in her own. "I'll leave if you want me to."

Against everything her Midwestern sensibilities ever taught her, she refrained from sending him away. "I don't want you to leave. I want you to explain."

Fenwick dropped his forehead into his hand. While he was sitting on the other end of the couch, he suddenly sounded far away. "First, and I mean this in the nicest way possible, I despise New York. I find it hard, dripping with false pretense, and ridiculously crowded. There is a reason I've stayed in Iowa all these years. Iowa doesn't try to impress you. Whether or not someone finds it to their liking, Iowa has a refreshing sense of authenticity and room to breathe. If... when... I finally came to see you, it for damned sure wasn't going to be for dinner at the New

York City restaurant of the week."

"Gee, tell me how you really feel," Madeleine responded sarcastically.

"Second, when I saw you would be performing *Années de Pèlerinage*, the parallel couldn't have hit me with more force than if the gravity of the earth itself shifted to pull me here. Liszt was madly in love when he wrote that collection of compositions. He had found an exquisite muse in Marie d'Agoult, and honored his love for her with music. Christ, Madeleine, the irony was torturous. I had to see you."

Reynold watched Madeleine draw in a slow breath and hold it for a single clarifying moment before she allowed herself to slowly exhale. He met her eyes, and was surprised when she was the first to speak.

"But the relationship didn't end well. Liszt and the Comtesse d'Agoult spent a tumultuous decade together. They loved and had children. But in the end, they parted ways. She was young, and he was complicated." Madeleine took a sip of wine to steady herself. Her trembling hand did not escape Fenwick's eye.

"So I've heard. Did they have regrets? That is the only relevant question, and in keeping with many of life's great mysteries, nobody knows the answer."

"More to the point," Fenwick continued, "One of the board members here, at The Hall, is an old friend of mine. I saw that you were scheduled to perform, and I contacted him. I told him that you were my former student, and asked him to make sure that you were comfortable here."

"That was kind, but I don't –"

"I inquired about your travel plans," he let his voice trail off and lowered his eyebrows.

"Why on earth would you do that?"

"I needed to know if you were traveling alone." He closed his eyes and braced himself.

"WHAT? Why would you…" her hands started to tremble, and she realized that she was still holding the rose.

"Because I never, ever would have approached you if you had reconciled with your fiancé, or if you were obviously involved with another man. It would have pained me, but I would have stayed away."

At 37 years old, Madeleine was nobody's fool. She didn't need a translation, but she did need a moment to think. In that moment, she went from stunned to angry.

"Do you know... do you have any idea how intimidated I was by you? For YEARS?" Her cheeks flushed pink.

"Yes. And for that I am gravely sorry, but I won't lie to you."

Madeleine stared at him, her eyes hardening, waiting for him to explain. She took a long drink of chardonnay to steady herself.

"I've never in my life gone about anything half-heartedly, Madeleine. I'm not the kind of man who does things halfway. Most people don't understand that and many people, understandably I suppose, dislike me for it. It's why I own one of the finest pianos in the world and live in a small apartment, rather than owning both a mediocre piano and an average house. It's why I would rather wait years for the opportunity to spend time with one exquisite woman than date average women every day."

"I don't know what to do with that, Reynold. I really don't."

"Have dinner with me."

At her silence, Fenwick shifted slightly toward her and, setting the rose in between them, took her hands in his own. He kissed her fingertips so lightly she may have imagined it. "Have you never wondered, Madeleine?"

She held her head high and glanced down at her hands in his. She felt the air transform around them, as if dated, outgrown roles were melting away. Reflecting on the past few years, Madeleine confidently recognized that she wasn't the kind of woman who does things halfway, either.

She raised her eyes back to his.

"Not clearly. At least, not clearly until last night."

She thought he would kiss her, but she underestimated Reynold Fenwick. He smiled, touched his forehead to her hands and fifteen minutes later they were seated in the far corner of a tiny restaurant listening to strolling string musicians. They talked, they laughed, they ate and drank. They enjoyed each other.

After several glasses of wine, Madeleine mustered the courage to speak what had been threading through her mind for the past 24 hours.

"I spoke with Derrick last night, after dinner."

"I'm not sorry your plans fell through," Fenwick stated with a wry smile, "but I trust he is doing well?"

"Of course. His career has been expanding spectacularly."

"An interesting comment from the pianist who just completed an invited stay at Béla Bártok." Fenwick chuckled.

"He and Ethan are very happy together."

"Happiness in love is a rare treasure, Madeleine. I trust we both understand that." His deep gaze made Madeleine flush.

"He told me... I don't exactly know how the conversation spun in this direction. He explained how you... communicated... in no uncertain terms that you never allow another living soul to touch your piano."

Fenwick let out a long sigh and looked somewhat relieved. "Well. That is the mystery that has been weighing on your mind? It's true. I'm sure you heard all about the unsavory incident." He did not clarify, nor did he look apologetic.

"I didn't really press for details," Madeleine lied. "But I'm curious."

"I had a brief errand to run, university committee nonsense, and told Derrick to work in my office until I returned."

"Work in your office?"

"We were using one of my current composition drafts to clarify a bit of theory. I don't allow my compositions to leave my office."

Oh my. "What a complicated man," Madeleine murmured more to herself than to Fenwick. He overheard nonetheless, and seemed vaguely amused.

"When I returned, he was at the piano. I suppose I was in one of my moods." Fenwick looked briefly embarrassed. Madeleine smiled.

"Does my temperament alarm you, Madeleine?" He suddenly looked worried.

"Not anymore. I'm all grown up now." Madeleine relished the look of lustful discomfort that crossed his eyes before he continued.

"I explained that my instrument is mine and mine alone. I would no sooner have him make music with my piano than I would expect him to tolerate my hands on his lover."

Madeleine had an urge to laugh at the lunacy of the comparison, but seeing that Fenwick was deadly serious, she ground one of her heels into her opposite foot and managed to compose herself. "But you allowed me many times…"

She simply stared at him, willing herself not to settle on the conclusion upon which evidence had triangulated. She tried to steady her breath.

"It was the only way I could tell you I loved you." He gazed at Madeleine steadily, as she gasped at his candor.

"I knew you wouldn't understand – I needed you not to understand. I needed you to be free to pursue your studies freely, without complication. I needed my respect for you, which called for uncompromised professional ethics, to remain stronger than my desire for you. If I was ever unkind, my dear Madeleine, it was only because I felt as if I was beginning to lose my will. Forgive me." The expression on his face was hopeful, and raw with unleashed emotion.

Madeleine was overcome. Suddenly, she burst into laughter, greatly startling both Fenwick and herself. "You were such an ass that last weekend I went to see Andrew! Not as much of an ass as he was, but – " Tears of laughter leaked from the corners of her eyes, as the pieces fell into place and Fenwick's unpredictable behavior during that final year of her studies suddenly made sense.

Fenwick shook his head, thoroughly embarrassed, but grateful that he wasn't hated. He nodded discreetly toward one of the strolling musicians, who led his partners into the first bars of a long, slow ballad. Fenwick stood and offered his hand to Madeleine. "Dance with me," he said.

They were a sight to behold. Her long, slender shape melted against his tall, strong frame as her glimmering gown swirled around the perfect creases of his midnight black tuxedo. Her body warmed as she felt his heart beat steadily through his jacket, and her pulse raced as she breathed in his exquisitely masculine scent. He planted chaste little kisses in her hair as he held her close, as if holding a treasure. Indeed, a treasure is what he finally held in his arms.

Back at the Corinthia, Madeleine wordlessly guided him onto the elevator with her. She leaned against him, arms entwined around his neck, with her eyes closed. When the slow climb ended and the doors opened on Madeleine's floor, Reynold Fenwick gently lowered one arm behind her knees and picked her up. He carried her delicately into her suite and quietly locked the door.

Throughout the warm Budapest night and into the next day, Reynold and Madeleine explored the first hours of a love that had finally been allowed to bubble to the surface, released from layers of policy and pretense.

János happily changed Madeleine's travel plans, so that Madeleine and Reynold could fly home together.

Spicy Chicken Strudel with Paprika Cream Sauce

Dough: Combine 2 ½ cups flour, ½ teaspoon baking powder, ½ teaspoon salt, ½ teaspoon paprika, and 1 teaspoon sugar in large bowl. Add 3 beaten eggs, 2 tablespoons olive oil, and 2 tablespoons water. Knead well (add another tablespoon of water if necessary) and let rest under a clean cloth for 1 hour.

Filling: Sauté ½ diced onion, 1 teaspoon diced Hungarian hot wax pepper (more or less to taste), and 1 teaspoon paprika in 2 tablespoons olive oil.   Remove from heat. Stir in 3 tablespoons sour cream and 2 cups cooked, shredded chicken.

Assembly: On a lightly oiled surface, roll dough into rectangle, approximately 14 x 8 inches. At 1 inch intervals along the long sides, make cuts two inches in toward the center of the rectangle. Place filling in a long, narrow stripe down the center of the dough. Lift cut edges on either side toward each other, working end to end, twist together, and lay flat. Your completed strudel will have a braided appearance. Sprinkle with paprika. Bake on a parchment lined pan in preheated 350 degree oven for 15–20 minutes, or until crust is golden. Slice and serve warm with sour cream.

38 YEARS

"OUCH! Darn it anyhow!" Years of experience as a clumsy cook had taught Annie that yes, yelling really did help. She felt the sharp sting before she saw the thin red line appear on the pad of her index finger. Shifting from foot to foot and perspiring, she set the paring knife next to the offending, half peeled apple on the cutting board and headed toward the utility room for the first aid kit.

"Annie?" Bryant found her rummaging around among the cleaning supplies and paper goods, the note of concern evident in his voice. His eyes widened when he saw the dishtowel wrapped around his wife's left hand.

"Just a shallow cut, don't worry," Annie muttered, hoping her words were actually true.

"Is there any chance," Bryant asked as he gently cleaned and bandaged Annie's finger, "that you might be taking on just a bit too much this holiday season?"

Annie glowered at her smug looking husband.

"Hey! Suit yourself," Bryant responded, raising his hands in the air in surrender. "All I'm saying is, they sell apple pies in town. Mighty fine apple pies, I might add. Pies that someone else slaved over, which we could all enjoy after Christmas dinner without you losing any appendages."

"If you don't like my baking, just say so." Annie knew she was being ridiculously childish, but for Pete's sake, she was hurt and deserved two minutes of sympathy.

"You said it, not me." Bryant winked playfully at his wife. "Hey, where'd your dad go? I thought he bought rock salt for the walkways, but I can't find it in the shed."

Well, here we go, Annie thought to herself.

"Dad?" Annie coughed uncomfortably, "Dad drove down to the florist in Sturgeon Bay to pick up white lilacs."

"Huh?"

"White lilacs."

"Why would he do that? The highway is an icy mess right now. I wouldn't drive down the peninsula for much of anything today. What's so darn special about white – what were they again?"

Annie closed her eyes and prayed for patience, both for herself and for Bryant. "White lilacs. He ordered a vase for Candice's suite. They're her favorite, apparently." Annie's eyes shifted sideways toward her husband.

"Huh? Why does my mother need flowers in her room? He's driving to the florist in this weather because…"

"If memory serves, you put a few miles on the car yourself before surprising me with a big night out last month. You drove down to Sturgeon Bay just for a box of my favorite chocolates. The gesture was much appreciated, by the way!"

"That's completely different." Bryant shook his head.

"Oh?"

"You're my wife. Plying you with truffles is shamelessly self-serving." Bryant reached for a dish towel and gave Annie a playful swat.

"Oh seriously, Bryant, don't be naïve." So much for Annie's patience. At least her sharp tone helped Bryant snap to his senses. Suddenly, his eyes widened.

"Please tell me you aren't suggesting that my mother and your father -" He let his voice trail off.

Annie's reply was carefully neutral. "I'm not suggesting it, I'm merely examining the evidence."

"Aren't they related now? Is that even legal?" Bryant's expression could best be described as horrified confusion.

"Don't be stupid, Bryant."

Annie looked carefully out the kitchen window, giving her husband time to absorb the same wacky revelation she was still trying to sort out herself.

"I didn't know… I didn't realize…" Bryant just stared at his wife, bewildered.

"Well, we've spent years hoping that your mother would have a change of heart and become friendly. Maybe we hoped too hard." Annie laughed weakly.

"You think this is funny? So, what, they're 'dating'? Like high school kids?" Bryant's face clouded over in an angry scowl.

"No, I don't think it's funny at all."

"Are you OK with this, this, whatever it is?"

"You know, I am. I had to think about it for a while, but I really am. Dad's been alone now for almost five years. God, I can't believe it's been that long. I guess I was too busy being the oblivious daughter to notice that my dad seems to be at his happiest when Candice happens to be here, and she's been 'happening' to visit the grandchildren an awful lot this last year."

Bryant took a deep breath. "That last part hadn't escaped me."

"As weird as it is that, well, she's not my mom, and she was pretty crappy to me when you and I were first married."

"I know, I know…"

"She was a raging bitch on wheels, actually."

"Finished?" Bryant asked in a tired voice.

"I think so, yes. I mean, she truly was. But she came around, and I try not to hold a grudge." Annie smiled just a bit too sweetly.

"How long have you known about this?" Bryant asked.

"Not long. I guess it all clicked for me around Thanksgiving when I saw them – really watched them – with the kids. Candice was oohing and aahing over Abby's school project, my dad was needling Danny about working up the nerve to try out for soccer, and when Josiah showed them his honor roll letter, your mom and my dad smiled at each other, equally pleased. They looked like 'Grandma and Grandpa,' and they are, just a bit unconventionally paired."

"You seem certain about this, Annie. Are you really sure they're a…"

"A couple? Yes, Bryant, I'm sure."

"Do I want to know how you are so sure?"

"I don't think so."

Bryant rubbed his forehead and walked back outside toward the shed. Maybe the cold air would help clear his head. He needed all the help he could get, if he was to face his mother. She was due to arrive for the holidays in just a few hours.

The next morning, Mr. Anderson was up with the sun. He crept in the side door of the main house with an arm full of split wood, intent on starting a fire in the parlor fireplace before beginning a giant batch of pancakes. He stopped right in his tracks when he spotted his daughter sitting at the kitchen table sipping a cup of coffee.

"My goodness, Annie, why are you up so early?" Mr. Anderson feigned normalcy.

"I could ask you the same thing, Dad." Annie offered her father an all-grown-up, wry smile. She dropped her amused look when her dad went a bit pale. Annie stood up, poured him a cup of coffee, and they both sat awkwardly at the table as the sun continued its slow creep over the horizon.

"Why do I feel an uncomfortable sense of *déjà vu*,

except that I'm sitting on the wrong side of the table?" Mr. Anderson drank a sip of strong, black coffee and waited.

"I was up late reading, and my mother-of-mischievous-children ears heard the outside door open and close. I looked out the window and saw you walking over toward Candice's suite. I felt bad that you were clearly trying to be, um, discreet. So anyway, this is awkward because I know you don't need my permission or anything... God, I don't really know how to say what I mean here. For what it's worth, if it's worth anything, I mean, I want you to know that I'm good with it." Annie looked down intently into her mug of coffee and didn't see her dad's eyes tear up. Suddenly, he was standing behind her with his arms hugging her shoulders.

"It means everything, Annie. Candice and I didn't really see this coming and we were concerned. She offered to stay away this Christmas, you know."

"What?" Annie looked truly stunned.

"She understands that she was unkind to you early on and she still feels guilty. Bryant is, or rather was, all she had in this world. She knows she handled it terribly. If anyone could understand that kind of mistake, I certainly could. If I ever felt like someone were taking you away from me, after losing your mom…"

Annie reached up and ran her hands over her dad's forearms.

"She's apologized many times. I'm over it, Dad. It was a long time ago, and I'm glad she's here. I'm glad you're happy. Bryant is happy for the two of you, as well. I think 62 is old enough to make your own decisions. You can stop sneaking around like teenagers, OK? I have enough children on my hands already." She smiled up at her dad, who leaned down and kissed her forehead like he used to when she was a little girl.

"Thanks, Annie. Want to help make pancakes?"

39 YEARS

"Goedemiddag. Winair vlucht 73 van Saint Maarten wordt kort komen."

While the intercom system at the tiny Juancho E. Yrausquin Airport was pleasantly clear, the words came too rapidly for Audrey's limited understanding of the Dutch language. Frustrated, she reflected upon the occasional incompatibility between her career path and her painfully slow language acquisition skills as she waited for the English translation.

"Good afternoon. Winair flight 73 from Saint Maarten is arriving momentarily."

Audrey smiled and picked up her pistachio-green bag and her bouquet of yellow tulips. The bag was a recent splurge from Oilily's Fantasy Flora collection. The tulips were for Pam.

Through the large, wall length window, Audrey watched the 19-seat, Twin Otter turboprop aircraft navigate over the steep terrain and land safely on the runway after its brief flight from the nearby island of Saint Maarten. If memory served, the flight took between ten and fifteen minutes, depending upon the speed of the wind.

After a few moments, the air stairs were lowered onto the tarmac and passengers began to disembark. Audrey watched impatiently as an older, distinguished looking African man dressed in traditional, bright blue kikoy wraps stepped gracefully down the stairs. He was followed by a young couple dressed in touristy beach clothes and flashy sunglasses. Honeymooners, she imagined. When a tall, fortyish woman with a short blond bob stepped onto the stairs, shielding her faintly freckled face from the equatorial sun with a colorful, wide brimmed hat, Audrey broke out into a broad smile. She waved excitedly from the window, then rushed over toward the door where the passengers were entering the building.

Pam stepped inside and caught Audrey in an enthusiastic hug, running a hand over Audrey's familiar coffee colored curls and leaving a simple kiss on her temple. Still smiling, Audrey moved reluctantly to hand Pam the bouquet and placed the palms of her hands on Pam's cheeks, fingers extended outward for show, and gave her a big, dramatic, Hollywood style smooch. Nobody paid them any particular attention.

"Welcome to Saba," Audrey said with emphasis.

"I'm not sure there's a more remote island anywhere on Earth," Pam teased. "If there were, I think you would have dragged me to it!"

"Is that a challenge, dear?"

"No. Nope. Not at all, Aud. I'd say three flights on two different airlines in twenty-seven hours is quite enough adventure for me!"

"Chicken," Audrey deadpanned. "Let's see. You're smack in the middle of the Caribbean islands, which I would guess have been visited by, oh, two-thirds of all Americans." Pam smiled and rolled her eyes. Audrey continued on, ticking off details on her fingers for emphasis.

Audrey sighed dramatically. "On your little trip so far, everything has been politically stable, communication has been in English, and nobody lost your luggage. You call that an adventure? We may as well have gone to Orlando."

"Yeah, yeah, I'm here, aren't I? Do I get a shower and a meal out of this arrangement?"

Audrey picked up one of Pam's carry-on bags and kissed her cheek. "I'll see what I can do."

"Unh." Pam grunted as a pillow landed on the side of her head, waking her from a dead sleep.

"Are you going to sleep all afternoon? I thought you were hungry."

"Time?" The question was muffled by the offending pillow.

"What?"

Pam tossed the pillow on the floor and propped herself up onto one elbow. "Yes. What time is it?"

Audrey answered Pam's glare with a sunny smile. "It's almost 7 p.m., my grouchy darling."

"Three flights, two airlines, twenty-seven hours. Remember?"

"I'm remembering… ah, yes," Audrey flashed a wicked grin, "I remember how the sympathy practically oozed from your veins when I had to shift gears from Fiji to Colorado overnight. My reward was spending the day in the company of approximately two million members of the Marquardt family, which included being hazed by Aunt Betty. Remember that, dear?"

Pam sighed heavily, flinging the comforter off of the bed and reaching for her glasses on the nightstand. "A fair point well made. She wanted to be here, by the way. She said she would have driven to meet us anywhere in the U.S., but if God wanted her to fly, he would have given her wings."

"That sounds like Aunt Betty, alright."

Pam pulled a brush through her hair and dug through one of her bags for a pair of sling back sandals to complement her white linen capri pants. One quick swipe of lip gloss later, she was ready to go. "Seriously, Aud, if I don't get a meal soon, I'm going to start chewing on my shoe leather."

"Relax, dear. We're having dinner right here at the resort, remember?" She glanced at her wristwatch. "In fact, our table is probably ready for us right now."

As the women walked across the grounds from their cottage to the restaurant, Pam was awed by the terrain. "I feel like I'm walking through a fantasy movie. Everything is so otherworldly. Even at my age, if a gnome or a fairy presented itself, I'm not sure I'd be surprised!"

"The greenery is unlike anything back home, that's for sure. Would you believe that the locals actually call this the 'Elfin Forest'?"

Pam watched the mist rising from the steep hills and noted the moss growing almost everywhere. A carpet of green presented itself on large, flat rocks and up the sides of trees. "I believe that."

"See that grove of trees over there?" Audrey pointed in the distance, down a steep hill to the left of the path.

"What are they?"

"Those are a highly endangered species of Mahogany. As far as I know, the species only grows in Saba."

"Why are they endangered? Let me guess – unsustainable logging, like the Rosewood trees in Madagascar?"

Annie smiled, knowing how Pam's penchant for ecological issues would lead her to fall in love with this island. "Actually, that's not the reason. The island's tiny size and extreme terrain have kept the population low, and the locals are excellent stewards of the land."

"Then what is the reason?"

"Fifty or sixty years ago, I don't remember exactly, a massive hurricane swept through the Caribbean and hit Saba directly. Almost all of the Mahogany were uprooted and destroyed. They've never recovered. Something about an imbalance is all I remember."

"Sure. New trees thrive under the protection of established trees. Without protection from the elements," Pam looked around at the steep hills and deep valleys, imagining how the wind might tear down the hillsides, "new trees sometimes don't stand much of a chance." She shook her head sadly, then glanced at Audrey.

"How do you know all of this, Aud?"

"Lunchtime small talk, I guess. I've met more than a few locals during my discussions with School of Medicine administrators these past two weeks. It's important that key stakeholders know Abbott College alumnae have been educated about respecting local cultures and ecologies if administrators are to welcome our graduates to their school and their island."

Pam nodded. "That makes sense. You're really good at what you do, Audrey. I mean that."

Audrey smiled and squeezed her partner's hand. "Thanks. This is a big step for Abbott, fostering an international relationship for pre-med graduates rather than for current undergrads. I hope it works out. Either way, my part in all of this is complete. Barring some sort of emergency, Dean Riley will handle everything else with the School of Medicine long distance. That means -"

"We're on vacation!" Pam and Audrey exclaimed together.

Promptly upon arriving at the restaurant, the women were escorted to a small table overlooking a high cliff. The ocean was visible in the distance, providing the perfect backdrop for a Caribbean sunset.

"What is that peculiar sound?" Pam asked.

"Frogs."

"Frogs? Seriously?"

"Saba is full of frogs, apparently. They aren't active during the day, but you can really hear them once the sun sets."

"I know I gave you a hard time about the travel,"

"Neophyte!" Audrey interrupted, teasingly.

"But this island is an interesting place. Even aside from being governed with common sense by the Netherlands, I mean. I'm glad we're here." Pam reached across the table to hold Audrey's hand, as a server opened a bottle of wine and discretely placed it on their table.

"Cheers to that! Wait, did you order this?" Audrey asked.

"No," Pam answered, confused, "but it's a nice New Zealand sauvignon blanc." She examined the bottle more closely. "It's one of my favorites, actually. Maybe it's included as part of our resort stay?"

Audrey simply shrugged, pulling her thin, pale green sweater over her shoulders to shield against the evening breeze. She handed Pam a glass and lifted one for herself.

"To us!"

Before Pam could respond, their waiter reappeared with two spectacular dinners. Each plate featured a lobster fished from local waters, accompanied by bright and fragrant chutney prepared from mangoes picked in the resort's own grove.

"I hope you enjoy. Save room for dessert!" The waiter exclaimed with a smile.

"I don't understand," Audrey said.

"Your dinner this evening is compliments of a 'Mr. and Mrs. Marquardt'. They wish you well tomorrow. Is everything to your liking?" The waiter looked back and forth between the women.

Pam smiled. "Everything is lovely, thank you."

As the waiter walked away, Audrey took a drink to steady herself. Pam's smile faded.

"What is it, Aud?"

"Nothing. Your parents... I just..."

Pam tried humor. "It's dinner, not the deed to a country. Very nice of them, yes, but why the watery eyes?"

"My parents don't even know." Audrey looked out over the ocean. A gentle hand rubbed her forearm.

"I thought you tried calling them," Pam said softly.

Audrey didn't answer right away.

"I was going to. Every time I thought about picking up the phone, the funeral came back to my mind. I can't shake it."

"You know I would have gone with you, right?" Pam asked.

"Of course. I hope you believe me, it would have only made things worse. By myself, it was just the silent treatment. Together, there might have been a scene – an awful, embarrassing scene at my grandmother's funeral. Can you even imagine?" Audrey's voice began to shake.

"I want you to be wrong, but unfortunately I believe you."

"I wasn't surprised that my father ignored me. Being flat ignored was easier than a harassing lecture would have been, I suppose. But my mom – she looked so tormented. She didn't say a word to me beyond a cardboard sounding 'Hello, Audrey'. My father would never allow it. But she kept watching me. I wrote our address and phone number on one of the memorial cards, and tucked it into her purse. She watched me do it. I was so sure I would have heard from her sometime this past year."

"Aud, I'm so sorry."

Audrey coughed out a watery laugh. "I don't mean to have a pity party. For goodness' sake, I'm almost 40 years-old. Nothing can possibly ruin this week. It's just, every once and a while a little hope sneaks in, you know?"

"There's nothing wrong with that, even if it hurts sometimes. Your capacity for forgiveness is one of the many traits that make you such a beautiful person."

The following morning, the women walked down the path from their cottage, through the mango grove, and into a misty clearing. In the middle of the clearing stood a large, weathered gazebo surrounded by lush tropical flowerbeds. Off to the side, a breakfast picnic basket waited. From the opposite direction, a smiling blond-haired man appeared. The minister greeted Pam and Audrey with a cross around his neck, hearty handshakes, and the full blessing of both his synod and the United Kingdom of the Netherlands.

Holding hands, the women bowed their heads and reflected earnestly. They listened to an ancient poem about the mysteries of life and love. The minister lifted their rings into the air for the blessings of God and the Universe as they turned to face each other. Holding hands, they exchanged vows.

"Pam, you are the love that I have always dreamed of and you are the half that completes me."

"Audrey, you are the light that I have always searched for, and you are the half that completes me. You're brightness is irrepressible and I am proud to belong to you."

Audrey chuckled softly. "Pam, your sanguinity is unshakable and I am proud to belong to you. I look forward to creating a loving home together, a sanctuary where we will be centered."

Pam looked around their surroundings pointedly and smiled. "I look forward to traveling the corners of the earth together and experiencing adventures where we will be inspired. Wherever the winds may carry us, you will always have a safe home in my heart."

Audrey blinked back a tear from the corner of her eye. "Wherever we may land, I will love you with my last breath."

"And I will love you, Audrey, with mine."

With damp eyes and glowing smiles, Audrey and Pam exchanged matching silver rings. They kissed in the sunshine and twirled each other around in the misty clearing, deliriously happy to be married at last.

40 YEARS

"Shhh, little one, just give me a minute, OK?" Madeleine's mother rummaged around fruitlessly inside of the refrigerator. With an exasperated sigh, she opened the freezer, removed a small bag of frozen milk, and set about thawing it in a bowl of warm water. As the milk thawed slowly, the baby screamed and screamed.

Mrs. LaBlange rocked the baby, who was quickly turning red with fury, deftly in one arm. "You're fine, little one. Please hush, so your mommy can sleep."

The baby apparently had other ideas, and began to writhe and thrash about in her grandmother's arm, kicking off her pink blanket and turning up the volume of her hungry wailing with each passing second. Only after Mrs. LaBlange managed to carefully pour the thawed milk into a bottle and offer it to the angry infant did the screaming cease. As the baby pulled frantically on the nipple of the bottle, her fists unclenched and the blotchy redness subsided from her chubby little cheeks. Mere minutes later, the bottle was almost empty and the screaming demon was replaced with a sleeping, fuzzy haired angel.

Mrs. LaBlange was too worn down to pay much attention as the lock turned in the door. Soft footsteps across the apartment floor and a pair of dull thumps on the counter told her that Maddie's old friend, Derrick, had returned from the grocery store.

"Wow, babies should come with a dimmer switch, or something. This one only knows 'on' and 'off'."

Mrs. LaBlange smiled weakly. "I thought you just walked in."

"The window's open. Little Miss Arianna serenaded everyone in the parking lot and half of Iowa City before she fell asleep." Derrick smiled and shook his head as he tapped the baby softly on her cute little button nose.

"Don't wake the dragon," Mrs. LaBlange chided. "Thank you for getting groceries."

"It was no problem. I grabbed Maddie's mail on the way in," Derrick added as he placed the envelopes on the growing pile by the sink. He gave the pile a long glance.

"I don't want to overstep, but I'd be happy to spend an hour or two sorting through all of this. I'd hate for her to slip behind on bills. On the other hand, maybe Maddie would prefer that I didn't interfere."

"My daughter needs all the help she can get right now, I'm afraid." Mrs. LaBlange rubbed the back of her neck with the hand that was not cradling her granddaughter. "You were the first person she called. I'd say that's all the vote of confidence you need."

Derrick nodded solemnly and sat down in the small kitchen to sort through Madeleine's mail. He found her checkbook on top of the refrigerator, and was relieved to see that it was recently balanced and flush with cash. Maddie had too many hurdles ahead of her already to add financial problems to the list.

"I'm glad she's sleeping at least," Derrick said absently as he subtracted from the ledger.

"I put a sleep aid in her tea," Mrs. LaBlange said matter-of-factly. Derrick's hand froze above the checkbook. His eyes widened, but he kept his mouth closed.

"Don't look so pious about it," Mrs. LaBlange snapped. Then, she pinched her lips and let her head fall. "I don't know what else to do. I don't know how else to help her," she whispered.

"She won't be alone," Derrick said. It really was all he could think to say.

Mrs. LaBlange snorted. "Do you how much work is involved in raising a child, Derrick? Do you have any idea? She'll feel alone more than you or she realize."

Derrick clenched his teeth. "Mrs. LaBlange,"

"Margaret. I think we can dispense with formalities, given the circumstances."

"Margaret, I know I'm not family, but Madeleine is my best friend. I love her like a sister. I flew halfway around the world, overnight, when she called. When I say she won't be alone, I mean that. I will do anything and everything I can to help her adjust. I promise you that."

As tears escaped from the corners of her eyes, Mrs. LaBlange carefully lowered baby Arianna into her pink bassinet and walked over to Derrick. She placed her hand on his arm. "I don't mean to be testy. You are a blessing, Derrick. Thank you for being here for her."

"I wouldn't be anywhere else."

"I had a bad feeling, mother's intuition, but I never thought…"

"Nobody could have predicted this, Margaret."

"I don't know what she was thinking. The age difference, the whirlwind romance…"

"Surely you aren't blaming Maddie?" Derrick tried to keep the edge out of his voice.

"No."

"Good, because that would be patently unfair." Derrick kept his voice soft, but his eyes were hard.

"She never listens to anyone," Mrs. LaBlange complained.

"I agree," Derrick laughed softly, "but your daughter is not a child. I happen to know that she highlights her hair to cover the grey."

Mrs. LaBlange looked mildly surprised.

"It's a deep, dark secret. I only know because I spent a lovely afternoon with her once at the salon."

Mrs. LaBlange sighed. "I'm not the bad guy here, Derrick, I just don't understand. If she would have taken her time, this might never have happened."

"Oh Mom. If I would have followed your timeline, I might never have had Arianna. I am 40 years-old and lucky to have her. I will never regret my beautiful daughter, not for one second, not ever." Madeleine's voice was more tired than angry as she stood in the hallway in her bathrobe and slippers, hair pulled back in a ponytail, eyes cloudy with sleep.

"I'm sorry we woke you," Madeleine's mother said quietly.

"You didn't wake me. I woke up in a pool of milk. Obviously I missed a feeding. I feel like I'm going to explode."

"Maddie, really, consider your audience." Mrs. LaBlange shifted her eyes pointedly toward Derrick, who only laughed.

"Here, Maddie. I cleaned it and think I assembled it correctly, but you might want to double check." He handed over her breast pump.

Mrs. LaBlange shook her head. "You sure are an interesting man."

Later that evening when Mrs. LaBlange and Arianna were asleep, Derrick set out a plate of his signature homemade orange hazelnut biscotti and poured Madeleine a scant half glass of wine. She breathed in the heady aroma and tasted the tiniest sip, intent on making her two ounce pour last as long as possible.

"You know your mother assumes you'll move back to Illinois, right?"

"Oh God. I'm not sure I can deal with this right now."

CARLY ELLEN KRAMER

"I know, Maddie, and I'm so sorry to bring it up. I'll drop it if you –"

"No, I'm sorry. 'Life goes on, que sera, sera, and all of that'. It's been a few weeks, and bless you, neither you nor my mother have even flinched about the upheaval all of this has caused. I need to get my act together and figure out what the hell I'm going to do."

"Do you want to go back to Illinois?" Derrick tentatively asked.

"No. I feel guilty saying that because it's probably selfish. My mother has been a rock these last few weeks and I know she and my father would welcome us home unconditionally. That said, my life is here right now. Arianna was born here, and her father... I can't imagine just walking away."

"Can we talk about something, Maddie, without you getting angry?"

Madeleine simply stared.

"You know Ethan and I aren't bound by geography, right? He telecommutes, and I fly a few times a month to..."

"No. Unh uh. Absolutely not. I would never turn myself into an anchor around anyone's neck."

"It was sort of Ethan's idea," Derrick continued, undeterred. "He mentioned on the phone that he missed Iowa City in a nostalgic sort of way, and pointed out that we could bank a ton of money if we sublet our place in New York and rented something out here for a while."

"No. You both mean well and I love you for it, but no."

"It would only be for a few months. We wouldn't sell our place or do anything drastic, I promise."

Madeleine's silence was encouraging.

"You're one of the strongest people I know, Maddie, but even you are going to need a little while to get on your feet. There's no shame in that."

"I can't stand the thought of people seeing me as less

226

than self-sufficient. It makes my skin crawl." Madeleine twirled the stem of her wineglass back and forth between her thumb and her index finger. She stared into the ruby liquid as if she were seeking wisdom.

"Nobody sees you that way. Geez, Maddie, I'm not a woman, a parent, or single, but even I know that being a single mother is going to be hard as hell. You have the next 18 years to prove how self-sufficient you are. Let your friends help for a few months."

"I'm terrified, Derrick."

"You're in transition, and transitions are terrifying. But intrinsically, you are fearless."

Madeleine drained her glass of wine and leaned across the couch to wrap her arms around Derrick in a sisterly bear hug and smiled. "Talk it over with Ethan. Really talk it over. If you decide you're up for an Iowa adventure, Arianna and I would enjoy the company."

"There's an apartment for rent two blocks away. I've already paid the security deposit."

Derrick's Orange Hazelnut Biscotti

Cream together ½ cup butter, 1 cup sugar, 3 egg yolks, and 1 tablespoon freshly grated orange zest. Add 3 cups flour, ½ cup finely ground hazelnuts, 1 ½ teaspoons baking powder, and ½ teaspoon salt. Mix well.

Shape dough into two rectangles, approximately 9x4 inches. Bake on a parchment lined pan in a preheated 350 degree oven for 20 minutes. Allow to cool slightly.

Cut rectangles on a slight diagonal into ½ inch slices. Place slices cut side down on a parchment lined pan and return to the 350 degree oven for another 15 minutes.

After biscotti have cooled, drizzle with an icing made from 1 cup powdered sugar and 2-3 tablespoons orange juice. Garnish with coarsely chopped hazelnuts.

41 YEARS

"Bryant, did you gas the car?" Annie yelled from the bedroom.

"Yes, and I double checked the air pressure in the tires." Bryant shouted up the stairs.

"Did you program the GPS?" She countered.

"Yes, it's still 381 miles to Iowa City. Still 7 hours, plus whatever you and Josiah manage to tack on for food and bathroom breaks. In between the gas station and the Garmin, I also met with our financial planner to update our will. Just in case."

"Very funny," Annie grumbled as she clamored down the stairs to greet her husband with a hasty kiss. Out of the corner of her eye, Annie saw a tall, lanky figure in a well–worn, red hooded sweatshirt dart across the hallway to make a break for the back door.

"Not so fast, Josiah. I want to double check what you've packed before you head out with your friends."

"Mom." He slumped his shoulders at the sound of his mother's voice and sent his father a pleading look.

"Sorry, son." Bryant laughed. "She needs someone to fuss over, and if her attention's on you, I get a break!" He winked at his son and headed for the back door himself. If

Annie's father was still cleaning gutters around the property, he'd no doubt appreciate some help. Bryant didn't think his father-in-law had any business climbing up and down ladders as long as Bryant himself was around, but he knew his place in the pecking order and kept his well-intended mouth shut.

"Great." Josiah grumbled under his breath. He turned to his Mom. "I love you, Mom, and I'm not trying to be disrespectful, but seriously."

"Seriously what?" Annie replied, her patience wearing thin.

"I'm 16 years-old. Almost 17, actually. My bag is packed because I am going to look at colleges, Mom. Colleges. We're only going to be gone for three nights." Josiah held his palms up for emphasis. "I need jeans and a hoodie, dress pants, a dress shirt, a tie, three pairs of clean socks, and three pairs of clean underwear. Please, Mom, tell me that you don't really need to see my underwear." He looked down at her and grinned.

Annie shook her head and tried to deflect her tears of nostalgia with humor. "Well, don't forget to pack Mr. Fuzzy. The first time you were away from home overnight, you called me at bedtime because you forgot Mr. Fuzzy. I had to drive him over, in the rain."

"I was seven but I'm sure I appreciated it, Mom." Josiah laughed and kissed his Mom's forehead. "If it will make you feel better, I'll pack Mr. Fuzzy. I'm sure he'll love Iowa. I'll be home by 11. Promise."

"Ok. Josiah?"

He knew this part of the Saturday night routine well. "No beer. But if I have a beer, I can call home for a ride, no questions asked. I love you, Mom."

"Have fun, I love you. Make sure your friends drive at the speed limit." Annie replied wearily. "We'll leave tomorrow morning at 8:00 sharp!"

"Abby, Danny, try to stay out of Grandpa's hair while

we're gone, OK?" Annie asked the tired looking teenagers who were sitting sullenly at the table, staring at her over bowls of cereal.

"There's not much of that left to worry about!" Annie's father laughed, running a hand over his partly grey, mostly bald head. "They'll be fine."

"Yeah, we'll be fine." Abigail said absently, rubbing her eyes.

"I'd have been just as fine if I didn't have to crawl out of bed for this." Danny muttered with a scowl.

"Danny." Bryant quietly admonished his younger son.

"Well, it's not as if Josiah's leaving for college forever. He's just visiting a college. He'll be back in three days, right? Or do I get his room now?"

"DANNY!" Annie scolded at a notably louder volume than her husband had used.

Bryant closed his eyes and silently wished he and Annie had allowed their younger children to sleep in. Josiah's high school graduation was still over a full year away, but Bryant knew his wife was already dreading the day when Josiah would inevitably leave the nest.

"Stay outta my room. Next summer it's all yours, bro." Josiah slapped his little brother on the shoulder while Annie frowned. Josiah grabbed his backpack off of the floor and picked up his violin case from the counter. "I'm all set. I'll be outside."

Bryant and Annie said good-bye to their sleepy teenagers and uttered a few last minute instructions. Annie hugged her dad and thanked him again for offering to coordinate everything at the Inn for a few days. She popped a little white pill into her mouth, swallowed it with a sip of water, and followed Josiah and Bryant out to the car.

"What time is it?" Annie asked, rolling her head around to stretch her neck. A quick glance outside the window told her they were still in Wisconsin, but the small farms and cherry orchards of Door County were obviously long behind them.

"11:20. You've been out cold for two and a half hours, darling." Bryant smiled but kept his eyes on the road.

"Sorry. It's the Dramamine. I can either sleep or throw up, so I guess I'm poor company on road trips either way."

"Does this mean we'll get to fly to Massachusetts instead of driving?" A hopeful voice chimed in from the back seat.

"Massachusetts?" Annie asked, with an edge of panic in her voice. She lowered her visor to peer in her mirror into the back seat.

"Yeah," Josiah replied, a bit unsteadily. "There's a music conservatory out there that I'd like to look at." Josiah looked at his dad in the rearview mirror. Bryant took one hand off of the steering wheel to rub his forehead.

"Massachusetts?" Annie repeated, bewildered. Then she focused her gaze on her husband, and she didn't look happy. "You knew about this?"

"Darling," he said quietly, with a note of caution, "Remember we told Josiah that we would support his goals, even if that meant selecting a program that is outside of our neck of the woods."

"Well, everything is outside of our neck of the woods, considering that we live near the tip of the Wisconsin peninsula. But Massachusetts… at least Iowa is a feasible drive." She was silent for a few moments. Both husband and her son had the good sense to leave her alone with her thoughts.

"I think you'll love the University of Iowa!" Annie suddenly exclaimed brightly, contorting her upper body so that she could face Josiah in the back of the car. "You know, I have an old friend who went to Iowa for graduate studies… she played piano. I don't know why I didn't think of that until just now." Annie frowned.

"Who?" Bryant asked, confused.

"Maddie. Madeleine LaBlange!" Annie's sharp tone implied that Bryant should have this information handy, as if Madeleine had been around every weekend rather than someone he hadn't seen in almost 18 years.

"Oh yes, Maddie. I remember your crazy friend Maddie. She's not the one who... you know, James..."

"Bryant!" Annie exclaimed, causing Josiah to laugh. He didn't know the backstory, but Josiah was plenty old enough to know when his parents were trying rather pitifully to hide a piece of juicy gossip. Bryant simply shrugged.

"No, that was Audrey, and anyway I can't believe you found that little gem worthy of filing away in your long term memory." Annie shook her head, but behind her dark hair she was grinning widely at the ridiculous memory of their best man and co-maid of honor disappearing for an hour at their reception. James had kept a remarkably straight face while explaining how he ran to the store for cigarettes, alone. Audrey had supposedly taken an important work call in the coat room. Uh huh. That didn't exactly explain why James's tuxedo jacket was crumpled. It certainly did not explain why Audrey's stockings were missing.

"Got it. Sorry. Maddie was the loud blonde girl with the preppy boyfriend then, right? I remember. He paraded her around at our wedding reception like he was one of the Kennedy men and ended up carrying her, inebriated, out to the car."

"Well, that's rich." Annie smirked at her husband.

"What?"

"Her boyfriend's name was Andrew. And if you calling him 'preppy' – at the age we all were – isn't the pot calling the kettle black." She began to laugh.

"Guilty. I guess I was pretty sure of myself at that age, too. Did they have a similar happy ending?"

"I assume so. I imagine they were engaged soon after our wedding. I remember being a bit surprised when I realized Madeleine's wedding must have come and gone and we weren't invited, but life pulled us in different directions, I suppose. I didn't exactly overexert myself to stay in touch, either."

Bryant looked at her sadly. "I didn't realize you were quite so out of touch with your old friends. Have you really had no contact all this time?"

"Mostly. I mean, I sent Madeleine a congratulatory card once, when I saw her name in the paper after what looked like a big performance. And I received a postcard from Audrey from some island or another."

"That's all?" Bryant asked softly.

"Well, no. After Mom passed, they tried to see me. Both of them, actually. But I was a mess. I just… it wasn't an opportune time for a reunion, you know?"

"I know. But, I think there's a difference between a 'reunion' – high school hierarchy, old flames, that sort of thing – and leaning on old friends when you need them." Bryant looked at her.

"You sound like a girl." Annie snorted at Bryant, but he noticed that she was sniffling just a bit.

"And if I ever acted like one of the Kennedy men, you can blame my mother." Annie stopped sniffling and laughed at Bryant's joke, as he knew she would.

"It's not fun to blame Candice for anything anymore, not since she retracted her claws and became, well, normal."

"Grandma Candice?" Josiah asked.

Now it was Bryant's turn to admonish Annie for her indiscretion. They had almost forgotten their oldest teenager was sitting three feet behind them. "Don't worry about it, Josiah. The truth is, and this doesn't leave this car, do you understand?" Josiah nodded before Bryant continued, "Grandma Candice wasn't always completely friendly to your mom, but Grandma came around."

Annie arched an eyebrow. "Something like that, yes."

Bryant smirked, and looked at his son in the mirror. "Grandma came around because I intervened and insisted that my mother treat my wife kindly." He gave his wife a wicked grin. "Much the same way as I imagine you will call your mother, if your future wife complains."

Josiah cracked up laughing as Annie gasped out loud. "Oh you mean, mean man!" Annie scolded her husband, punching him lightly on the arm.

"We offer private scholarships to help defray costs, but they are highly competitive and applications have a firm November 1st deadline of the year prior to admission. We do our best to lock in the most talented music students early." Dr. Euvgeni Drakova smiled encouragingly, but the room full of parents looked collectively apprehensive.

"Our well-qualified, financial aid counselors will be happy to schedule private consultations with each of you and your son or daughter, of course. They will be happy to walk you through the long list of government-backed student loan options, including both subsidized and unsubsidized loans, depending upon qualifying income levels. If the maximum allowable loan amounts under these programs are not sufficient," Dr. Drakova spoke a bit faster as the anxiety level in the room dialed up a bit, "there is also a parent loan program through which loans may be guaranteed by the parents rather than the student. And of course, there are always private loan options. Our counselors will be happy to answer all of your questions."

A young, perky woman wearing jeans and a University of Iowa sweatshirt poked her head into the fearful room. "We have just completed our residence hall tour and question and answer session with a group of this year's freshmen students. Parents, you are welcome to join your sons and daughters in the atrium for refreshments before continuing on to your chosen departments."

Bryant and Annie looked at each other with relief,

happy to be excused however temporarily from the looming financial reality of having a child, and soon multiple children, in college. They gathered up their heavy folders of applications and miscellaneous resources, and headed out into the large, noisy, open atrium.

"Mom! Dad! Over here!" They didn't need to take a single step to see that Josiah had stars in his eyes.

"How was your tour, son?" Bryant asked.

"Awesome! The dorms are great! One of the freshmen buildings is brand new, with a bathroom and kind-of a living room, where you can put a TV and a microwave in between each pair of private rooms. Everyone says dorm rooms are small, but these are about the size of my room now, without a nosy little sister or brother barging in every few minutes!"

Bryant arched an eyebrow, but Annie just smiled. "When I was in college, there were three rooms around each central area. I had crazy suitemates, Maddie and Audrey. We became good friends. They were my maids of honor when your Dad and I got married."

"Cool. Do you still see them? Maddie and Aubrey?"

"Audrey, not Aubrey. And, well, we tried to stay in touch for a while…" Bryant's arm came over her shoulder and pulled her close.

"Your Mom was just talking about trying to see them again, weren't you, darling?"

"Uh, I have an appointment in the music department in a little while. Since I don't exactly know where that is," Josiah stared at a campus map, and then turned it sideways to stare for a moment longer, "maybe we should get going?"

The trio found the music building after only one minor detour, and what a building it was. The behemoth structure was actually two, five story red brick buildings connected with a corridor almost large enough to be considered a building unto itself. The marble staircases with heavy oak bannisters, brass railings, lead glass windows, wrought iron light fixtures and ceramic tiled floors were all spotlessly clean and in perfect repair. This was obviously a music department with both a rich history and a well secured future. Josiah was bedazzled.

As Josiah trotted off ahead of his parents, Annie whispered to Bryant. "The buildings housing the music department here are larger than the entire campus of Abbott College. Imagine the resources they must have at their disposal. No wonder it was so important to Josiah that we visit early."

"He's a smart kid, Annie, and damn good at the violin. And whether we like it or not, he won't be a kid for long. Let's try to make the transition as comfortable as we can." Bryant gave Annie's hand a reassuring squeeze.

They followed Josiah up a wide, winding staircase to what should have been the third floor violin wing. Instead, they wandered around rooms full of percussion instruments, lost.

"Can I help you?" The freshman who asked could spot a touring high school student from a mile away, having been one himself fairly recently.

"I have an appointment with the Coordinator of Violin Studies, and I thought her office was right here, but I must be mistaken." Josiah looked embarrassed.

"Ah, easy mistake. This is Building A. Violin is on the third floor of Building B. Just take the stairs back down to the first floor and walk straight through the piano wing. You'll see a big sign directing you through the corridor to Building B. And my name is Brad, up here in percussion, if you have any questions."

"Thanks, man." Josiah nodded toward Brad and took off down the stairs.

Winded, Josiah slowed down once he reached the bottom of the stairs. As he meandered through the piano wing, parents marching dutifully behind, he grimaced. "Duh, this is Building A. All of the rooms end with an A. Nice if I would have noticed that before I walked up all those stairs."

"Before WE walked up all those stairs," Annie corrected, her feet already angry at having been crammed into dress shoes for the occasion. "These must be practice rooms," she noted, peering into an endless row of tiny, sparse rooms barely large enough for the pianos they housed. A petite woman with dark hair and Asian features sat at a piano in room 121A, an intense look on her face and a frightful number of cans of Diet Mountain Dew perched on her window sill.

"And these rooms are obviously for professors," Bryant stated, nodding to the other side of the hall. The doors were much more widely spaced and built of more substantial wood. Most of the doors were closed. A custodian was tidying one of the offices, the open door allowing the Andersons a glimpse of a sunny room decorated in a soothing, effeminate pastel palate.

"Can I help you?" A tall, distinguished looking dark haired man asked in the direction of the trio, obviously a doe-eyed prospective student and his nervous parents. He had a soft spot for nervous parents.

"Um…" Josiah cleared his throat, straightened up, and began again. "I'm on my way to the office of the Coordinator of Violin Studies. I understand it's on the third floor?"

"That's correct. You'll find Dr. Peterson to be very personable. Don't be nervous. And if you change your mind and decide to play piano," the professor joked, "Come see me. I'm Dr. Stanley."

"Thank you, Dr. Stanley! I'll keep that in mind." Josiah again trotted off down the hall, as Annie and Bryant flashed grateful smiles at the kind professor.

Further down the hall, from one of the faculty offices, Annie heard the distinct sound of a baby giggling. Annie had an embarrassing soft spot for babies, so much so that she had one of the suites at the Inn renovated to accommodate new parents. The Babymoon Suite, it was called, designed to offer overwhelmed moms and dads a luxurious place to honeymoon with their new babies. Annie's father indulged her despite his conviction that it would become an unrentable space. Lo and Behold, the Babymoon Suite, complete with a crib, changing table, and play area in addition to the already present and decidedly scrumptious king size canopy bed and Jacuzzi tub, became one of the Inn's most popular rentals.

Bryant smiled, understanding that Annie would simply not be able to resist poking her head inside of the office door to ogle the source of the noise. Sure enough, Annie crept up ahead to look. She was rewarded with a drooling, cherubic smile from a sandy blonde haired baby girl standing on her mother's lap and looking out over her shoulder. Annie hardly noticed the man kneeling in front of a bookshelf in the back of the room, surrounded by boxes. Annie made a silly grin and waved at the tiny girl.

"Hi!" The baby squealed enthusiastically. "Hi! Hi!"

"Hi!" Annie replied, still waving unashamedly. The baby's mother began to turn, her blonde hair catching the light.

"I was just passing by and your baby is beautiful." Annie smiled, then froze.

Annie and the mother stared at each other.

A moment passed.

"Oh. My God." It came out as barely a whisper. Bryant looked at his wife, confused, and saw a tear form in the corner of her eye.

Without warning, the blonde haired woman leapt off of the chair and practically flung her baby at a stunned, still Bryant.

"ANNIE! OHMYGOD!" Madeleine squeezed her arms around Annie with a strength that only a lifelong, pick-up-where-you-left-off friendship would allow. Both women fell apart in a tearful mess. The commotion caused Josiah to turn back, and he and his father stared at each other helplessly. Bryant turned his stare toward the startled baby, now struggling in his arms. The baby started to cry, and was finally plucked out of Bryant's arms by the man who had been packing boxes in the back of the room. Even as the baby calmed down, Bryant grew increasingly certain that this was some sort of practical joke, and looked around for a camera crew.

"Madeleine?" The man holding the baby inquired with a baffled expression, his eyes moving back and forth between the tearful women and the equally bewildered Bryant, all the while gently bouncing the baby on his forearm.

Madeleine efficiently rubbed the mascara that had trailed down her cheeks sideways all over her face, turned her head back to the familiar man, and tried to explain. "This is Annie, my old, old friend –"

"Easy there, girlfriend, I'm not that old!" Annie interrupted, wiping away tears of her own.

"Annie is my friend from my Abbott College days. OH! That means you're BRYANT!" Before the words were out, the blonde haired mascara mess threw herself at Bryant, who was catching on as quickly as he could muster.

"Maddie! NOT the maid of honor who disappeared with James. How could I forget!" He hugged her back, sorry that the man holding the baby was still completely in the dark.

"We were best girlfriends," Madeleine explained. "Hell, we ARE best girlfriends." She looked at Annie somewhat tentatively, and Annie vigorously nodded her approval. "There were – are – three of us. We've just been out of practice for a while."

Annie looked at the man who obviously wasn't Andrew. He was about their age, but didn't resemble a Kennedy in any way.

"This is Derrick, my dear friend, and my daughter Arianna." Madeleine beamed. Then she noticed the teenager practically hiding behind his father. Madeleine's eyes nearly popped out of her head. "Is this... no...

Annie?"

"This," Annie began, in what felt like one of the proudest moments of her life, "is our oldest son, Josiah. He's a junior this year, and an excellent violinist."

"Mom," Josiah interrupted, embarrassed.

"He's looking at the violin program here at the University of Iowa as a potential college choice!"

"I'm... speechless." And Madeleine truly was.

"Uh, I have an appointment with the Coordinator of Violin Studies," Josiah interrupted, looking at the time on his cell phone, "in five minutes."

"Oh my goodness, you need to get to that," Madeleine announced. "You're here for the night at least?" She looked at Annie expectantly, her hands still on Annie's shoulders.

"Yes, absolutely!" Annie said.

"There's so much to talk about. I'm overwhelmed. I'll need to clear my head but I'm not letting you escape. Let's meet for dinner – will 7:00 work for you?"

"5:00, 8:00, whatever. I can't believe it's really you!" Annie was positively beaming.

"Take your son – I can't believe that's your son, Annie – to his appointment. I need to get Arianna home for a nap, but I'll leave directions to the restaurant with the department secretary. He's just down the hall. We'll catch up in a few hours, as much as that's possible!" The women shared a long, joyful hug and went their separate ways.

Bryant and Annie spent the remainder of the afternoon discussing Josiah's impressions of the university. His meeting with the coordinator had included introductions to several faculty members, all of whom were exceptionally welcoming to the impressed and intimidated teenage boy. At 5:00, they left Josiah with an admissions counselor in the lobby of one of the freshmen dormitories, and drove back to their hotel to change for dinner.

"Darling, you look lovely, but the expression on your

face suggests that you just swallowed something awful." Bryant looked at his wife bemusedly. He couldn't help noticing how she gave the tie of her emerald colored wrap dress an extra cinch before climbing into the car, or how she fidgeted with her matching earrings, which she had previously professed to be comfortable enough to forget she was even wearing.

"Do you have a hot date I don't know about?" He smiled at her, trying to put her at ease.

"I'm sorry," Annie frowned.

"He'll be fine, you know. The overnight experience is designed and chaperoned by admissions counselors. They won't let anything happen to Josiah, because they know they'll lose the chance to swindle us out of a million dollars over the next few years." Bryant scowled at his own joke.

"It's not that."

Bryant gave her a silent, I-know-you-better-than-that look before returning his eyes to the road. Annie smirked.

"Ok, it's a little of that. He just doesn't feel old enough for us to leave him on a college campus in a strange city."

"Well, you know what they say about Iowa City. You won't find such heinous crime or debauchery anywhere else."

"Oh stop it. He's growing up. I get it. I left him there, didn't I?"

"After an embarrassing number of hugs, hair ruffles, and terms of endearment, yes. And the poor boy took it all in stride, because he loves you."

At that, Annie offered a genuine smile. "I know you're going to think this is ridiculous, but I'm nervous about seeing Madeleine tonight."

He did think it was ridiculous, but he kept quiet. "Why is that?"

"Well, look at her." Annie frowned as she said it, and Bryant knew to tread lightly.

"Huh?" When in doubt, feigning ignorance sometimes worked in his favor.

"She looks fantastic, and successful, and… I'm being ridiculous, I'll get over it."

"Would you feel better if you ran into her at the Speed Dragon, and caught her with a cigarette in one hand and a cheese Danish in the other? While she was purchasing a fifth of whiskey at 11 a.m. as her dirty kids ran all over the convenience store?" Bryant winked at his wife.

"Maybe," she laughed. "Maybe I'd be a little less aware of being, well, the same. Plus an extra ten pounds of more of the same."

Bryant knew there was nothing to say to this. They had been down this conversation thread many, many times. "We're here, darling." He parked the car, kissed her cheek, and walked around to escort her inside.

It took a moment for their eyes to adjust to the dim lighting in Ray's Steakhouse on the outskirts of town but Annie and Bryant felt at home right away. The place had the feel of an old school supper club reminiscent of many older establishments in Door County, right down to the unapologetic, wood paneled walls, gold veined mirrors, and ample chairs upholstered in padded black vinyl. The pianist in the bar to the left was crooning an old Tony Bennett ballad with earnest conviction. The place was perfect.

"Annie, Bryant, over here!" Madeleine called from a corner table with an enthusiastic wave. After a complex round of hugs, handshakes, and cheek kisses, Bryant and Derrick pulled out chairs for the women and joined them at the table. The silver relish tray complete with green goddess dressing made Annie smile.

"First things first," Madeleine declared primly. "You have a grown son!"

"Almost grown, not quite grown," Annie corrected, flustered. "But yes, Josiah is 16 now, and makes us very proud."

"And you have another child, yes?" Madeleine pressed.

Annie's eyes expanded as she realized exactly how

much catching up there was to do. She filled Madeleine in, to the extent of which politeness would allow, on the antics of her three children. The pride Annie felt in her family shined through her eyes.

"And your dad? Is he well? I tried to get in touch with you, but... I'm really sorry about your mom, Annie."

Annie's smile faded a bit, but she recovered. "Thank you. Dad's well. It's been a few years. I can talk about it now. I'm sorry, too. I wasn't... I wasn't in a good place to reconnect. We help run the Inn now, Bryant and I."

Madeleine looked confused. "Over the summers?"

"No, I work there full time, and Bryant helps darn near full time, when he's not working for a subsidiary of Tribune at a local office. We left Chicago. We moved to Cherry Harbor the year after Mom passed, and haven't really looked back since."

"No offense, but I really can't picture Bryant – sorry," she conceded, acknowledging Bryant for the first time in several minutes, "trading corporate America for the back roads of Door County." Madeleine shook her head, before turning her attention fully to Bryant. "You must be quite a guy. I guess you were worth the ugly blue dress I still have photos of, and the five pounds I gained downing a gallon of ice cream with Audrey as she attempted to eat through the horror of a hook-up with your best man."

Bryant raised his hands in the air in a posture of complete innocence, as Derrick chuckled politely. "I didn't realize there was history between all three of you."

Madeleine tried her best to bring Derrick abreast of her undergraduate years with Annie, and the antics of their wedding eighteen years earlier. An hour and two bottles of wine later, the years which had elapsed felt fewer and fewer.

"I need to visit the ladies room," Annie declared, reaching for her purse.

"I'll tag along, for old time's sake!" Madeleine chimed in. The men looked at each other and simply shook their heads.

The brightly painted restroom was empty when they entered, and the slightly tipsy women scurried into bathroom stalls.

"Bryant seems wonderful, Annie. You know what they say about marrying young."

"And we certainly did that!" Annie confessed.

"But you two, you really pulled it off." Madeleine talked through the walls of the stall, while fumbling with her dress.

Neither woman paid any attention when the outer door opened and two more women entered.

"Thanks. He's the love of my life. And you've clearly found yours. Derrick looks at you with such adoration, I'm giddy for you!"

Madeleine laughed. "Oh, it's not like that at all. It's... a story for another evening. I don't imagine I'll be garnering much adoration these days anyway, since I'm old enough to be wearing Spanx under this dress. Speaking of which, I'll need a moment to untangle and reconstrict myself here."

A tall woman in an embroidered indigo skirt and gauzy caftan top stood at the counter, touching up her eye makeup and pinning her hair. Her voice carried over to the petite, dark haired woman in the champagne colored, tulip skirted dress who had entered the third stall. "I hope you don't mind Aunt Betty joining us for dinner. To be honest, I can't believe she drove so far just for dinner. She said the fact that our travel conference at the U of I coincided with our anniversary was the perfect excuse for a celebration. I realize Iowa is a bit closer for her, but seriously, it's not like it's a convenient drive."

"Don't be surprised. She loves you enough to come all this way in her old age," the voice of the woman behind the door caught for a moment, "and it's nice to celebrate our anniversary with family."

Something in the woman's voice made Annie pause.

"Honey, are you feeling OK?" The woman at the counter asked.

"I'm fine, I guess I'm just feeling a little nostalgic today. I'll be right out. Don't keep Aunt Betty waiting."

"I'll be right outside. And Audrey? I love you."

Annie felt the air freeze in the ladies room. Surely it was only the wine and the nostalgia of encountering Madeleine, and this couldn't possibly be...

"Audrey Navarro?" The question was barely a whisper, and it came from Madeleine.

A small gasp. "Who is that?"

"No!" Annie managed that one, tiny exclamation before fumbling with the lock on her narrow door.

"What on earth was that?" Derrick interrupted his small talk with Bryant and turned his head toward the back of the restaurant. At the sound of the screaming and yelling coming from the ladies' room, both Bryant and Derrick stood up to investigate further.

They followed the commotion through the hallway, past the restrooms, and into a separate, smaller dining room. All eyes were on the boisterous group of five women at the center table. Madeleine was being hugged enthusiastically by an elderly woman in a shockingly bright green, knee length dress. Annie and a woman in a champagne colored dress had both sets of hands locked together as if they were long lost sisters. A tall woman stood just behind them, beaming, her hand on the shoulder of the somewhat stunned looking woman holding onto Annie. Derrick and Bryant stood back, not at all willing to step into a mob of inexplicably emotional women.

The woman in champagne had quiet tears running down her face. She leaned her head against the woman in ivory and quietly said, "I've been thinking of my family a lot today, you know? And now, well, I'm speechless." She gazed in wonder at Annie and Madeleine as if they were apparitions, and let out a choked sob. "I almost can't believe it, but here you are."

When Madeleine and Audrey started to cry and more patrons began to stare, Aunt Betty intervened. "For Pete's sake, ladies, it's an anniversary dinner, not a funeral. Pull yourselves together. I didn't drive all this way with my bad hip just to watch people blow their noses all night." She motioned for one of the nervous looking waiters, who hastily began moving chairs to create a table for seven. Bryant and Derrick understood that they were to gather what they wanted from their own table and come join the emotional party. They didn't understand what was happening, but neither man felt particularly inclined to question the bossy, white haired woman wearing the prom dress.

The restaurant proprietor was sympathetic to the happy situation and allowed the party to linger after closing while the staff cleaned the kitchen. Several hours later, Bryant drove his inebriated and emotionally exhausted wife back to the hotel.

"You don't think dad will mind that I offered a few rooms next month, do you?" Annie asked around a yawn.

"Are you kidding? He'll be delighted that you've reconnected with your girlfriends. To be honest, I think he's been worried that the Inn is isolating for you."

"There was a time when it would have been. Now, I can't imagine living or working anywhere else. It's so much a part of us now, even if it feels like too much to manage sometimes with so few staff." She smiled at Bryant. "I'm so excited that they're coming up, I can hardly stand it. I wouldn't even mind if Pam's eccentric aunt tagged along."

"She was a real piece of work, wasn't she?" Bryant laughed.

"Audrey and Pam... I honestly had no idea. I never would have guessed." Annie said, reflectively.

"I guess things didn't work out with her and James?" Bryant smirked.

"Oh knock it off," Annie scolded. "That was a lifetime ago. We have so much to talk about."

"Are Madeleine and Derrick…?" Bryant asked.

"No, I don't think so, but Maddie didn't seem ready to elaborate. I noticed how, aside from discussing her career related travels, she was content to let everyone else talk. We have a lot of catching up to do."

"And you will, darling, you will." Bryant leaned over to kiss his wife quickly before returning his eyes to the road. A heady combination of wine and memories lulled Annie to sleep within minutes.

Green Goddess Dressing

The highlight of any old school steakhouse relish tray is Green Goddess Dressing. In a blender, combine ½ cup mayonnaise, ½ cup sour cream, ¼ cup chopped fresh parsley, 1 clove chopped garlic, 1 tablespoon fresh lemon juice, 1 tablespoon dried *herbes de provence*, and 1 anchovy (optional). Blend until smooth. Serve chilled in a cut glass bowl surrounded by crinkle cut carrot sticks, celery sticks, green onion stalks, radishes, and black olives. Green Goddess Dressing is also delicious with breadsticks.

42 YEARS

Audrey gently stirred the large, bubbling stockpot full of tart red cherries and cane sugar with a long wooden spoon while a canning pot full of mason jars and water boiled furiously on the adjacent burner. She still couldn't believe that Annie had been purchasing cherry preserves for the guests' breakfasts for years, but smiled to remember how delighted Annie was to learn how Audrey had mastered food preservation techniques during her many years of travel. Since Audrey began helping in the kitchen, the breakfasts at the Anderson Inn had become somewhat famous. Guests seemed to slather homemade preserves on everything, which for Audrey was a source of pride. She and Annie were even beginning to run a few preliminary numbers to see if offering a Sunday brunch for non-overnight guests might be profitable.

Audrey thought back to that first, fateful trip to the Inn, mere weeks after the amazing run-in with her college girlfriends in Iowa City. As she had hoped, she and her former suitemates were able to pick up where they had left off almost twenty years earlier. Liberal pours of cherry wine lulled them right back into tipsy giggles that somehow didn't clash with the faint lines around the women's eyes. Much to Audrey's relief, Pam got along famously with Audrey's old friends. Both Bryant and Mr. Anderson seemed genuinely thrilled to see Annie so social and happy. Everyone, of course, was madly in love with baby Arianna.

Only two weeks later, Annie invited everyone back, and unveiled her proposal. It sounded outlandish at first, the idea of moving to Door County. But as Annie pointed out, Pam was already telecommuting, and Audrey was looking for a new direction. Madeleine was simply waiting out the remainder of her lease. After that, she didn't have a concrete plan, only the realization that she couldn't travel easily with a baby. Her half-hearted job search had paid off, sort of. The state school near her parents had offered her a reasonable if lackluster teaching position. Wearily, she concluded that returning to Illinois would probably be best for Arianna, even if it meant abandoning her performance career indefinitely. Annie suggested that perhaps Madeleine would be willing to help out at the Inn during the busy tourist season, in exchange for happily provided childcare during the winter performance tour.

The clincher was Mr. Anderson's explanation that the Inn was becoming too much for himself, his daughter, and his son-in-law to manage. They needed additional staff, but offering competitive salaries would be untenable to the bottom line. He could, however, offer comfortable living accommodations in the spacious, three story, six bedroom main house, complete with profit-sharing and a built-in family. As Mr. Anderson saw it, the arrangement would be a wonderful way to make his daughter happy and prevent a difficult decision about whether or not to sell the Inn. After a few weeks of frank, long distance discussions, everyone decided to give the arrangement a one year trial before committing to a co-ownership agreement.

Lost in her thoughts of how the last year had unfolded, Audrey went through the motions of filling hot, sterilized mason jars with a funnel and ladle, carefully wiping off the rims, centering flat sealing lids over the wide jar mouths and securing the lids in place with screw bands. When the first batch of twelve jars was full, Audrey used insulated jar tongs to carefully place the jars into the boiling water of the canning pot. Audrey was efficient, and had her workspace gleaming again before the twenty minute processing time in the water bath had elapsed.

"Crash!"

The kitchen door flew open and slammed into the wall just as Audrey was attempting to gently transfer a sealed canning jar of cherry preserves from the water bath on the stove to the cooling rack on the counter.

"Auntie Au-rey! Auntie Au-rey!" The small, wide eyed girl implored. "Pease cherries?"

Any irritation Audrey may have felt over having to rid the counter of a broken jar and a ruby colored mess was washed away by the joyful plea of Arianna, who delighted in eating cherry preserves by the spoonful, and knew exactly whom to beg.

Mr. Anderson appeared in the doorway, looking winded and sheepish. "Sorry, Audrey. Miss Arianna and I were taking a walk in the leaves while her Mommy plays piano and she must have smelled the cherries from outside of the window. Her little hand slipped out of mine and she took off like a dart." He went to scoop up the small child, who was busy frowning at the toes of her tiny red sneakers, her pigtails drooping forward across her ears.

"It's OK, I've got her." Audrey was rewarded with a bright smile and a hug around the tops of her knees. Mr. Anderson stifled a yawn and proceeded to make himself a cup of tea.

"Ari, no running away from Grandpa, OK?" Audrey put on her serious grown-up face for the little girl.

"K."

Audrey smiled and carried the little girl to the booster chair at the kitchen table. When she snapped a bib over the Arianna's shoulders, the little girl squealed. "Yay, cherries!"

"Hi, Ari!" A teenage girl with fair skin and long hair in loose curls skipped into the kitchen and waved at the little girl.

"Abby! Abby!" Arianna exclaimed, dripping cherries onto her bib.

"Finish up, kiddo, and I'll read you a story and tuck you in!"

"I wuv you, Abby!" The little girl exclaimed. Audrey washed Arianna's face, kissed her forehead, and sent her off with her big sister at heart.

As soon as the girls left the kitchen, Annie appeared with a serving tray laden with dirty wine glasses, cider mugs, and small serving plates. She carefully deposited the tray onto the counter nearest the dishwasher, and hurried off to the pantry. Bottles clinked together gently behind the pantry wall.

"Done?" Audrey enquired.

"Almost. Two pairs of guests have charmed Madeleine into a longer performance, and are actually dancing in the parlor. I should bring out one last bottle of wine."

"Sure, why not. Maddie loves it, and you'll likely get repeat business for the effort."

"We'll likely get repeat business, you mean. We're a team now." Annie served up a slightly chastising smile, as if they had previously visited this topic. Then she was back in the parlor, pouring wine for their guests with a smile.

"Do we have another extension cord?" Bryant shouted down from the top of the tall ladder.

"I thought there were four hanging in the shed, which means there should be one left. I'll go check. Stop trying to be a hero and take a break, will you?"

Bryant laughed. "Good idea. In fact, I think you should be up here, balanced precariously in the night sky against all of these arbor vitae. If memory serves, this was your bright idea!"

"Ah, the guests will love it and you know it. I'll be right back!"

Bryant climbed down to survey the boxes full of long strings of white holiday lights. They were over halfway finished, he estimated, and he hadn't broken an ankle yet. Pam was right, the Inn looked fantastic in the fall and winter months when the tall arbor vitae glittered with lights, but the darn shrubs – if you could reasonably call them that – were almost fifteen feet tall.

"Here ya' go, one last extension cord at your service! Do you need me to run to the hardware store for more?" Pam asked sincerely.

"No, we'll make do. Jerry's probably closed the store for the night by now anyway. And if we had more, you'd probably have me climbing around the gutters like a monkey, stringing more lights." Bryant grimaced at the mere thought.

Pam laughed. "Hey, it was just a suggestion! It's your place!"

"You keep saying that, and you're going to get me into trouble with my wife. Two words: profit sharing. It's a team effort and, if I may say so, we all make one hell of a team."

Pam smiled reflectively, as if she were mulling over an important thought. "Audrey is… different… since we moved here, in all the best ways. I knew it hurt her that her family didn't embrace us, but I guess I didn't realize how sharp that was."

"I can't imagine," Bryant offered. He really couldn't.

"It's important to Audrey and I both that we pull our own weight around here and I hope you'll be straight with me, Bryant, if you need anything at all from either of us. Audrey would be embarrassed if she knew we were having this conversation, but she doesn't talk about this as a job or a living arrangement. She talks about how she now has a family."

Bryant nodded, somewhat at a loss for words. "When

Annie's mother died, I thought we might end up here and to be honest I was apprehensive about it. Now, I can't imagine living anywhere else."

"Her dad is quite a guy," Pam said.

"Yeah, he really is. But for as happy as Annie was to come home to her dad and the Inn, she didn't really have girlfriends here. She has a lightness about her now which I haven't seen in a while."

"Are you done, or do I need to call an ambulance?" Annie yelled from the front porch.

"We're done for now," Bryant yelled. "Be right in."

"What happened in here?" Madeleine asked, noting the broken glass in the sink as she went for a glass of water.

"Just dropped a jar, no big deal," Audrey called from the utility closet where she stowed the mop and bucket.

"Is there any wine left? Open, I mean?" Madeleine wondered aloud.

"Check with Annie," Audrey responded, wandering back into the kitchen.

"Check about what?" Annie asked from the side door adjoining the parlor.

"Wine," Madeleine persisted.

"I have a few half bottles left from your evening concert, I'll bring them out," Annie offered. Bryant and Pam walked in through the back entrance, rubbing their hands on their red faces to warm up.

"Save them as refills for tomorrow's concert, darling." Bryant insisted. He suddenly turned back toward the back door and entered the utility closet.

"But – " Madeleine began to protest.

Bryant returned with two bottles of wine retrieved from a hidden location. Madeleine furrowed her brow quizzically, while Annie rolled her eyes.

"This," Bryant began dramatically, waving his right hand across the bottles draped in his left arm, "is wine. Annie, I love Door County. Audrey, I love your preserves.

But wine, I'm sorry, is made from grapes. It's made in a faraway land known in some circles as 'California'."

Madeleine began to laugh as she went to the buffet table for stemware.

"Please, darling," Bryant implored Annie, "save the tourist wine for the tourists. Tonight we will drink like dignified people." Bryant took a theatrical bow, to the applause of Madeleine, Audrey, and Pam. Annie rolled her eyes again but was smiling. Bryant swiftly uncorked the bottles and poured five glasses. "To us!" He toasted.

"Don't be a snob. I really like cherry wine," Annie grumbled good-naturedly. After a brief clink of glasses, everyone moved into the parlor to settle into more comfortable furniture.

Almost immediately, Madeleine began to absentmindedly rub her shoulder, then her eyes. Annie noticed that her wine glass was already empty, and shot a quizzical look at Audrey, who shrugged her shoulders. Suddenly, a shrill screech from upstairs broke the silence.

"Unka Bwyant! Unka Bwyant! A mon-ser, Unka Bwyant!" Arianna sounded panicked.

"Be right there, pretty girl!" Bryant yelled, already heading for the utility closet.

"I've got it," Madeleine sighed, her voice weary with fatigue. "I'm so sorry she's not sleeping well." she apologized to the room.

Bryant reappeared, looking absolutely ridiculous. He was wearing a hardhat and had a flashlight on his hip, jammed between his belt and the waistband of his jeans. He was carrying an aerosol can of air freshener with enough authority that it may as well have been a firearm.

"Sit down," Bryant admonished Madeleine. "You forget that 'Uncle Bryant' is a professional monster hunter!" As the room began to laugh, he bounded up the stairs to the little girl's rescue.

"Maddie, honey, are you OK?" Annie asked, her voice full of concern.

"I don't know what I would do without all of you." Madeleine's voice was barely a whisper. Annie and Audrey were at her side in an instant.

"You've been working too hard, and you need a break," Annie offered. "You can't work in the reservations office all day, and then put on your party face and give parlor concerts every night. It's too much."

Madeleine wiped a hand restlessly over her face and shook her head. "I miss Reynold so much around the holidays, I feel like my heart is breaking all over again."

Audrey wrinkled her forehead, and pulled Madeleine in for a hug. Pam discreetly excused herself, realizing that the three old friends needed a moment together. Awkwardly, Annie recovered her speech in time to offer "And here we are, carrying on like fools about wine and other such trivialities. Of course this is hard for you. I'm so, so sorry, Maddie."

"I thought this year would be easier, and maybe it is, a bit. I'll get there."

"Oh honey, take all the time you need," Annie said, wrapping Madeleine in a hug while Audrey refilled wine glasses.

"We're here if you want to talk about it, you know." Audrey let the offer linger as she handed her still grieving friend an unfashionably full glass of California cabernet.

"When Reynold died, it completely gutted me. I don't know how else to describe it. I loved him with…" Madeleine's voice caught in her throat, and she drank a long sip of wine. "He was the love of my life."

"Arianna was only three months old, for God's sake. We were newlyweds. I was still healing, and chock full of nursing mother hormones. Reynold had been complaining of headaches, but we both thought it was simply the hideous sleep deprivation that comes with having a newborn. He laid down with a particularly bad headache, and… I just couldn't wake him up. The doctors said the aneurism took him quickly and he passed in his sleep."

Madeleine let her head fall into her hands, silently, as her shoulders began to shake. "I'm sorry, I know you've heard all of this before."

"Maddie, I would give anything to have been there for you. It sickens me that we weren't there for you." Annie's eyes teared up as she apologized to her friend.

"Oh Annie, we had been out of touch for darn near two decades, there's nothing to feel bad about. Derrick was there less than 24 hours after I called him. I don't remember calling him." Madeleine smiled faintly. "He bribed a gate agent in London, and was on a flight within an hour. I honestly think I would have died without him there to hold me up." Talking about it made Madeleine stronger but reduced Annie and Audrey to silent tears.

"It was divine intervention by my guardian angels that I found both of you in Iowa City that day. I will believe that with my last clear thought on this earth. Derrick was helping me clean out Reynold's office so that his replacement could move in. How do you replace Reynold Fenwick?" Madeleine laughed dryly.

"Derrick and Ethan had been living nearby for months, and, while Derrick was too gracious to ever bring it up, I knew he would need to return to New York soon. The thought paralyzed me."

Annie and Audrey simply held Madeleine's hands while she talked through her memories. "I had found a more suitable apartment for Arianna and I, down the block from a quality child care center and near a park with a playground but our living room was small." Suddenly, Madeleine choked out a sob. "I was going to sell his piano, because I simply didn't know what to do with it."

The three women looked at the magnificent piano in the parlor, where Madeleine entertained the guests of the Anderson Inn. Annie suddenly realized how important those intimate evening concerts were, not only to the unique ambiance of the Inn, but to Madeleine herself. What Annie had worried was a burden, was actually a healing balm.

"You know, I've never been a believer in guardian angels. Suddenly, I couldn't be more convinced of their reality than if they were birthed from my own body." Audrey nodded vigorously in agreement with Annie's spoken sentiment.

Annie continued, "When I was a little girl, I used to wish for a sister. Who knew that I'd find two of them in my forties?" The three women shifted from tears of grief to tears of happiness and levitating laughter.

"It's safe now, you can come back," Madeleine called into the kitchen. Bryant and Pam appeared, somewhat tentatively.

"Enough dwelling on the past, at least for today. We have a Christmas to plan, yes?" Madeleine stood up, resolved, and walked to the reservations office for her day planner.

"Do you mind if I comp a room in early April for a few nights?" Audrey asked around the sprig of mistletoe she held in her teeth. She held a large pine and holly wreath against the front door of the main house, her arms aching as she waited for Annie to secure it with a large, red velvet ribbon.

"You know that's fine. That's practically a dead month for us anyway and hosting friends and family is one of our perks. Who's coming?"

"I talked to Dale, my good friend from Azores, this morning."

"I remember," Annie offered. The ribbon was just a bit too wide for the nail in the door and kept slipping. Audrey was leaning into the door for support, and was beginning to groan in protest.

"He called to wish me a Merry Christmas, and then dropped the bomb that he's getting married. Dale, married. Stranger things have happened, I suppose!" Audrey laughed at the idea of her friend, the confirmed bachelor, morphing into a married man. "Anyway, I thought it'd be a nice gesture to offer a suite as a wedding gift."

"Absolutely! We'll put together one of our honeymoon baskets, with gifts from local businesses around Cherry Harbor. They'll love it!" Annie took particular pleasure in tending to the needs of personal guests, as the Inn itself was such a source of pride. Finally, Annie managed to secure the hulking wreath to the door. Audrey rubbed her aching biceps.

"What's next?" Audrey asked, having lost track of the day-before-Christmas chore list they were slowly whittling down.

Annie looked up into her head, sorting through the whirlwind of holiday tasks. "Well, Pam offered to go into town and brave the grocery store today, so that's done, and God bless her." Audrey laughed, knowing how much Annie hated frenzied store crowds. "Bryant and Danny are moving firewood to each of the guest rooms, and Madeleine is busy making Hungarian strudel today while Abby and Arianna have a doll party."

"You mean, Madeleine is busy tearing up the kitchen I just cleaned." Audrey groaned.

"Or that, yes." Annie laughed. "Really though, she can't possibly make more of a mess than you managed with that soufflé last night!"

"Hey now, I may have dropped the first bowl of egg whites, but my second attempt was rather fabulous. I vaguely remember someone sneaking the chocolate crumbs out of the soufflé pan before washing dishes." Audrey said with a smirk and a raised eyebrow.

"A fair point," Annie said. "But why on earth didn't you just use the electric mixer? The bowl snaps right onto the stand."

"That's just not how I learned, I suppose."

Christmas Eve morning, the kitchen was bustling with enough activity that an outside observer would never guess the Inn was actually closed for business for the week. The large, cylindrical coffee pot was brewing noisily away while a large slab of breakfast ham warmed in the oven and griddle after griddle full of pancakes were transferred to the restaurant-style warmer. Individually and in pairs, the family began a slow trickle into dining room.

"You're an awesome big sister," Madeleine whispered to Abby, noting how the teenage girl had indulged Arianna's wish for matching Christmas nightgowns. Seeing the toddler and the sixteen year-old side by side, it was hard to say who looked more adorable in red flannel, bedecked with giant, iron-on Christmas trees. Abby picked up the little girl, who squealed with delight and offered a big kiss.

"Well, you're an awesomely ridiculous-looking big sister," Danny joked. "Where's a camera when I need one?" Abby simply glared at her annoying little brother who, at 15, knew exactly how to get under her skin.

"Where's Josiah?" Danny asked. He may have been too cool to admit it, but Annie knew he missed his older brother.

"I'll wake him in a few minutes. It's winter break. He's catching a few more Zs," Bryant stated as he strolled into the kitchen in bare feet, wearing a blue sweatsuit with the Chicago Bears football logos plastered everywhere.

"Let him sleep," Danny said dismissively. "More pancakes for me."

"Son, you've lived here quite long enough to ditch the Bears clothing, already. Get yourself some respectable green and gold!" Mr. Anderson knew that Bryant wore that goofy outfit just to draw a comment and smiled with fondness at his son-in-law. When Candice walked in, impeccably groomed as if it were dinner time instead of 7:30 a.m., Annie's father walked over and joyfully kissed her cheek. Candice tipped her head so that her lips grazed his, as Annie and Bryant smiled.

Josiah came stumbling into the kitchen in a pair of

warm-ups with the letters I-O-W-A plastered down the side. He leaned over to hug his mother, who patted his scruffy chin and reached up to ruffle his hair. "I could smell ham, and knew I better get here fast in case Danny was awake. I'd like something to eat other than pan drippings." Josiah air punched Danny, and sat down between his brother and sister.

Audrey and Pam darted into the kitchen, dressed up and wearing coats, to offer a round of hugs and Merry Christmas exclamations before filling their travel mugs with coffee. Madeleine looked both startled and concerned. "You're leaving for Christmas?"

Pam smiled. "Nah. We'll be home for dinner. Maybe even lunch." She grinned at Audrey, who looked slightly sick.

"What's going on?" Mr. Anderson inquired. "I can't have one of my girls unhappy. It's Christmas Eve morning!"

Audrey looked as though she didn't know where to begin. "We're meeting my parents for breakfast."

A stunned silence filled the room. Everyone knew about the non-relationship between Audrey and her parents. She hadn't seen them in years.

"They, ah, they asked to meet Pam. I said 'No.'"

"And I said we should try," Pam filled in, holding Audrey tightly in one arm around her waist.

"My mother asked if they could drive up here."

"Of course they can!" Annie chimed in. Audrey glared at her.

"Of course they cannot." Audrey kept her voice low but there was no mistaking the finality in her tone. "I told her I didn't know if I wanted to see them, that they can't just expect to waltz back into my life, and anyway it's Christmas and I have plans with my family. Here."

"My mother didn't argue. She apologized. She said she understood if I never wanted to see her again, but she wanted me to know that she has had a change of heart and she would do anything for a chance to see me and meet Pam."

"Wow." Madeleine whispered.

"That was a week ago." Audrey said softly.

"And you didn't say anything to any of us?" Annie asked incredulously.

"I tried to just push it away and not deal with it for a while. But my father called the next day. I haven't talked to my father since…" Audrey's voice broke. Madeleine and Annie were up in a dash, offering hugs of support.

"He told me that he respected my hesitation, and would respect my space. He even acknowledged that I would likely want to protect Pam from them and swore that he and my mother would both be on their best behavior." Audrey smiled weakly at Pam.

"He asked if I would be willing to meet them for breakfast today. They would drive as far up from Chicago as Pam and I were comfortable, to be convenient for us without us having to invite them into our home. 'Just breakfast, and then we'll leave,' he promised. How could I say 'no' to that?"

"Do you want me to drive you?" Mr. Anderson asked earnestly. Audrey almost started to laugh at the absurdity, but caught herself when she realized that might hurt her surrogate dad's feelings.

"Thank you, but we'll be fine. It's just breakfast. We're meeting them in Sturgeon Bay. I'm willing to see them, feel them out a little, but I really don't want them up here. Not yet."

The hopefulness that crept into those last two words made Annie's heart lurch. Damn them if they hurt Audrey again, Annie thought bitterly. Then she thought of her own mother-in-law, presently holding hands with her father.

"People can change," Annie said simply. "Good luck. When you come home, even if it's in an hour, there will be wine!" Audrey and Pam both laughed.

Mr. Anderson stood up and put a hand on each of the women's shoulders before they left. "I hope everything goes well. You're brave to open yourselves up to them, even for breakfast. I love you. We'll celebrate Christmas tonight, as a family. Drive safe."

Audrey and Pam smiled and headed out into the winter air. No guts, no glory.

A few minutes later, the doorbell rang.

"What did they forget this time?" Madeleine muttered, hovering over the sink to rinse plates and worry about Audrey. Annie had to turn her head away to smile.

Mr. Anderson walked through the kitchen and parlor toward the front door, and motioned for little Arianna to join him.

Arianna squealed. "Unka Derrick! Unka E-fan!" A dish clattered into the sink.

"Baby girl!" A man's familiar, booming voice exclaimed. When a shadow filled the doorway, Derrick plucked the little girl off of his chest and handed her to Ethan.

"Madeleine. Merry Christmas, Madeleine." Derrick opened his arms as Madeleine ran forward to fill them, eyes glistening.

"We wanted to surprise you. I guess we did!" Derrick laughed as Madeleine looked from him to Ethan to Mr. Anderson, who held up his hands in a gesture of mock innocence.

"Not really. We're just cheap, and Mr. Anderson offered us a free holiday stay." Ethan shrugged noncommittally, making Madeleine laugh.

Bryant went to the coffeepot to fill mugs for the men, whose noses were still red from the freezing cold air. Annie glanced into the parlor at her old friend, who looked blissfully happy. From the corner of her eye, she caught the increasingly comfortable sight of her father and Bryant's mother enjoying the commotion of a house full of children and grandchildren.

Suddenly, Annie started to laugh. And laugh, and laugh, and laugh. Bryant set down the steaming mugs and walked over to her, smiling.

"What on earth is so funny?" He asked.

"Everything. Nothing. Nothing turned out like we planned, did it?" Annie was shaking her head and trying to catch her breath.

"What do you mean? Christmas?" Bryant looked confused.

"Not just Christmas. Everything. The whole twenty years!"

"Annie, have you been drinking eggnog?"

"Ha! Eggnog. We're supposed to be drinking eggnog in Chicago. In our big house on Lake Drive filled with all of your stuffy Tribune employees whom we're hosting at our pretentious holiday gala!" Annie laughed at her own joke, while Bryant arched an eyebrow.

"Our 1.8 children were going to be business students at Northwestern, because why would anyone ever leave Chicago? We would pay their tuition in full, of course, because I would run all of the labs at the hospital by now, and my parents," Annie's voice hitched briefly, and then just as quickly recovered it's humor, "would have long since sold the Inn and invested the piles of profits!"

Bryant thought of the pile of invoices sitting in the roll top desk and frowned. He thought of the long list of maintenance projects that would necessitate hiring a full-time handyman come spring. Ruefully, Bryant wondered how they were going to work a handyman into the budget, and hoped reservations would be steady come spring. Then he looked around at the boisterous holiday scene. A slow smile started on his face, and he waited for his wife to continue.

"I should be opening Christmas cards from Maddie and Audrey right now. I wouldn't have seen them since college, of course, because we'd all be too important for such trivialities. Madeleine should be singularly focused on her music, and Audrey – if her early 20s were any indication – should be ruthlessly pursuing her conquest of a long list of single men in Chicago!"

Bryant grabbed one of Annie's arms and spun her around into a joyful embrace. He kissed her neck below her ear, while Danny walked past and muttered "Gross."

"I'm sorry life hasn't gone the way you expected, Annie," Bryant chuckled into her ear. "Care to make any predictions for the next twenty years?"

Annie snorted, and then turned her head to kiss her husband. "I wouldn't dare! I love you, darling."

EPILOGUE

18 YEARS

"Looks like you're the first one here, sweetie!" Mrs. LaBlange nervously rubbed her hands together as she looked around the tiny dormitory suite. Behind her, a tall, skinny blonde girl pushed a shopping cart full of bags and boxes through the crowded hallway and over the threshold of the door.

"That's the idea, Mom. Get here early and pick out the best room." Tucking a few stray hairs back into the bright pink scrunchie securing her ponytail, Madeleine abandoned her cart and made a quick sweep through the suite. She wrinkled her nose at the cinderblock walls but nodded with marginal approval at the size of the bathroom. Noting that one of the three bedrooms had more sunlight than the other two, she quickly ran back to the cart.

"Hey Mom, can you help me make this bed?"

Mrs. LaBlange grabbed a stack of purple bedding and joined her daughter in the sunny room. As soon as the bed was made and a few boxes were shoved onto the shelves,

Madeleine reasoned, her claim on the room would be staked for the year.

As Madeleine and her mother unpacked bags and boxes, a plump, stern looking, middle aged woman marched down the hallway followed by an ornery looking, green eyed girl.

"One of your roommates has already arrived, Audrey." The woman tucked a bobby pin into her hair bun and gathered up her long skirts to scoot past the cart which partially blocked the doorway.

"Oh, here, let me move that," Mrs. LaBlange said to the other woman, just as Madeleine returned to the cart for another bag. "I'm Margaret, and this is my daughter Maddie," she offered with a smile.

"Pleased to meet you. I'm Mrs. Penelope Navarro, and this is my daughter, Audrey." The stern looking woman smiled and motioned for her daughter to step forward.

"I hope she's a short, fat girl," Audrey mumbled under her breath, nervously tugging on one of her chin length, brown curls. She had plans for her first semester of college, all right, and they didn't involve much homework. When Audrey caught a glimpse of her tall, thin, blonde, smiling roommate, she snarled inside of her head and vowed to apply for a new room assignment as soon as was allowed. Audrey had no intention of rooming with a boyfriend stealer.

"Hey! I'm Maddie. Nice to meet you!" Madeleine offered a glowing smile at her new roommate.

Audrey choked back a scowl and managed to croak out "Hi. I'm Audrey. Which room's mine?"

"There's two left, take your pick!" Madeleine answered, too excited to even register Audrey's reticence. Madeleine scurried back to her room, while Audrey checked out the rest of the suite.

"I can't believe my little girl is in college now!" Mrs. LaBlange said to the other mother, laughing and shaking her head.

"It is hard to believe, I know. As my husband reminded me this morning, all we can do is pray that we have raised our daughter with a strong moral compass to help her make righteous decisions and stay pure in the eyes of God." Mrs. Navarro nodded her head solemnly.

"Oh, er, yes." Mrs. LaBlange replied awkwardly, a bit taken aback by the strong words but quickly sizing up the advantages of her daughter spending her freshman year of college with a religious girl.

"Is anyone here?" A pair of friendly brown eyes in an olive skinned face framed with long, dark hair peeked into the doorway. Her smiling parents stood, holding hands, a few feet behind.

"C'mon in! I'm Maddie, nice to meet you!"

"Hi! I'm Annie, and these are my parents. I'm so totally excited to finally be here!" Annie motioned to the shopping cart next to her parents. "Which room do I get?"

"You'll need to ask the other girl, 'Aubrey' or 'Audrey' or something. I'm not sure which one she took."

Audrey appeared a few feet behind Madeleine. "You can take whichever room you want. I don't have a preference. I'm Audrey." She smiled as sincerely as she could muster. *And I don't plan to spend more than two weeks in this suite, anyway*, she thought to herself. At least the third girl wasn't another towering blonde.

"Cool. That's nice of you!" Annie grinned from ear to ear, her shoulders raising up a bit as she smiled.

"I'm a biology major," Annie offered. "What are you guys studying?"

"Music," Madeleine answered. "I play piano."

"You mean music education, right Maddie?" Mrs. LaBlange corrected with an almost imperceptibly tightened smile.

"Yes," Madeleine said with a long sigh. "I am interested in performance piano, and will also be pursuing a teaching license." Facing Annie and with her back carefully to her mother, Madeleine rolled her eyes to convey that there was more to the story. "Got it," Annie's lightning fast wink seemed to convey.

"What about you?" Annie asked the green eyed girl.

"I'm undecided." Audrey said simply.

"But she's considering religious studies." Mrs. Navarro offered pointedly.

Audrey stood around the corner from her mother and slapped a palm to her forehead. "I'm considering international business, but I'm undecided."

"Interesting," Madeleine said with a smile, but she was disappointed. A science nerd and a business enthusiast weren't exactly the roommates she had in mind. But hey, these girls were only freshman year roommates. They just needed to keep quiet, not steal, and clean the bathroom every once and a while. After spring semester ended, they'd probably never see each other again.

Friendship Bread

Combine 1 cup milk, 1 cup sugar, and 1 cup flour in a mason jar. Cover with a coffee filter and secure with a rubber band. Leave jar on countertop and stir daily for one week.

After 1 week, pour contents of jar into a large bowl. Add 1 ½ cups milk, 1 ½ cups sugar, and 1 ½ cups flour. Stir until well combined. Return 1 cup of this mixture to the jar, cover as before, and save for next week. Place 1 cup in a large mixing bowl to use in the recipe below. Give the remainder to friends.

To the 1 cup of Friendship Bread starter in the large mixing bowl, add the following ingredients: 1 mashed ripe banana, 2 eggs, ½ cup applesauce, ½ cup oil, ½ cup milk, ½ cup sugar, 1 teaspoon vanilla, 2 teaspoons baking powder, ½ teaspoon baking soda, ½ teaspoon salt, 1 small box instant chocolate pudding, and 2 cups flour. Mix well.

Pour batter into 2 loaf pans which have been greased well with butter and dusted with sugar. Bake in a preheated 325 degree oven for 1 hour or until a toothpick inserted near the center comes out clean. Keep 1 loaf to enjoy. Give 1 loaf to a friend.

ABOUT THE AUTHOR

Carly Ellen is a food traveler and writer who loves incorporating delicious recipes into her stories. She has a minor obsession with French boulangeries, and is sublimely happy with a fresh baguette and cup of espresso in any European cobblestoned square.

Visit Carly Ellen's blog at **crowdedearthkitchen.com** for hundreds of fabulous recipes, free book giveaways, and more!